To Dance in the Glen

The Glen Highland Romance Book One

Michelle Deerwester-Dalrymple

Talia—
Happy Reading!
Michelle H
3/25/2023

Read More!

Want a bonus ebook about Gavin and learn what happened before he and Jenny met? Click the image below to receive *The Heartbreak of the Glen*, the free Glen Highland Romance short ebook, in your inbox!

Click here: https://view.flodesk.com/pages/5f74c62a924e5bf828c9e0f3

The Glen Highland Romance

To Dance in the Glen

Michelle
Deerwester-Dalrymple

Contents

Prologue: Northern Highlands 1296

THE THRUM OF THE horses' hooves on the ground made the earth vibrate in announcement. The horsemen scattered all about the land, searching for a woman who had been missing for nearly a day. The woman's husband, Laird of the clan MacLeod, Colin MacLeod, was beyond distraught, bordering on insanity in his search for his wife, the Lady Caitir MacLeod of MacLeod. A tall, strong, beautiful woman with hair blacker than the night sky and the most piercing blue eyes a soul had ever seen, it was rumored that God himself crafted her body in addition to her soul, carving her out of the most coveted jewels found on earth -- sapphires, diamonds, onyx.***

More than her appearance, however, was her very nature. While she practiced Catholicism as all good Christians did, she was raised with a deep-rooted belief in the old religion and tied it to her Catholic beliefs. She used herbals and prayer to heal the sick, advice and prayer to help the souls of clansmen and women who came to the Laird for help. She was genuine and honest and would give her very last shift to a poorer soul if they needed it. It was oft said that she kept Colin grounded since Colin, though he was a full-grown man reaching nigh two score of years, could still be a rash and hot-headed man much of the time. However, just a movement or gesture from Caitir was usually enough to calm the storm that was her husband. All these reasons and more made her the most loved person in clan MacLeod.

No one, however, loved her more than Colin. He was infatuated with her and did everything in his power to spend most of his waking moments in her presence. He scheduled hunts, farming, even his business for accounts on Market Day around Caitir and how often he could be with her. Friends and family made jokes about how Caitir led Colin around by his nose, or other body parts, but instead of growing angry, Colin laughed at the comments. He knew them to be true.

But today, it was not laughter that Colin felt, it was anger and concern, more concern than he had ever felt in his life. Even more than when his oldest had fallen off a tree and landed awkwardly. They feared that the future Laird would be crippled from a broken leg, but it turned out to be naught more than a twisted ankle, and the lad healed fine. This time, however, there was little hope that all would be fine.

The English had pushed farther and farther north at the insistence of King Edward Longshanks, and the sufferings of the Scottish people had increased thousand-fold. Men were slaughtered, women raped and maimed, children beaten, attacked, orphaned, or even killed. The recent events had sickened Colin, and while the English had not come as far north as Lochnora, they had come close. Now he feared that they had come too close after all.

Caitir had left that morning to find marigolds, which she claimed were good for headache and for keeping bugs off other plants. While Colin was not inclined to disagree with her either way, he worried for her health. She was over six months full with their fourth child, a late baby since Ewan, their oldest was nigh on 15 years. They both hoped for a daughter this time, and Caitir had told him she could feel it. She had not felt like the bairn was a girl with her other pregnancies, and they weren't, so Laird MacLeod and his wife were confident in this omen. She had been inside so much, sewing bunting for the bairn while a steady rain fell outside, but that morning the sky was clear, even if a misty fog hung low. Caitir convinced Colin that she was fine and would not go too far past the main road south of Lochnora, so he had naught to fear.

When she did not return for a midday meal, Sarah from the kitchen asked Keith (since called "old Keith" after the birth of his son, "young Keith," much to "old Keith's" chagrin) if he would bring a lunch to the Lady Caitir as Sarah had not seen her leave with any food, and what woman with a babe could go more than a few hours without any food? Old Keith rode off quickly and headed south, expecting to see Caitir walking back towards the keep. Soon though, he realized something was amiss when he reached the edge of the land of clan Lee and still had not seen Caitir, either on the muddy dirt road or anywhere in the grasses and trees close by. Without pause, Keith reined his horse around and rode at breakneck speed back to Lochnora, screaming for Colin at the top of his voice.

Colin was already overwrought at Caitir's disappearance. He knew deep in his heart that something was not right and assembled several men to ride into the woods south of Lochnora to search for his wife when Old Keith rode up in a panic. He told Colin that he had ridden all the way south to Lee land and saw no sign of Caitir, only of riders traveling the roads. Now Colin paled in fear, afraid that the English had come farther north than ever before. Afraid that his beloved wife had encountered them.

Colin split the search parties into two groups, one to head directly south with himself, and the other to ride with Old Keith toward the southeast in case Caitir walked far from the road. Colin thought this unlikely, but he was not a man to make assumptions. He wanted the whole of the area searched, and they would not ride home until she was found.

They split off south of the road that led north to Lochnora and south into the land of Edmund Lee and his clan. At one of the more recent Market days, the Lees had told Colin of sighting the English just south of their holdings, and that was too far north in Colin's consideration. He had heard of the atrocities of the English, and had a wife, sons, and a clan to care for. Any sighting of English skin was too much. All of this plagued Colin's mind when he heard shouting coming from the woods to the east.

Old Keith had his group spread out within hearing distance to better cover as much land as possible. When he heard one of the younger men in his group (was it Simon?) give a loud screech, Old Keith rode to the man's aid, only to discover the most gruesome sight he had ever laid eyes on. They had found Caitir MacLeod, wife of Colin MacLeod of MacLeod, mother of three sons, and beloved of the clan MacLeod, and Old Keith's first thought was how to hide her before Colin approached.

The English had found her. Caitir slumped at the base of a tree, her shiny black hair now matted with dirt and blood. Her golden dress had been ripped from her, and her chemise torn up the middle, exposing her pale flesh. Her breasts were stark in the clouded afternoon sun, and there was no doubt in Keith's mind that she had been raped. However, the obviously violent rape was not the reason for her death. That was a result of the giant gash in her abdomen where her babe had lain warm and protected until this day. There was so much blood, Old Keith had no doubt as to the fate of the unborn child, and he heard Simon gasp, "oh GOD!" then turn and sick up his morning meal into the bushes near his horse. Old Keith dismounted and walked over to the young man when his eye caught upon more blood under some brush only a few steps away. Peering closer, Old

Keith then saw the second most gruesome sight of his life. Not only had the English killed the mother, the gash in her stomach was more than a death blow—it was to remove the unborn child from the belly of the mother. Old Keith felt his gorge rise as well, with the full horror of the scene falling on his head. *She had been alive when they cut the babe from her. Oh, God save us. God save her.* Old Keith quickly unwrapped his plaid from his shoulders and covered the bloody, dead babe in the bush. *I canna let Colin see this,* he thought to himself. *'Twill kill him as sure as I stand here.* He then turned to the others who were immobile with horror.

"Quickly!" Keith yelled to them. "Take your plaid and cover the body! Quickly, before Colin comes and sees!"

He'd barely completed his command when hoof beats resounded in the woods behind him. He turned and saw Colin approach with his small band. Colin pulled his horse up to a halt, then dismounted, silent the whole time. Keith moved toward him, but Colin put up a hand to stop. He moved toward his wife slowly, as if trying to understand why she lay there on the cold, hard ground. Then he knelt to her, and placing one arm under her head and the other on her slashed belly, Colin pulled her body to his chest and cried out-- a loud thundering cry of all the pain and anguish and horror that one man could contain. Then he lowered his head into that once shiny hair and cried like a child.

The men surrounding him did not know what to do. They waited patiently for the Laird of their clan to slow his tears. They watched as Colin removed his plaid from his shoulders and covered his wife as best he could with one hand, then placed that hand under her legs and lifted her to his horse. Silently he rode back towards Lochnora, slowly, with his proud head lowered in defeat.

When they reached the manor at Lochnora, Colin placed her body on the table amid the keening and wailing of the women in the house. He kissed her blue lips then stood back, watching her as Alyce began to wash the body. Alyce's small daughter, Jenny, stepped forward with a thistle brush and began to work on Caitir's hair. Then Old Keith came in, a small bundle in his arms. He placed the bundle on Caitir's body, then stood back to the shadows to gauge Colin's reaction. The Laird's face twitched, and his eyes flashed with anger and pain, but he didn't move or make a sound otherwise. Father MacBain rushed in and spoke to Old Keith first, who recommended a quick funeral, burying mother and child together. When Father MacBain approached Colin to confirm, Colin made no acknowledgement of hearing the priest's words. Father MacBain left Colin's side to begin preparations for the funeral, which were to take place the next day.

Colin watched the preparation of his dead wife and child, staying with them the entire night. He did not leave their side, even when the clansmen took the body to the cemetery. Colin followed his wife's body through the misty rain. He watched silently as both his wife and the babe were laid in one coffin, then lowered into the ground. As Father MacBain spoke, Colin reached down, grasped a handful of the grainy black dirt, and threw it into the grave. He stood and looked up to the sky, the light rain wetting his hair, beard, and face. Then he turned and marched back to Broch Lochnora. He went to his chambers that he had shared with his wife, closed the chamber door, and secured it against any intruders. He stayed in that chamber, undisturbed, for six days. Not Keith, Alyce, nor his own sons could entice him to leave that chamber.

When he emerged six days later, the robust Colin MacLeod was a sickly old man. He commanded his things to be removed to a separate chamber, and he never entered his old chamber again. Colin MacLeod was a different, changed man from that day on.

CHAPTER ONE

An Auspicious Beginning

THE YELLOW AND WHITE kitten peeked its face from beneath a shady bush and caught Meg's eye. Enamored with the little cat and its pretty face, Meg bent down to collect it. The kitten, however, had other plans and scuttled deeper into the bush. Not to be put off, Meg ventured farther under the leafy branches, and found the little rascal cowering against the roots.

"Ye wee *screb*," Meg scolded. "Get ye here, and I might find a bit o' food for ye."

The kitten tried to shy away deeper, but Meg was quick to grasp the kitten's scruff, and pulled it from the bush. The kitten rewarded her with a scratch on her hand.

"Vicious wee thing, ye are," she cooed softly to the kitten. She petted the small, frightened animal, and soon it was purring, cuddled against her. Meg placed the kitten in her sack, and let it sleep in the hidden comfort of her bag. She then reclined to take in a last look of her quiet little demesne before heading for home.

Lochnora was a small village that the MacLeod clan had inhabited for generations. In the Western Highlands, the land was tough and the soil rocky, but mountains, lakes, and wooded lands made it a paradise for those who sought to see it as such. It was also fairly close to the sea, and if Meg closed her eyes, she was sure she could smell the tang of the ocean though she had never seen it. Meg had never been farther than a short walk from her father's house, which is why Meg's private little glen was a treasure to her.

Meg found the little brook, that formed a small loch of a pool, several years before. Perfectly shaded from the heat of the day, and from the under-used road that led past her father's croft, she often came to her private Eden when she wished to be away from her brothers and sisters. The eldest of six, she was oft left to tend to the younger Lachlans, including the bairn, Innes. She found that coming to this "little Loch," as she dubbed it, quieted her mind, and a bath in the small pool rested her body. Time was fleeting, however, and she had to return to her responsibilities long before she felt ready. Today was no exception.

Brushing the dust from her plaid, Meg took up her sack, checked on her fellow traveler, and worked her way toward the path to her home. She longed to stay in the quiet glen, content with her thoughts and the view of the green and heather but knew that her mother would soon notice her gone. Not wanting to alert her father, nor have her private garden intruded upon, she traipsed through the bushes to the main road.

As she focused on her path home, she neglected to glance back on the less traveled path, lost in thought. This far north of the village, 'twas rare to have any travelers on this road. It was only the sound of hooves that disrupted her reverie, not the guffaws of the Englishmen on the horses. She turned and paled when she saw who approached.

"Well, men, it looks like we have a Scottish lass here today," announced the largest of the men.

All three looked unkempt, as if it had been years since their skin had touched water, not the typical month that most men forgo. Knowing she was in trouble either way, and proving, at least to herself, that she was as brave as the mightiest Highland warrior, she glared at the man who spoke of her, then darted off into the woods. Her skirt made it difficult to run, and she hiked it up over her knees to run faster. Brambles scratched her feet and branches caught at her skirts and hair. She could hear them following her through the brush - and they sounded very close.

English deserters! she thought and cursed softly to herself. *If I hadna tarried so long in the glen.* As of late, soldiers who had left Longshanks' army had been terrorizing northern lands, even the MacLeod lands, as if their clan did not have enough to worry about, what with the conflict with Clan MacKay. At first, the English rogues had only stolen crops and livestock, but they had recently grown more worrisome and aggressive, attacking crofters, and had maimed Ramsay's oldest son, causing him to lose the use of a hand. King Robert the Bruce was too busy keeping the English at bay and trying to keep peace among the clans to worry himself over a few English army stragglers, and these stragglers pressed that advantage.

Meg only stopped running when the hand on her shoulder threatened to crush her bones. She was caught by these dirty Englishmen. Now she had another worry. She hoped that whatever entertainments they desired with her would last only a short while, for she had been absent too long, and soon her mother would send one of her sisters to find her. Meg knew she had the strength, if not the courage, to face what these rogues had in mind, but she would do anything to protect her family. She spun to face her captors.

"English dogs! Lay your hand off me!" she screamed at them as loud as her quivering voice could manage. She was yanking away, trying to pull herself free when an arrow caught one of the men in the arm, knocking him from his horse. With the Englishmen's attention diverted, Meg seized the opportunity to run for the meager safety of a near-by bush. Three men burst into the small clearing, two of them obviously younger than the third. The third man was older than her eighteen years, but not much. From her hiding spot, she watched as they seized the fallen man and attacked the other two. With one of her attackers dead from an arrow to the chest, another Englishmen managed to ride off away from the village into the horizon. The three young men were able to subdue the third.

The three Scots paused to catch their breath and bind the captured man so he could not escape. They stood panting for a moment before they spoke.

"Ewan," said one of the younger men, "what are ye goin' to do wi' him?"

The oldest of the three looked thoughtful for a moment, evaluating the Englishman. This afforded Meg an excellent opportunity to take in the one called "Ewan." He was much taller than the other two, and much wider through the chest, which told her that he had reached manhood while the other two were still young men, probably just having reached an age of five and ten or so. The oldest did bear a striking resemblance to the younger men, which told her that they were probably brothers. They all had rich black hair, and Ewan's hair was long enough to reach his shoulders in ragged waves. However, it was his eyes that caught her attention - such a shade of blue she had never seen on a man before. Meg saw he held a bow - obviously the one that felled the Englishman, and since it was quite an accurate shot from atop a horse, she assumed he was an expert marksman as well.

"Weel, Ewan?" continued the younger, much to the aggravation of his brother.

"Christ, man! Can't ye shut up and let me think?" The older brother's voice was strong and rich, and his response hinted at a deep anger, whether towards the Englishman or his annoying brother, Meg didn't know.

They wore the MacLeod plaid of black and red with hints of yellow, and the three brothers looked exceptionally muscular, especially the oldest, since he was in full manhood. The hair on Ewan's strong legs was as dark as the hair on his head, making his skin look sun-kissed, as though it were Beltane, though it was only early spring.

At that moment, the little kitty decided to make his appearance and leapt out of her sack in front of the bush she was using for cover. Without taking a hand off their prisoner, all three brothers turned in her direction, dirks and swords in hand. Still shaking, Meg stepped out, scooped up the kitten, and faced her would-be rescuers.

"Well, now we ken what the English rats were after," the third brother finally spoke. They looked her over with obvious scrutiny, trying to piece together what had happened, or almost happened, in the road.

"And ye are?" asked the oldest.

"Meg Lachlan of Clan MacLeod. I live wi' my family no' far from this road."

"Lachlan? Is your Da a farmer and ye mother the midwife?"

"Aye, they are," Meg answered warily. "And ye are?"

The one called Ewan glanced at his brothers, and they all smiled. The oldest looked back at her and replied, "Aye, well, I guess we can't all recognize the MacLeods of MacLeod, now can we?"

His voice was stern, but the subtle laughter in his eyes was lost on Meg, who was embarrassed and slightly ashamed that she had been unable to recognize the sons of her Laird. Regarding them now, she of course noticed that their plaids and tunics didn't appear worn, and all their weapons looked as though they had recently been forged. Even their horses resembled finery, now that she cared to notice. These weren't mere crofters; these were the sons of her Laird. 'Twas almost an insult not to know them.

"Oh, forgive me. I dinna ken ye," Meg responded, flustered. The dark-haired man laughed loudly, in an almost condescending manner.

"I'm Ewan MacLeod, and these two are my brothers, Hamish and Duncan," he said, with a short gesture towards the two younger men. He then looked her over, and she suddenly felt out of place in the presence of her Laird's sons, with disheveled hair, dusty clothes, and an unruly kitten in her hand.

"What were ye doin' out here, by yourself?" he asked.

"Weel, I was walking, and found this wee *screb* of a kitty here, and then the English were upon me." As she spoke, she realized she sounded simple, as if she were a wandering idiot, but she did not want the Laird's sons to know about her private glen, or that she had been lingering there alone.

"Well, let's get ye home then," Ewan said offhandedly, as though she were another chore on his list of many. Ewan and his brothers were lifting the Englishman they captured onto Hamish's horse when she started to protest.

"No, that is no' needed. I just live up the road."

"Hamish, Duncan," Ewan called over his shoulder to his brothers, not taking his eyes off Meg, "take the *Sassenach* back to the castle. Make sure he is well supervised. He is no' to get away."

Meg thought that was a lot of responsibility to put on the younger MacLeod lads, but decided not to comment. Ewan was sure to know his brothers well enough. He helped lift the prisoner onto Hamish's horse, and then the two young men sped off. Ewan turned to her.

"Weel, lass, let's see ye home."

"Oh." She was caught unaware, not expecting to be escorted home by the Laird's son. "Well, I live down the road, ye see, so 'tis no' necessary."

"No' necessary?" Ewan sounded incredulous. "After ye are nearly ravished by English scoundrels? I think no'."

Grabbing her around her waist, he lifted her onto his horse then swung up behind her, nudging the horse forward. He wrapped one arm around her and held the reins tightly in his other hand. She marveled at how well he handled the beast. Not having been on a horse before, she awed at the height and speed at which she traveled, and shortly they arrived at her family's small croft.

The croft was typical of most clansmen and women, with short, squared-off sides and a single open door. The wood and peat roof hung low, helping to keep in the heat during even the coldest winters. Meggie's croft, however, was much farther off the main road to the village and up to the Laird's house. It was the northernmost croft of the clan, surrounded by large tracts of grass and trees, buttressed by rock, which was fortunate for Lachlan who mainly raised some sheep and goats. At the front of the croft sat a trough of water for easy household access and heaps of peat to throw on the fire when necessary. Ewan caught sight of a small garden off to one side, where the family raised some onions and cucumber.

Overall, the croft was fairly isolated in this location, so Ewan could understand how a family could feel secure in their surroundings. That left Meggie more open to an attack upon her person. What Ewan could not understand was how such a large family, like Meggie Lachlan's, could fit in so small a house. Perchance it made them closer as a family?

Meg began to wiggle in an attempt to slide off the steed, but the Laird's son grasped her more tightly around the waist and held her atop the horse. He moved his arm up and grasped her breast as he forced a rough kiss on her unyielding lips. Straining against him, she pushed at his chest until he pulled away. He grinned at her with a boyish look on his face, as though he had done nothing wrong. Meg straightened her clothes, then shifted in the saddle and slapped Ewan as hard as she could. She finished her slide off the horse, angry as a bee. She glared up at his feigned surprise and whacked him on the leg for added good measure.

"What?" he asked innocently.

"What do ye *think* ye were doing?"

His grin widened. "I'm the Laird's son, soon to be the Laird. Most lassies would be honored to be in your position." He was almost leering at her. Her eyes widened in an appalled glare.

"An honor, ye say? In the eyes of the Lord God, 'tis a sin! My mother says that a woman's body is a privilege, and that privilege is for her husband only! Ye would no' put your hands on an honorable woman that way!"

"The position ye were in with the English might indicate ye are something other than honorable," he insinuated, lifting one raven-black eyebrow.

Her own pale eyebrows rose nearly off her face at his statement. "How dare ye? Ye think yourself so great that women should lose their honor 'acause ye are the Laird's son? Ye leave your less than honorable hands to yourself."

She stormed off just as her father turned from the side of the croft. Connor Lachlan was an older man who often felt and looked older than his true age. Years of work herding goats and trying to maintain the few crops to keep his large family fed and pay taxes and tenant fees had bowed his legs and caused his back to slump. His hair had gone almost all gray, and he was starting to lose some off the top of his head. His clothes were always worn and dirty, no matter how often Elspeth washed and patched them. Lachlan held a makeshift shovel in his hand, and Meg was relieved that he did not witness the altercation with the Laird's son. Her father immediately recognized the lord of the demesne.

"Milord MacLeod," her father addressed the Laird's son with respect. "To what do we owe this honor?"

Ewan smirked at that comment. "Your daughter encountered some English scoundrels down the road, and fortunately, I happened along to rescue the damsel in distress." He turned and flashed his smile at her. He could see she was embarrassed, pink as her cheeks were, and he liked how it made her glow. Her skin was almost the same color as her reddish blonde hair when she blushed.

"Ooh," her father started. Fear crossed his features, but Meg smiled at her father to relieve his worry. Meg took her father's hand and patted it like one would a child.

"Father, the brash and brawny Ewan MacLeod was a great savior. I was naught in any danger." She turned towards Ewan and gave him a small curtsey. "I thank ye, sir, for your rescue." Then she swirled in a huff and retreated to the safety of the croft where her mother stood near the doorway. She heard Ewan bid leave of her father and ride off. Meg's mother looked worriedly at her daughter, wondering what trouble had followed her home this time.

"Wee Meggie, pray tell me that ye are no' in trouble this time. I heard a man's voice outside."

Meg knew her mother was worried about her daughter's innocence. As a young woman, the best both Meg and Meg's mother could hope for her was a well-to-do crofter to ask for her hand, which would never be an option if Meg's innocence was in question.

Meg smiled at her mother to allay her fears. "Worry not, mother. 'Twas the Laird's son himself who escorted me home."

Meg's mother raised her eyebrows in disbelief at this -- her mother had heard about the escapades of Ewan MacLeod.

"He was a true gentleman, mum," she assured her mother, who had three daughters to worry about: Mairi, who had seen 12 summers, and wee Anne, who had not yet seen 10 years. However, 'twas Meg who worried her the most. After 18 summers, she had yet to find a suitable husband. Now going into her 19th summer, her mother prayed nightly that a decent groom would be found. She had talked with mothers and grandmothers at market days, asking after sons, grandsons, nephews, and cousins. Thus far there had been few prospects for the daughter of a poor crofter, but the prospects would be even fewer if gossip surfaced that the Laird's son had been seen with Meg. Elspeth bit her lip with worry. She handed Meg a wooden bowl and spoon, and Meg took them, silently stirring the ingredients together.

While Meg's mother sat at the table and fretted about her daughter, Meg's father was relieved to see the Laird's son leave the croft. Meg herself did not know why she defended him to her parents. Perhaps 'twas out of gratitude for saving her from the English; mayhap 'twas out of respect for the dying Laird. Everyone in the demesne knew about the sickness that was slowly ebbing away the life of their current Laird, Colin MacLeod, leaving most of the land's control to his sons, particularly the oldest. Ewan would soon be the new Laird of the clan. Impetuous, wild, and counting the days until he would be in full control, Ewan spent most of his time with either his claymore or a woman, and the tales were well known among the lands.

Later that day, Ewan caught up with his brothers, who told him they had thrown the English bastard into the dungeon, but since he was unconscious, he was not talking. Ewan decided to approach his father.

The Laird MacLeod of Lochnora lay on his bed, as he had for months since deciding to give up his battle with the coughing disease. It had been troublesome since his stay in the English towers, with too many wet drafts and too little warmth. With the death of his wife, so also died his will to live. His only regret was that the cough was taking so long to consume him. However, the extended length of his death sentence did afford him the opportunity to continue to train his son, who would all-too-soon be Laird.

Ewan, he thought to himself, calling up the image of his eldest son, now a strapping barbarian of a man who bore a striking resemblance to Lady Caitir. Ewan was his greatest pride and his gravest fear, for his son was headstrong, impulsive, and had no misgivings about defying authority, or spitting in the face of tradition. He worried at first about granting Lairdship of the keep, and of the small clan, to his overly headstrong son. Recently, though, his eldest had begun to show the makings of a great leader. Colin knew he would rest well in the afterlife with his wife, should God so desire. Now, if Ewan would keep his hands off the lassies and find himself a wife.

Colin MacLeod had heard that his sons encountered some English vagabonds on MacLeod lands, and this concerned him. While the MacLeods of Lochnora did not have much in the way of land or title, Colin wanted to keep what they did have. His was little more than a keep, and he had no close connections to the King Robert the Bruce, but Colin and his sons were proud of their small demesne. He had hopes that Ewan might take a wife with a bit more privilege than himself, but that seemed to be proving unlikely. On the tail of this thought, Ewan burst through his father's door like a rough wind.

"Hello, Father," Ewan greeted him with a smile. He always tried to be cheerful for his father, who was as large as Ewan, but had seemed to shrink as of late.

"Hello, my son. I have heard news that ye captured one o' these English scrappers and that he now resides in our dungeon. Did I hear the truth?"

"Aye, Father, ye have heard naught but the truth. He was wi' two others, and I would like to get their names from him before we kill him." With regards to the English, Ewan bore the same fierce hatred as his father, for his mother's death came at English hands, a sin far too great for Ewan to ever forget.

"Well, ye may have to induce him, if ye will, to talk. The English usually need a bit o' incentive to loosen their tongues." Colin grinned at his son over the innuendoes.

"What I can no' believe is that the English were this far north. We have no' had much trouble with the English since."

"No, not since," Colin repeated quietly, and Ewan was sorry that he had alluded to his mother's death.

"What did they want?" Colin asked.

"I dinna ken," replied Ewan. "They were quite taken with a slight bonny lass they encountered off the road. I think they meant to make sport o' her and I was compelled to intrude. Excellent reason, me thinks, to dispose of the English, especially those on our land."

"Who was the lass? Did ye ken her?"

"Aye, the midwife's eldest daughter, caught tarrying too long unawares. Wee Meggie Lachlan," Ewan answered with a smart grin on his face.

"Ahh, no' so wee as I think. She is but a score of years, aye?"

"Aye, Father, but whilst I tried to make her one of my 'petty indiscretions,' as ye so call them, she spurned me, claiming purity for her future husband," Ewan snorted.

"Ye have met your match in such a lass then. Her good mother is raising her well. Ye still have your pride in check after such abuses, my son?"

Ewan flashed his father a grin that so strongly resembled his mother's, Colin was taken aback momentarily, and his heart skipped.

"Aye, my pride will heal. 'Twas but a minor insult."

Colin raised one eyebrow at his son. "A minor insult? From such a bonny lass, I would think ye were permanently damaged." Colin laughed heartily and followed that with a series of coughs. Ewan's eyes narrowed, and he changed the subject before this father coughed himself to death before his eyes.

"Do ye think they will return again, Father? What could they want with us?"

Ewan was not unaware of Lochnora's political insignificance. This truly did not bother him, for Ewan had no interest in having his life run by the crown, but if the English were near, that could mean something else altogether.

"I dinna ken if we will see them again. Mayhap ye scared them away, but I would wager they will return. Through our MacLeod lands is the most direct route to reach more northerly ports, and with John of Argyll an English sympathizer, we can no' guess what they would do."

"Aye, Father, I think ye are correct. They are like leeches, no? When you spot one, ye ken that more are around, sucking at your life." Colin laughed softly at his son's comparison. "Then I will put a message out to be wary of English stragglers, and for women to take company when leaving their homesteads."

Pride swelled in Colin's chest at his son's decisiveness, and he was once again assured that Clan MacLeod would be in capable hands when he passed on.

CHAPTER TWO

Between a Rock and A Hard Place

EDWARD MONTGOMERY ACCOSTED CONNOR Lachlan as he herded his sheep towards the small pen behind his croft. Montgomery was taller than most Englishmen, which made him as tall as many Scotsmen in the Highlands. His yellow-gold eyes never smiled; instead, they reflected an inner coldness. He was a man of war and weapons and known for his success as a cold-hearted mercenary, often hired out to conduct some of the worst atrocities known to man. A ragged scar on the side of his face, from temple to jaw, testified to the slaughter this man had seen.

Here, in the Highlands, however, he had been told to rein in some of his ruthlessness. His employers did not seek death upon these people, only the land itself. Killing was to be the very last resort. In Montgomery's opinion, his employers should let him kill them all and have God sort them out, but for the price, he would obey his employer's instructions, for now.

A powerful man with chestnut hair, Montgomery controlled every situation, and within his realm of influence, his word was law. He inspired fear into nearly everyone he met. Lachlan had sent his eight-year-old son, Able, home with word to his wife that he would arrive shortly and to have the eventide meal ready. The appearance of Montgomery made Lachlan glad in his decision to send the boy ahead.

"I hear your eldest daughter had a brief encounter with some of my associates this day." Montgomery grinned at Lachlan, who groaned inwardly. Montgomery leaned easily against a sapling, as one neighbor greeting another. His horse was busy chewing on the sparse grass nearby. However, as an aging father with a comely daughter, Connor felt his skin crawl at Montgomery's appearance and comment.

"Aye, but she managed to remedy the situation well enough," he replied.

"Yea, I also heard that the Old Laird's son took it upon himself to rescue your lass. Quite fortunate, aye?"

"Ye promised that my family would no' be harmed," Lachlan remarked pointedly.

He now regretted his encounter with Montgomery and the blackmail means by which he became associated with the English. A poor attempt to protect his family, he should have known not to trust this man, or the English at all.

"Well, that was an oversight, I guess we can call it. I don't think my men knew it was your daughter."

"And now they ken, and will leave her alone?" Connor despised the sound of begging in his voice but would not let these men wreak havoc on his family.

"Well, there is the problem, you see. You have not been very forthcoming with information regarding the MacLeod movement as promised. We think you may need additional incentive to acquire this information."

"No' my daughter!" Connor Lachlan's heart stopped beating momentarily. Montgomery laughed lightly.

"Not how you think, old man. We found it interesting how the Laird's son took interest in your wee Meggie and believe that might help us in our cause."

"I do no' understand ye, man."

"'Tis simple enough. If we trouble your bonny lass, perchance the Laird's rebellious son will take it upon himself to ensure her safety, and where better than the safety of the Laird's own keep? Once there, she can bring you news of anything she hears."

"Ye canna mean to make my own lass a spy? And within the Laird's own keep?" Connor gasped, shock apparent in his voice.

"Well, she doesn't have to know she is a spy, now does she? She can be an unknowing player who provides you with what you need to keep your family safe, aye?"

Connor was quiet. He was trapped. To say no could mean he would be brought out as a spy, a treasonous offense, and suffer his family to the mercies of these English brigands. To say yes would mean to sacrifice his daughter. He stared at the ground, weighing his options. If the Laird's son did not take in his daughter, then the situation might work out to his favor. *Perchance.*

"Aye. Jus' be kind to her. Dinna take advantage of her. We will see if my bonny lass becomes a favorite of the Laird's son."

Montgomery reached for his horse and mounted up. "Excellent decision, Lachlan. A pleasure as always." Montgomery tipped his hat, tugged on the reins of his horse, and rode away. Lachlan stood amongst his sheep, offering a prayer to God that the Laird's fickle interest in women would prevent his daughter from coming to harm. He then turned back to his sheep and herded them home.

Connor walked into his small croft and found Meggie and her mother sitting at the table. His other children were scattered about the room, with the babe in a cradle near the hearth. His gaze turned toward his eldest child, who looked so startling like her mother. Her hair was not quite brown, not quite red, with highlights that made her hair a molten bronze. She had hazel eyes that could be the color of soft leather when content, or if angry, green as the grass after the rain. The most he could have ever hoped for her was to find her a decent husband, maybe the son of another local farmer, and now he was willing to risk her innocence, her life, to save his family, and admittedly his own self. It was treason -- he could be hanged -- but it was his *family,* and he was a poor old man with no recourse. What else could he do to protect them? He tried to justify his decision. *'Tis in the best interest of my family.* But somehow, this brought him no reprieve. He walked over to his wife and sat at the table.

"What is there for sup this fine eve?"

The English were honest in their plan. Every day, a sickened Lachlan would usher his daughter out of the house for one errand or another - helping herd sheep, milking goats, drawing water from the well, retrieving small animals from the traps - to afford the English the opportunity to accost her.

One evening, near gloaming, Meg was pulling the bucket up from the well. It was a warm evening, summer seemingly arrived early, and Meg rested the bucket on the edge of the well, wiping her sweaty hair out of her eyes. She tugged at the ragged scrap of linen that held her hair back and tried to refasten her hair. With a sigh, she gave a useless wish for a fancy ribbon with which to tie her hair into a fashionable queue. Something long and silky and colorful to bind her hair securely had long been a dream of hers. She had seen some girls and women purchase them at the village when she went with her mother to market, but not many could afford such luxuries; usually, ribbons were only purchased for a wedding. Once she saw a merchant's family pass through the village, and all three daughters had a rainbow of ribbon in their hair. Meg knew her thought was but a vain one, one that would cause her mother, if she heard Meg voice it, to chastise her. "We are beautiful in the gifts God gives us," Meg could hear her mother's voice echo in her head. Sighing again, she grasped the bucket and was straining to lift it when she felt rather than heard someone behind her. She left the bucket on the edge of the well and spun around.

Looming over her was a mildly handsome man, brown-haired, a scar on his cheek. Behind him were three more men, much worse for wear than the one directly in front of her. She recognized one of the men from her attack in the glen, but when she opened her mouth to scream, the large man clapped a hand over her mouth. The force of it caused her to shuffle backwards, and she heard the water bucket as it fell off the edge of the well and hit the water. The man grasped the back of her shoulders to steady her and watched as his shining eyes roved over her form. His hand tasted like dirt and smelled of horse and sweat. Meg tried to stop trembling but couldn't, and when the man leaned in close, what little control she had left slipped away.

"My men were right," he spoke with a tight English accent. "You are a tasty bit of baggage." He pressed his face close to hers, his breath steaming in her ear, and she squeaked in protest.

"I could have you, here and now," he breathed, his voice barely above a whisper, "and no one would save you this time. Not your mighty Laird, and certainly not your father. Where would you be then, lass, eh?"

Suddenly he shoved her way, pushing her down to the ground as he laughed with his men. He turned and spit in her hair, then slipped away into the night while Meg lay gasping in the dirt. She stayed on the ground, trying to regain herself when she heard her father calling for her in a panicked voice. In a crazy moment of annoyance, she realized her hair had come loose from the linen strap again.

Connor Lachlan raced to his daughter as the men rounded the far side of the thatched stable. Only when Meg heard the horses ride off did she stop shaking. Meg took several deep breaths as her father patted her back in a weak effort to comfort her, and she slowly felt herself calm down. Her scrap of linen lay in the mud of the spilt bucket. Connor watched as she regained composure, then, as she adjusted her hair out of her face once more, he retrieved her fallen bucket out of the well and filled the small pail. He took the pail in one hand and Meg's hand in the other to walk her home.

Connor escorted a tear-stained Meg into the house, where Elspeth, his wife, glared at him. Sometimes he wondered if his wife did have the gift of second sight and saw right through him to what he had permitted to come to pass. Elspeth sat her daughter down and retrieved a cup of milk for her, holding her hand in reassurance. Aside from a dirty shift, she was unharmed, and Meg assured her mother as such. Casting another glare at Connor, Elspeth helped Meg behind the curtain and put her to bed. After checking on her other children in a panicked mother's response to danger, she turned her anger on her husband.

"Ye must do something, husband," Elspeth pleaded, not understanding why Lachlan did not see the danger in his daughter's situation. When he didn't reply, she grabbed his arm imploringly. "Please," she begged in a ragged whisper. For the first time in their marriage, Connor turned away from his wife and left her scared and wondering.

⇛⇛⇛ ⇚⇚⇚

Elspeth was more than upset at the interest the English had in her daughter; she was afraid for Meg's safety. Why would the English harass her daughter? Meg was a bonny girl, yes, but to what end did the English want with her? Not one Englishman had violated her, though she had been threatened. There seemed to be no reason for their interest, and the fact she could not guess their reasoning decided for her. Since her husband, the girl's own father, felt no inclination to assist, Elspeth needed help from a higher power. In a bold move, she set out the next morning to visit the Laird to see what he could do. Given the MacLeod's weakened state, she met with his son who was presently Laird by proxy, destined to take over clan leadership after his father passed into the next world.

Ewan strode into the front hall. He was tired - he had not slept well the night before. His thoughts had drifted from his father to the recent problems with the English to the copper haired lass he had met days before. He had fallen asleep late and was awake early to skirmish with Gavin, his man-at-arms and long-time friend. He must not have looked too worse for wear, since Elspeth gave him an approving once-over before she approached him.

"Master Ewan?" she queried. Ewan paused and studied the woman for a moment.

"Aye. Ye must be the midwife - I met your daughter when she found herself in a bit o' trouble." He paused and raised an eyebrow at her. "Ye will be wanting to discuss her encounters wi' the English?"

Ewan had wondered how long it would be before Elspeth and her husband requested an audience regarding their daughter. If the rumors were correct, and Elspeth's presence assured him that they were, Meg's incidents with the English had increased, both in number and unfortunately, in severity. Elspeth proceeded to tell him of the events of the preceding night and then beg for help.

"An additional guard near the road, a warning throughout the land, something. Please, milord," she pleaded. "'Twould mean the safety of my wee Meggie."

Ewan raised his other eyebrow at this, remembering Meg's previous encounter with the English scoundrels, her large eyes wide with fear, leaves and twigs in her hair from running in through trees. He also recalled her reaction to his trying to take some pleasure in her -- short of the slap in the face, she told him his advances were not wanted. She seemed strong, standing up to both him and the English, and it maddened him to know that. As much as he liked to play the hero, he had not rescued her as much as he thought he had.

"Aye. We will send out some more scouts, to look out for this band of English, and to assist those who might encounter them. And ye try to keep Meggie closer to home. Would that satisfy ye?"

Elspeth nodded, more than happy with the Laird's son's decision. He could have turned a cold heart to the plight of her daughter, but instead took his clanswomen under his protection. Ignoring the possibility that Ewan could have an ulterior motive, Elspeth was certain that he would be a grand leader indeed and told him so.

"That would be more than generous, milord. Ye are a great man to do so."

Ewan crossed his arms over his broad chest and gave the midwife a sidelong appraisal. He'd heard the rumors about her gift of second sight but tried to dismiss it as petty, ancient beliefs. However, those ancient beliefs were not too far in his past - his own mother believed in many of them - and maybe this woman had a gift after all.

"A great man? Would ye know that to be true, Midwife Lachlan?" he questioned her. Elspeth raised her sharp green eyes to the young man, evaluating the intent behind his question. He could be trying to flush her out as a pagan, but many already knew of her, and probably so did the Laird's son. She had heard that the Laird's dead wife was a believer in the old ways. Maybe he was trying to elicit knowledge for his own peace of mind. Elspeth looked him in the eye.

"Aye, milord, ye shall be a great man indeed. Unorthodox, worrisome to a few, but ye are a man who will always do what is right, which may not be what is proper, ye ken? Your people will always trust ye as long as ye give them leave to do so."

Ewan smiled at that, wondering if she knew how close to the truth she came. He nodded to her. "Anything more?"

"Nay," she smiled at him. "That is all, my young Laird." She turned and departed, leaving Ewan to ponder the meaning of her last words.

After the midwife left, Ewan paced the room for a time, recalling the incident with the English outlaws and the midwife's daughter. Meg - that was her name. He remembered flowing hair, and how she looked like a wood sprite standing up to the fearsome English. Stubborn, she was, as he also remembered how she rejected him when he brought her home.

Soon, the small demesne would be his responsibility. He had promised the midwife that he would guard his land and all its inhabitants with more scouts, and who better to assist in that endeavor than the brawny son of the Laird himself? It would give him something to do during the day and show his clansmen that he was a man who meant what he said. Most politic. And if he happened upon a wood sprite in distress, what better than to be her savior from a terrible fate? Ewan rushed up the stairwell, bellowing out his brothers' names as he went. They would be ecstatic to spend the next few days hunting English scoundrels.

Ewan stumbled upon such a fortunate event just two days later.

CHAPTER THREE

When Opportunity Knocks

AFTER SEVERAL SMALL EXCURSIONS near the croft, Meg took it into her head to venture to her secluded area in the glen to bathe. Headstrong? Yes. Meg figured if the English thought she was still near home, they would ride there to confront her. The glen itself was hidden off the road well enough; the chance of discovery was slim. Also, she noticed that the men didn't really seem to try anything now, mostly making empty threats. Meg thought it odd behavior all in all. Plus, she craved a bath and felt it worth a small risk to get it. 'Twas near Beltane, and while the weather was warm, the water retained the last remnants of winter chill and gave Meg cause to look forward to the oncoming May Day celebrations.

Though not sanctioned by the Church, many of the local priests and clans people still remained somewhat true to the old ways, and Meg's mother was one of them. In fact, her belief in the old ways was one of the reasons why her mother became the midwife for this area and was often called to assist outside of the MacLeod lands. Her mother had taken it upon herself to teach her children about the old ways, so they would not be lost among the new religion that had overrun Scotland. Many had already fallen far from the older religions, including Meg's own father, but most women in the area still encouraged the old ways with children, and Beltane, now called "May Day" was still celebrated with much fanfare. Perhaps this half-year celebration of awakening and fertility would lead to her meeting a husband and being fertile with him.

Spending what little free time she had found to rest her body and mind by the small pool, Meg decided that a bath would be just what she needed. Meg kept her woolen kirtle and plaid close to the bank, knowing she would want to rush into them after bathing in the chilly water. Clad only in her shift, she waded into the loch, gasping as the pool's chill soaked her legs. Once she was accustomed to the temperature, she ventured in farther, shivering as cool waves caressed her skin. She splashed the cold water on her face and over her hair, and then, feeling chilled to the bone, she waded back to her clothes.

She put her hand on the pile of skirts when she heard the horses ride into the glen and halt near the pool. *Oh, this is most unfortunate,* she thought to herself. She did not even have to look at the ragged red cloaks to know that the horsemen were English. At least she did not see the tall, scarred man from before. *That's looking on the bright side, at least,* she thought.

"Well," started the man closest to her, "what have we here? A mermaid perhaps? Or a silkie?"

"Nay," called another, "a local wench laid in wait!"

Meg slowly gathered up her clothes, trying to cover herself while drawing as little notice as possible to her state of undress.

"Here, my lady," the first one said, nudging his horse closer to her, "let me help ye with your gown."

He reached down and grabbed the skirts out of her hands, leaving her with only her plaid shawl to cover herself with. She could feel the shift cling to her skin and did not want to imagine what view she was granting them. Meg dared not look at the men. She had a vague notion of what when on between a man and a woman, her mother had helped explain a bit on that, but she had more often heard of women who were forced by men -- usually Englishmen, their reputation not without reason. Forcing a woman seemed to be almost a pastime for the English, and now Meg was caught in a state of undress, her shift clinging damply to her curves, and surrounded by several men.

Her mother didn't raise her none too daft, and she groaned inwardly in a panic, realizing that she may be a victim of these English men. If she had a dirk with her, she would have used it on herself. 'Twould be better than bringing the shame of this on her parents. But as it was, she was weaponless, and at their mercy. She could only hope that if she were quiet and compliant, they would be done quickly.

The Englishman then swung down from his horse, casting her clothes to the side. Meg stood rock-still as the brigand approached her. He grabbed her hair, forcing her head back so he could stare into her face. From her position, she could look him in the eyes, which were dark brown and hidden under bushy brows of a similar color. His scraggly beard barely hid cracked and browning teeth. His top tooth was missing.

"As pretty as one o' your silkies, eh?"

He patted her cheek. His breath reeked of stale ale and fish. Compliant or not, Meg decided she had to fight. Her mother did not raise a sapling. Grabbing his hand from her face, she spat on him. He loosened his hold on her hair in shock, and she took the slight opportunity to try and flee. Too slight of an opportunity, for his hands were still wrapped in her hair, and he yanked her back roughly. She yelped at the pain.

It was a scream that Ewan heard when he was on the road, close to where he had last encountered the midwife's daughter with the English. His horse picked its way quickly through the woods as Ewan followed the source of the noise.

He stopped short. Through the brush, three English were enthralled with some activity before them. Ewan changed his angle, deftly stepping through the dense underbrush, and saw another man wrestling with a scantily clad woman. He weighed his options. Four on one was not good odds, but he had the element of surprise on his side, and from the way the lass was fighting, he figured that maybe he could count on her for at least minimal support.

Hiding in the brush, he drew an arrow from the quiver, aimed, and hit his target. One of the horsemen fell awkwardly. The other two reacted quickly, and Ewan managed to land another arrow in the arm of the second horseman. The man who had been wrestling with the lass lost his interest in her and turned his attention toward the attack, following the third horseman. As Ewan aimed a third arrow, he hoped to fell this one and meet the footman man to man.

The third arrow hit its mark, and the man fell to the ground in a swirl of tarnished red. *What pathetic warriors these English are,* Ewan thought as he leapt out of his hiding space behind the bush. He grasped the hilt of his sword, running toward the man on foot, when he saw the lass lift a rock.

Meg had no idea what happened as she fought off her aggressor. With one leg wedged between hers, one moment he was trying to lift the hem of her shift, and the next he was gone. She saw him turn towards his cohorts, reaching for his sword. Meg did not know what had stopped the attack on her, but she was probably better off with whoever was attacking the English and decided to seek her own small vengeance. She worked her hand around in the grassy bank of the pond, grabbed a good-sized rock, and grasping it as firmly as she could in her position, bashed it on the back of her attacker's head. He fell hard. She noticed another man with a bloody arm scampering with his horse and ride off.

Suddenly, a flash of plaid emerged beside her.

"Are ye alright?" Ewan put his arm around her to steady her. She looked up at him, and he registered who she was.

"I'm well," she told him, before she fainted at his feet.

When she opened her eyes, she was gazing into a cerulean sea. Her eyes came into focus, and a handsome face floated above hers, blue eyes filled with concern.

"Are ye sure you're alright?" he asked. She blinked and sat up quickly. Her head swam, and she placed her hand on her head to pull her thoughts together.

"Aye."

Then she looked up and realized 'twas the same man who had rescued her before, and an awkward sensation skittered over her back. Ewan's shift was dirtied from the scuffle, and the pommel of his claymore stuck up from the scabbard strapped to his back. His plaid was not draped over his shoulder and she remembered her undressed condition. Glancing down at herself, she saw that he had covered her with his plaid. She suddenly felt like a shamed little child, forcing him to take care of her. Meg apologized.

"I am sorry, milord. I did no' mean to have ye involved. Ye did no' have to . . ." she trailed off, unsure of what to say. She glimpsed his face and noted his look of shock.

"Didna have to? Lass, if I hadna, what do ye think would have happened? I dinna care to think of what would have happened had I no' been involved." He paused for a moment. Her head had dropped downward, as if she were cowering from him. A rogue smile tugged at his lips.

"After all, Meg, I recall what happened when I tried to get a simple kiss. I did no' think ye would take to four men, none of which were ye husband."

Her head snapped up at him, astonished.

"Ye remember me?" she asked quietly.

"Aye, who could forget such a bonny lass as ye?" He gave her a wry look, then smiled widely. A fierce blush colored her cheeks at his flattery, and then she returned the banter.

"Flattery, eh? Well, ye already know it won't get ye verra far."

He chuckled at her reply and found himself reaching up to touch one of her damp, bronzed curls. Now that she was safe, and awake, he realized how worried he was that the English may have harmed her. It came with a stab of ire towards the English, as thoughts like these always did, but seemed to be a fresher anger this time.

"Aye, weel, maybe more than flattery. Ye are verra bonny. No wonder the English were taken with ye."

That blush brightened profusely at his compliment, and she turned her face away from his. 'Twas then that she noticed one of the Englishmen close to them, slumped over in his own blood. She searched about to find two more dirty red clumps among the brush. He had killed to save her, a lowly crofter's daughter. Again, she was a burden. Wrapping the plaid tightly around herself, she averted her eyes. Her private glen was no longer private. The beauty of her glen had grayed from its earlier bright green, and she shivered.

"Thank ye, for rescuing me. I really didna want English company this day." She paused. "Again, ye didna have to," she said quietly. He took her chin in his large and surprisingly warm hand and lifted her face to his.

"Aye, wee Meggie, I did." He gave her another warm smile. "If it worries ye, then be glad that ye gave me a reason to kill the English. 'Tis always a joy for me."

She pulled her chin out of his hand. "How did ye find me? 'Tis a fairly private glen, or so I thought." She looked accusingly at the Englishman piled next to them.

"I heard ye scream from the road. 'Twas no' far off, so I followed the sound."

"Were ye with your brothers on the road?"

"Nay, they are off patrolling elsewhere."

"Patrolling?" Her brow knitted in confusion. He debated whether or not to tell her the truth and decided that lies would serve no purpose.

"Your mother paid me a visit a few days past, concerned for ye. She said that the English had been trying to make sport of ye, and I guess she was rightly concerned. I didna want ye or anyone else to come to harm, so I sent out guards to watch o'er the land."

While she was surprised to learn that her mother had sought out the Laird, Meg was not noticeably shocked over her mother's actions. Her mother was a woman of action, while her father seemed much more passive.

"Guards, aye. But why were ye out as well? Surely ye were not patrolling?"

"Ye are surprised at that?"

"I guess I am."

"Why? What do ye think I do all day? Sit in the parlor sewing?" She laughed at the thought of him sewing in a parlor, and his ears tingled at the sound of her tinkling laugh.

"Weel, nay, I thought that, being the Laird apparent, ye would have more important things to do than patrolling." That awkward sensation returned, and she hoped he didn't think she was insulting him.

"What could be more important than the safety of my clansmen?" He paused for a moment. "Or clanswomen, for that matter." This time his smile was a wide grin, and she was relieved that he was not insulted.

"Again, I'm sorry. I didna think of it that way," she told him honestly. "What will ye do about them?" She nodded towards the dead men.

"I'll send my brothers for them. They will be happy to have some exciting dealings with the English, I think."

They were still sitting in the tall grass. Ewan took Meg's hands in his and gave her a soft look.

"Are ye sure ye are alright? Ye weren't harmed none?"

She sighed. "No, I am quite well, my pride bruised a bit, 'tis all. Before your intervention, I was certain I would no' be well. I may have roughed up the man a bit, but I havena been attacked before. He was larger than I, and I was fair certain I was about to become a disgrace to my family." Meg paused. "I have never hurt someone like that before," she said quietly. "I wasna sure if the rock would do anything. And I was verra frightened."

Ewan looked intently into her bright green eyes. "Well, ye did verra well, for someone so frightened. And dinna worry at all. Ye are safe now, wi' me." He kissed her hand in a gallant manner.

"My dear lady, I will now see ye home," he said with a grand gesture. She laughed softly.

"Aye, milord, this maid thanks ye." She cast her eyes down at herself, covered only in his plaid and her chemise. "A moment to straighten myself?"

Ewan jumped up, raced over to the bank of the lake, and retrieved her clothes.

"And being the gentleman I am, I willna take the advantage t' watch ye dress."

He theatrically covered his eyes and turned his back to her. She laughed again and went a bit deeper into the woods to finish dressing. She returned shortly, handing over his plaid. He led her to his steed that munched absently at the grass, waiting for Ewan's return.

"Ye well remember Fire Foot?" He introduced his horse. "He will no' seem so daunting if ye pat his neck."

Meg reached her hand to the beast's neck and tentatively patted the horse's soft hair that was a shiny black, much like his master's.

"Why did ye name him Fire Foot?" she asked.

"If ye look at his hooves," Ewan gestured toward the horse's legs, "They are verra light, and his hair is so verra dark. When he was birthed, I imagined that, if we saw him run, his feet would look like they were on fire."

"So, he doesna run like his feet are on fire, then?" Meg asked cautiously.

"Only if I wish for him to," Ewan replied.

"Weel, dinna ask him until after ye have returned me home and I am off the beast. Agreed?"

Ewan laughed heartily. "Agreed."

Helping her onto his horse, he lifted himself up behind Meg with ease. She marveled at his movements. His body was warm behind her, almost shockingly so since she was still chilled from her swim in the loch. Without another look at the bodies they left behind, they began to ride toward her home.

"I trust ye will be more of a gentleman than ye were last time?" she asked, a hint of humor in her voice.

"Aye, a bit," he replied with a small laugh.

⤜⤜⤜ ⤛⤛⤛

Once they reached her croft, Ewan slid off the giant horse, and in one swift movement, brought Meg down gently as well. He held her hand in his and turned her face up to meet his gaze.

"A reward for the hero, perhaps?"

"Sir, ye said that ye would be more of a gentleman –"

"Aye," he interrupted, "A bit."

This time he kissed her gently, holding her face in his hands. Meg could not believe all the softness that he put into that kiss. Last time he was forceful and rough, like the man himself, but this time he was gentle and light, and Meg lost herself in the wonder of such a kiss. Then he pulled away, smiling down at her upturned face.

"A just reward for saving your honor, I should think."

Her eyes were as soft as her smile. "Aye, a just reward."

He turned and swung himself back up onto the horse, then leaned down, speaking to her quietly.

"I will do everything in my power to keep ye safe."

She found herself blushing at his statement, despite herself, and did not take leave to the croft until he rode off.

She encountered her mother when she walked into the small house. The midwife's face was strained with worry, and Meg realized how late in the day it was. She also realized how she must look, her hair still damp, unkempt and in disarray, with damp, dirty clothing to match. What must her mother think of her?

"Christ's love, my child!" Elspeth cried, rushing to her daughter. "Where have ye been? Did ye no' see how late in th' day it is?" Meg untangled herself from her mother's strong embrace.

"I'm sorry, Mother. But I ran into a bit o' trouble by the road."

She decided to tell her mother what happened, since it was only by her mother's precaution that she escaped unscathed.

"A bit o' trouble?" Elspeth paled. "What trouble? No' the English again?" Elspeth drew her arms to her chest in a panic. It looked to Meg as though she was holding her own heart.

"Aye the English, but I was no' wounded, thanks to ye."

"Me? Why me?" Elspeth, flustered and confused, was still in a state of worry over her daughter's long absence.

"Weel, I was by the road, after taking a wee dip in a little pool nearby." Meg ignored her mother's stern glance at that. She knew her mother did not like her bathing alone, especially far from home. "I was dressing when I was set upon by the English. I think they would have had their way wi' me. Suddenly the Laird's son himself was there. He took them down and halted the attack on me."

Elspeth noticed the delicate look in her daughter's face when she mentioned the Laird's son. Everyone knew of the youth's penchant for young women, and Elspeth dreaded that her daughter might fall amongst those ranks.

"And the Laird's son brought ye home?" The concern in her mother's voice was unmistakable.

"Aye, Mother. He took me home, straightaway."

Elspeth took her daughter by the hands.

"I was so worrit for ye. It is unsafe for a young maid," she paused. "Especially when the English or a certain Laird's son is near," she spoke with emphasis.

"He was a gentleman, Mother. Ye need no' worry about that. I keep ye words strong in my mind and close t'my heart."

She gently squeezed her mother's hands to reassure her. Elspeth's face softened, as it often did when her eldest was near. She knew her daughter was true of heart and strong of mind. But the midwife also knew that her daughter was naught but a woman, and strength or a true heart only went so far in men's harsh hands.

"I am still naught but a maid, mother. Dinna worry yourself over my honor."

Elspeth smiled at Meg. "Aye, but with that young Laird sniffin' about, ye might see why I have reason for concern."

Elspeth returned to kneading bread on a small table. Meg sat next to her, grabbing a lump of dough for herself.

"Mother, how do ye ken when ye care for a man? I mean truly care?"

Elspeth paused as she chose her words.

"Sometimes there is a moment, ye ken, and ye can say to yourself 'aye, I love this man.' But I think that when ye truly ken, ye dinna have to ask yourself if ye love or no'. Ye just do."

They worked quietly for a while, and then Meg ventured another question.

"Mother, when the English found me by the pool, I was certain I was going to be attacked, so I tried t' tell myself t' just accept it, and no' be afraid. But I was." Meg paused for a moment. "I ken that it wouldna be the same if I were taken against my will. But, if it were my husband, and I loved him. Mother," Meg stopped kneading and faced Elspeth. "What is it like? When a man takes his wife as a husband should, what is it like?"

Elspeth was speechless and breathless. She was unsure if 'twas proper to tell her daughter, to be descriptive or give a vague response. She flicked her eyes toward her daughter. Meg spoke quickly to cover her embarrassment.

"I mean, men ken what happens. They see it wi' animals in the barn, or learn at a very young age, before a maid for certain. Oft times, a maid doesna ken until she weds. I think 'tis best if I ken before that. What is it between a man and his wife?"

"Weel," Elspeth began slowly, "when a man and woman wed, he takes her into his bed to lie wi' her."

As she spoke, Elspeth decided there was little harm in her daughter knowing what went on in bed. She was sure to learn soon enough. *Better to prepare her,* she thought.

"When they lie together," she continued, beating at the dough, "the man holds his wife close. He kisses her, tells her he loves her. When they are both excited, they are a little breathless, and the husband's manhood rises. Ye ken what manhood is?" she asked her daughter.

"Aye, what wee Innes has between his legs."

"But only quite a bit larger," Elspeth said, becoming more comfortable with her daughter. Her doughy fingers left the bread and played with a crease in her skirt as she spoke. "And when a man becomes excited, it hardens so he can do his job. He then presses it between his wife's legs, and they are verra close and intimate. Now, it hurts the first time a man takes his wife, 'acause she loses her maidenhood. But after that, if the husband is kind and loving, it can be verra wonderful."

Meg leaned in close to her mother. "Is it that way between ye and father? Wonderful, I mean?" she asked wistfully. Elspeth looked at her daughter earnestly.

"Aye, my sweet. Verra wonderful."

After leaving Meg, Ewan ambled towards home, relaxing into Fire Foot's slow, steady gait. Since Meg's croft was north of the village Lochnora and northeast of Broch Lochnora, it was a long way before he reached the keep. The entire time his mind spun in circles, from images and thoughts about Meg to the English in the area. *What were they trying to accomplish?* Trotting through the gate, Ewan led Fire Foot to the stable, unhitched the horse and wiped him down. He then went to his father's chamber to let him know of the recent encounter.

"So, ye caught them, eh, my son?" the Laird ventured.

"Aye, Father. But one rode off injured, and two are dead. I dinna ken if there are more, or if we got the whole band in one turn." Ewan paused, his forehead pinched in deep thought. "I think it best to err on the side of caution and believe that more English will follow."

"So, ye let one get away? How did that come about?" asked MacLeod, eyes full of mirth.

"Weel, it wasna entirely my fault," stated Ewan, his hand on his chest, feigning an affront. "The wee lass was only occupying one o'men, and I did take down two. One was only injured and rode off. I would have taken down the third, but 'afore I had the chance, Meggie knocked him on the head wi' a rock."

MacLeod was quiet. "Meggie, is it?" he asked.

Ewan found himself blushing and was upset that he revealed himself so to his father.

"Ye said that she was no' petty indiscretion, my son."

"Aye, Da, I did say that. I did no' lie to ye. I havena touched the lass."

"Did I no' teach ye that lying is a sin?" MacLeod grumbled.

"Weel, I dinna think a quick kiss for a reward would count for what ye are thinking." They were both silent, with only the sound of MacLeod's raspy breathing breaking the quiet.

"Da," Ewan began, "How come ye didna find another woman after mother died?"

"Why do ye ask? Is it your business?"

"I like to think that 'tis my concern to see my father in good spirits. I ken ye are a man, with natural tendencies, if ye will. Why did ye no' find another woman to be with?"

"Do ye think it is that easy, to replace one woman wi' another?" Ewan was silent at his father's subtly angered tone.

"No, Da, I dinna think that. No' at all."

MacLeod sighed heavily. Could it be that his son was ready to put aside his numerous indiscretions and marry? But to whom? *Wee Meggie. A crofter's maid. Lord in Heaven, ease my burden.*

"None could replace your mother, in my heart or in my bed. Some women make a mark 'o your heart, son. A mark so deep and strong that it scars ye for life. Your mother did that for me, and I will carry that mark to my grave. I only hope that I will be meeting your mother again verra soon." MacLeod was quiet for a moment. "Have ye found a maid like that, Ewan? It's no' the crofter's daughter, is it?"

Ewan remained reticent. He was unsure of how to respond, not knowing quite how he felt about Meg.

"Ye realize it would be imprudent to wed her. Ye need to find a woman of your station, my son."

"Aye, and where would I find such a woman? There are no eligible maids whose lands border ours that I could wed, but for the MacNally's. In truth, I dinna fancy an arranged marriage wi' a woman I dinna care for. And I willna burden myself wi' the creature Elayne, God save me. Is that too much to ask?"

"Nay, it isna too much. Ye will be Laird soon, my son. A position like that, people oft overlook imprudence, ye ken. What of McNally's lass? She would be a good match, at least politically."

"The Harpy? Why would ye curse your own son with such a woman? Nay, I ken what ye are saying about prudence."

"Does she care for ye, my son?"

Ewan grinned awkwardly.

"Who? The Harpy? Nay, Father. Wee Meggie, that could be a problem. I dinna think she likes me overmuch."

MacLeod laughed heartily.

Ewan approached his prisoner as he had for the past few days, with anger in his heart and death on his mind. He wanted nothing more than to torture and kill the English bastard where he lay, chained to the stone wall. He could not, however. Not until he knew why the English were hiding on his land, and what their interest was in the young crofter's maiden. 'Twould also help if the man would wake up. He had been unconscious since Hamish and Duncan brought him to this cell.

Today, he was finally awake and had been well for more than a day. Ewan thought it time for a visit.

Ewan placed the tip of his broadsword into the fire, and pressed it against the bastard's back, smiling at the yelp of pain it elicited. The Englishman sat up, and Ewan drew low, his face close to his prisoner's, his eyes flashing a reflection of the fire and the anger burning inside him.

"I tire of waiting. I dinna care if ye have any knowledge or your English friends. I have decided that on this day I will torture ye, slowly and w' the utmost pain, until I decide to kill ye," Ewan spoke slowly to the man. "Now, I will kill ye quick if ye decide to speak what ye ken. I may even choose to return ye to the wilds alive and let ye fend your way back to England if what ye say is of true merit." Ewan paused slightly, letting his gaze wander back to the fire.

"Now, do ye feel more firebrand on ye? Or will ye tell me what ye ken?"

The Englishman said nothing. When Ewan raised his sword to the fire, the man began to speak slowly and haggardly.

"You know, MacLeod, your lands are not many," Ewan could almost hear the man's sneer in his voice with this statement, but let the *Sassenach* continue. "But they lie best with access to coast and John of Argyll."

At that name, Ewan bit back a curse. Argyll was known for his association with the English, and his assistance long aided them against Robert the Bruce. And now that Scotland was rid of English rule, Argyll would work to reestablish it. The pieces were coming together for Ewan, and he did not like the picture they created in his mind. The *Sassenach* spoke again.

"With your land under English control, albeit informally, Argyll and England could work with ease to move in and out of the Scottish Highlands, wreak havoc, and perhaps reclaim the throne. 'Tis all I have heard."

Ewan brooded over this statement. He let the words sink in, trying to decide between the truth and lies. What the man said did contain a ring of truth. MacLeod lands did have good access routes to the coast, with a major road not too far inland that served well for traveling. English armies could easily sail to Argyll, if they built some manner of port off the craggy cliffs, then gain access to the heart of the Highlands through his land.

"So why do the English play with a lowly maid? Will she give access to my land?"

"Nay. 'Twas our intention to force your people off the land with threats and destruction. We could not kill all of you outright without inciting another war. But with no one left on the land, 'twould not be worth much, and you could be disposed of easily."

"Easily, eh?" Ewan asked him. The man gave a grim smirk in response.

"Why do ye tell me all this?" Ewan demanded. "Have ye no loyalty? Or is the price of your hide worth more than a few coppers from the English?"

The Englishman turned his face up to Ewan's. His red, sunken eyes were as dingy the rest of him. His entire body slumped in defeat.

"I have no loyalty. I took the coins for my sister in Lancashire, for her sick son. You would kill me leastways. I figure you earned the right to know what is happening on your land."

"Is there anything else ye would tell me?" Ewan pressed. The man looked away for a moment, then returned his gaze to Ewan.

"Aye. Two things. The man you are looking for is Montgomery. Keep your eye on the glen where we found the lass."

Ewan nodded. "And the second?"

"I have no future in England, either as a restored prisoner or a turncoat," he said softly, his eyes flicking to Ewan's sword at his side. "Please kill me quickly."

With that, Ewan stood. After a quick prayer for mercy for the *Sassenach*, Ewan did as the man asked. He then bent low to the body and said softly, "Ye confessed before the moment of truth. I think God will forgive ye your sins. May ye find peace that ye did no' have here."

Ewan paused a moment before leaving the cell, trying to make full sense of what he'd learned. These English came, but not many. They were instructed to threaten and maim, not kill. The MacLeod clan was a small one that could, many seemed to believe, be easily overcome. Even the access to the sea was an odd desire, since the land access itself was very small.

Originally intended as a point of agreement between two clans, the MacNally's ceded the small strip of land to Ewan's great grandfather as a precautionary manner. The MacLeods were farmers and breeders, growing oats and raising sheep and goats; fishermen they were not. The access point allowed the MacLeods the ability to fish if drought or disease ever forced their hand, but thus far it had not – they traded for much of their fish – rarely traversing all the way to the sea.

Ewan was puzzled. Did Argyll, or whoever was behind these schemes, think that so small amount of coast was worth so much? Or did they mistakenly think the MacLeod's land stretched farther along the coast? Either way, Ewan thought the plot poor indeed and destined to fail. A small clan mayhap, but within it beat the heart of great and powerful warriors.

Overall, he decided not to give these pathetic attempts and this poor plot much measure. His clan would dispatch with these English, and there would be no further traversing of MacLeod land, he was sure. He shook his head to himself, mystified.

Ewan stepped into the hall and encountered Gavin outside the cell, waiting to hear what, if anything, Ewan had gleaned from the prisoner.

"Weel," Ewan began, "the English want our land. He says that Argyll is behind it, but I dinna ken who is leading these scavengers on our land or where they are."

"Will ye tell your father?" Gavin asked. Ewan shook his head.

"Nay, he has more to worry him than some English deserters on our land. If we canna keep our land, what manner of Scots are we?"

That night, Ewan, unable to sleep, paced his chamber trying to organize his thoughts. With his father's sickness, and now the issues with the English deserters, the last thing he needed was to have his head swimming with visions of a crofter's maid with flowing hair. But her visage would not leave his mind. And the kiss they shared -- he now felt like a swooning schoolboy instead of a man of five and twenty!

And her encounter with the English earlier, the thought that she could have been seriously harmed, or killed, enraged him, almost as much as when he thought about his mother's death. Knowing that the English were still out there, and she was unprotected. What if next time - *There wouldna be a next time if I were there.* That prospect stuck in his mind, along with the knowledge that he could not spend all his days tracking her, as much as he liked the thought. *But, if she were here, a guest in the keep, she would be protected. And near.* Now, that was a novel idea. He could bring her to the keep, *and woo her? Make her love me?* He liked this idea, and all the possibilities that went with it.

His father would be upset but understanding. He knew Ewan to be a bit rakish and would relish Ewan getting married, regardless of the lass. Ewan thought of the marriage he remembered between his mother and father. *Is that why father doesna push me into marriage? He kens the value of being in love with a good woman, even one without stature?*

Ewan caught himself with that thought. Did his father see something Ewan couldn't? How strong were his feelings for the wee maid anyhow? *Verra strong.* Ewan resigned himself to that fact. He was smitten by a young lass.

Would Meg be as understanding? After all, it was for her protection. He smiled to himself. He would travel to her croft on the morrow, explain the circumstances to her father, and bring her home. *Home.* The fire in his mind eased a bit, and he sank into the mattress, sleep coming more easily to him now.

Ewan had his father's blessing to retrieve Meg from her father's house the next morning and didn't fail to notice the suppressed grin on Colin's face. As he rode toward her croft, he noticed how warm it was and realized that it was only four days until Beltane. Ewan cringed inwardly at the thought. Ten years ago, to that day, his mother was killed not far from home. He pushed the thought as far from his mind as possible, instead relishing that he would be seeing his wee Meggie soon.

Meg was helping her mother build a fire outside the cottage in the mist when he arrived.

"Mistress Lachlan, Miss Lachlan," he addressed them as he swung down from the horse. "Might Lachlan himself be at home this day? I would like to have a word wi' him."

Elspeth gave her daughter a look of panic and went around the back of the croft to retrieve Connor. Meg stayed rooted where she was, eyeing the Laird's son. He was wearing full highland regalia, complete in black plaid, striped with red and yellow, fastened at the shoulder by a beautiful brooch with an emerald center. His black hair appeared freshly washed, the tiny braids at the side clean and neatly kept. Even in the sticky weather, he seemed to gleam.

Meg looked down at her stained skirts and suddenly felt unkempt. However, these were the cleanest clothes she had, her only other skirts boiling in the wash. They had been stained when the Englishman knocked them from her hands.

"What are ye doin' here?" she asked, averting her gaze.

"Weel, I am here t' speak wi' your father," he responded noncommittally. Meg became curious. *Why is he dressed so formally?* she wondered. *And why does he want to see my father?*

"And why would the Laird's son want to see a lowly crofter's father?" she shocked herself at how informally she spoke to him. *When did I become so intimate as to be informal?* Ewan flashed a toothy smile at her as he noticed Connor Lachlan approach. Lachlan paused in front of Ewan, blocking his view of Meg, waiting for him to speak.

"Might I have a word wi' ye, dear sir?" Ewan addressed him.

"Aye, my Laird," Lachlan responded, casting a glance back at his daughter. Ewan led Connor aways down the road. Elspeth watched her husband walk away.

"What do ye think he wants?" she asked her daughter in a low voice.

"I dinna ken," Meg replied softly.

"Your father, he has been preoccupied as of late," Elspeth told her. "I worry for him. I'm curious to learn if this meeting involves the reason for his distraction."

Her face was strained with worry, and her eyes did not leave the two men conversing. Meg reached out for her mother, placing an arm around her slender shoulders to steady her.

"Have strength, Mother. I dinna think it involves ye or your practices. I have no' heard anyone call ye a witch." Elspeth laughed at that.

"Aye, just a few generations ago, I would have been a priestess. Now I could be condemned a witch." Elspeth smiled at her daughter. "Seems sad, no'? But your father accepted me, and my beliefs in now ancient rituals, even as much as I profess the Church. I dinna think he would tell anyone, if not for my sake, then for his own."

"And ye do well to hide your practices during midwifing, making them seem as though they come from the church, that I have seen. Your worry is misplaced, I believe." Elspeth became gray at Meg's comment.

"Then why, my daughter, does the Laird's son visit your father now?"

As if to answer that question, Ewan and Connor began to walk back towards the cottage. Meg stood with her mother, her red-gold hair forming a sunburst halo around her.

She wore her hair mostly loose, the drab linen failing to keep her hair tied back, and it gave Ewan a sense of intimacy to see her more casual look near home. Each time he had seen her, that glorious hair had remained unbound, and he vowed that she would keep it that way, regardless of conventional beliefs on covering a woman's hair. Tresses that beautiful should not be hidden away. His breath caught at the beauty she was.

Lachlan spoke first. "Meggie, my dove, I've been told by our Laird's benevolent son that ye have encountered some problems with the English deserters nearby. Is that true, daughter?" he asked, unable to hide the strain in his voice and on his face. It seemed that within the past few months, he had suddenly become an old man, which frightened her. What could be the cause of his strain?

Meg was silent, and Elspeth began to speak for her.

"Connor, she told me that she--"

"Wife," Lachlan commanded softly, "I am asking our daughter. Meg, have the English accosted ye again?"

"Aye, Father," Meg replied quietly.

"Why did ye no' tell me?"

"I dinna want to worry ye, Father." Her voice was barely above a whisper.

"Worry me?" Lachlan took Meg into his arms, hating himself for the charade, and hating the English for hurting her and forcing him into this charade. He had never felt so lowly as he did the moment he held his daughter and lied to her. "Ye would no' worry me. I would have taken care of ye, my dove."

Meg smiled up at her father, nervously flicking her eyes toward Ewan.

"Then what does he want, Father?" she asked. Connor sighed heavily.

"He has a solution that will protect ye and your honor from the English. He has offered to take ye into the walls of the manor grounds and keep ye safe until the English brigands are captured."

And my neck stretched for treason, he added to himself, but it would be worth it to keep his family safe. The shocked look on both his daughter's face and his wife's conveyed a different belief. Elspeth regained her voice first.

"Connor! Ye would send your eldest daughter into his hands to spare her honor? Christ's blood, man! Are ye daft? And ye speak of her honor?"

Elspeth was in a panic. She was about to see her eldest, beautiful daughter, handed over to the greatest rogue in the Highlands. Her daughter's honor at the hands of the English was the least of her worries compared to her honor in the hands of the Laird's infamous rake of a son.

"Wife," Connor called sternly once more.

Ewan caught the panic in her voice and attempted to alleviate her fears. He bowed toward her, taking her hand in his.

"Please trust me in the knowledge that I mean your daughter no harm. I vow that ye will no' have to fear her honor while in my care."

He spoke openly, trying to convince Meg's mother that her daughter's safety was of the utmost concern. After all, she didn't know that he was interested in marrying her, not seducing her. Elspeth paused for a moment, then turned toward her daughter, still stunned at the offer.

"Well, my daughter, let us go pack your belongings."

Meg was too stunned to respond. Ewan wanted to force her away from her family, that she loved more than life itself, to provide himself with the opportunity to molest her? Take advantage of his power and force her into his home? Elspeth had to drag her into the cottage.

They gathered together Meg's few belongings. The brush her mother made for her. Her nightshift. Another drab scrap of linen for her hair. Some dried flowers she was keeping. The woolen plaid from her bed.

Packing her things into a small basket, she included the unruly kitten she had brought home and covered it with a square of cloth, securing the top with a leather thong. She left a small opening where the kitten could peek out and breathe, but it seemed content to curl up on her belongings and sleep. Meg wished she could feel as unconcerned as her cat. She couldn't even bring her other dress, for it was in the wash, but it really didn't matter. Her other dress was nothing more than a ragged kirtle over the long shift she presently wore, and she wore it when she had work in the stable or out in the field. In fact, she was glad she couldn't bring it; she would be embarrassed to be seen in it, truth be told.

Meg felt tears sting her eyes as she carried her few items outside. 'Twasn't right for Ewan to abuse his power as future Laird this way. Yet she was at his mercy, and, as she glanced at the tears on her mother's face, so was her mother.

Elspeth took the basket and walked over to Ewan while Meg hugged her father good-bye. With an aggravated glare, Elspeth placed it into Ewan's hands, grasping his arm. She spoke forcefully.

"I beg ye, dinna ruin my daughter's honor. Please."

"Mistress Lachlan," he said softly, "I vow that your daughter's honor will no' be ruined."

"Do ye care for her then?"

Ewan glanced over at Meg. He knew the midwife's question held more than it seemed. Some rumors about her were correct and he wondered how much Meg had told her about their encounters. Was it possible that Meg cared for him more than she could admit? He looked down into the stricken eyes of Meg's mother.

"Aye. I care for her verra much." He turned from Elspeth, securing the basket onto the horse.

Meg approached them, clinging fiercely to her mother.

"I dinna want to leave ye," Meg sobbed.

"Be strong, my daughter," Elspeth cooed. "He cares for ye, and he will do well by ye." She held Meg's face to gaze in her eyes.

"Keep my words strong in your mind and close t'your heart. Understand?"

Meg nodded. "Aye, Mother. I can swear t'ye on that."

Elspeth kissed her daughter's cheek and moved to stand next to Connor. Ewan took Meg's hand and helped her onto his horse. He swung himself up behind her, putting his arms around her to grasp the reins. He then leaned in close to her ear.

"Are ye ready, my wee Meggie?" he whispered, his breath blowing warm on her ear.

"Aye," she whispered back, lying. "I'm ready."

Ewan smiled to himself and flicked the reins.

≫≫≫⟩   ⟨≪≪≪

They rode quietly at first, and Ewan could hear her sniffing; she was obviously crying yet trying to cover it.

"Are ye well, lass?" he asked in a kind tone.

"Aye, I am fine. I have no' been away from home before. I am a bit frightened." *A bit frightened?* she thought. 'Twas understating the matter. She couldn't comprehend why the Laird's son would retrieve her to stay at his manor house.

They reached the outer grounds of the keep. Meg had been quiet, so unlike their previous meetings, and Ewan tried to speak to her again.

"Thank ye for packing so little. I will send someone for the rest of your belongings."

Meg snorted awkwardly in retort.

"Ye are obviously no' well informed about the life of a crofter's daughter. 'Tis all I have."

"All your belongings fit into this one basket?" he asked incredulously.

Over a year ago, a cousin of his had visited from Edinburgh, and she had enough trunks and valises to slow the carriage considerably. It took himself and his brothers two trips up to her room to unload all her packages. Several of his "indiscretions," as his father called them, had ribbons and brushes to spare, looking glasses, several skirts, chemises, personal kitchen items, handkerchiefs, and more than Ewan could not begin to name. Ewan naturally assumed that all women had a penchant for belongings, simple or not.

Was Meg's family so poor that they couldn't afford anything -- even handmade items? Or did she not care about such frivolities? He noted the scrap of worn leather holding some strands of her hair and believed it to be the latter.

Meg twisted slightly and raised an eyebrow at him, as though weighing the merit of his statement. Should she take it as an insult? Or was he used to women who had toiletries and clothes to make themselves feel better? Her mother had taught her that the simplest pleasures were the best, and nature had these pleasures in abundance. She preferred flowers to toiletries, the scent of grass and fresh water to smelly perfumes.

The only thing she could have wanted that was not made in nature was ribbon for her hair. Though her mother told her that her hair was like the sunset, the most beautiful image in nature, and needed no adornment, she was still jealous of other girls in the market who wore even the most plain ribbons of sky blue, wine, and pine green. However, she didn't have time to dwell on such thoughts while working, and the jealousy passed quickly.

Unconsciously reaching her hand up to touch the drab piece of cloth holding her hair, she turned away from Ewan without responding. Meg was on the verge of tears as it was, her eyes as misty as the weather, and she was afraid the tears would spill over if she spoke. Fortunately, Ewan did not press her, and they rode the rest of the way to the keep in silence.

CHAPTER FOUR

On Being a Guest

So few people rode out to her house, aside from her father, that the road from Meg's croft became more distinctive as it led toward the village, then to the Laird's manse. The clans people claimed it was not a full castle, but to Meg, it might have well been. Never in her life had she been in a place as large as the Laird's keep. It even had a name, Broch Lochnora, for goodness sake!

It may have lacked the heavy fortifications or size of a castle, but it was set off from the main road, with a low stone wall surrounding most of the immediate landscape. The open gate beckoned visitors. From the gate, she could see the keep itself, where the Laird and his family lived. Several, large open areas near the house and the stables farther back buzzed with activity.

Off to one side of the manor, near the doorway to the kitchen, Meg supposed, some well-established gardens flourished with fruits, vegetables, trees, and several flowering plants. How her mother would have loved so many plants that close to the cottage! Meg could hardly wait to walk through it, to see what grew there, when she remembered her situation. Who was she to prance around the Laird's gardens? Perhaps Ewan would set her in the kitchens, then she could have access to the gardens out of necessity.

A groom met them in front of the keep, and Ewan swung down, his powerful legs landing with grace. He assisted Meg as she slid from the horse, grabbed her basket, and handed the horse over to the groom. Ewan then escorted a wide-eyed Meg into the manor.

Meg had never been to the Laird's grounds, let alone inside the walls of the keep, and she could not stop herself from staring. Ewan, who knew that his home was not as awe-inspiring or decorative as other holds, was pleased by Meg's reaction. It gave him a new appreciation for what he had, and he smiled at her eager reaction.

The front hall led directly to the great room, and the rest of the keep spread out from that room. Several tables in the great hall focused toward a central table on a raised dais. An immense tapestry of a stag hung behind the raised table. She could see where one hallway led to the kitchen in the back, and a second hallway led to another room. Two stairways, one on each side of the hall, led to chambers upstairs. Ewan nudged her forward.

"Would ye like an introduction to the keep, or do ye need to rest first?" he asked her. Meg's brow furrowed. *Rest? I have no' done anything!*

"An introduction would be lovely."

He walked her around the kitchens, let her peek into his study, and then escorted her upstairs. Once on the second floor, he showed her the solar with its impossibly large fireplace, led her past the chambers for his father and brothers, and indicated a door near him.

"These are my chambers, and if ye need assistance in the eve, ye can find me here." Meg's wide-eyed, shocked expression told him what she thought of *that* insinuation. Ewan shook his head.

"Nay, I mean ye no harm or disgrace, but should ye need me, I want ye to be able to find me." He smiled widely at her. "Just knock."

Her face broke into a wide grin.

"I can no' believe how big everything is! And ye and your brothers each have your own rooms!" Ewan laughed at her excitement over the simplest things. "What room is this?" she asked as he walked her past a wooden door that was bolted shut on the outside with thick iron bars. Ewan's face clouded a bit.

"'Tis my mother's chambers, dead these past ten years. My father prefers to keep it as 'twas before she died. He moved out of the chamber shortly after we buried her, no' wanting to be reminded of her in the room they shared."

They continued to walk towards her chamber in silence. He swung open the door, and Meg stood in the doorway, staring into the room. Her first impression was the room was the stuff of dreams. Furs covered the large bed, pushed against the side wall, with the MacLeod plaid draped atop the furs. A dainty table next to the bed held candles. A small chest nestled against the wall, and a dusty, unlit fireplace lay cold across from the bed. In the corner, a stand supported a metal basin for water, and bright tapestries hung on the walls. The cloth in front of the windows had been pulled to the side to let in the light of the afternoon, brightening the room.

Ewan admitted that it was rather plain for guest quarters. Mesmerized, Meg stepped into the center of the room, eyes as wide as saucers, unable to look at everything at once.

"And this is to be my room? Alone?"

"Is something amiss?" asked Ewan. "Is there something ye require to stay here?"

"Nay," she breathed. "I can no' believe that I am to have all this room to myself. 'Tis larger than most of my cottage!"

Again, he had to smile at her enthusiasm over a mere room. While he thought it quite plain, she reveled in its largess. And to be truthful, it was one of the smaller chambers of the keep, but he was pleased that she thought so much of one small room. He began to admire the goodness she found in simple things.

Ewan took a small step into her room, setting her basket on the floor when a furry face peeked out from under the cloth. Meg scooped up the kitten, displaying it to Ewan and reminding him it was the one she found on the day she first encountered him. Ewan said she should name the scruffy thing *Dragh*, Gaelic for "trouble," since wee creature was the reason she first had trouble with the English. He placed a clean linen in an empty basket nearby, to serve as a new home for the troublesome little *screb*.

"Well, 'twill be time for the midday meal soon. If ye like, ye could get settled a bit, and then meet me in the great hall, and I will show ye the rest of the grounds."

He felt rather like a shy lad asking her, not a Laird-to-be in his own castle, and this flustered him slightly. Meg did not seem to notice. She was busy inspecting the coverings on the bed.

"Aye, 'twill be fine," she responded in a disinterested tone.

With a smile on her face, she turned suddenly and gave a quick bounce on the bed. The straw gave, if only slightly, and Meg knew she would sleep very well that night. Used to only a flat pallet in a small room with her other two sisters, the large bed piled with furs and plaids in a room all her own seemed like heaven.

Ewan watched her movements. He couldn't take his eyes off her as she played in the room, investigating it, and though he knew he should leave, give her privacy, he was riveted to his spot by the door. He did not want to move for fear that she would notice him. When she finally turned her attention to the window with the view, he stepped softly back through the doorway, pulling the door as he went.

While she excitement over her adventure coursed through her blood, Meg worried more so about Ewan's true intentions. She knew about his reputation in the village, and while she had never heard of anyone escorted to his home, she was still hesitant around him. Aye, he was handsome, far more than most, and aye, he was strong and very charming. And 'twas easy to see how women swooned for him. Meg sensed herself falling for his charms, especially when he kissed her only the day before. She, however, would not allow herself to become another one of his conquests, regardless of how attractive he was or how he made her heart race.

She scanned the large but relatively barren room. The liveliest part was the attractive MacLeod tartan thrown over the bed. Retrieving her basket near the door, Meg began to unpack her few items. Once those were in place, she began to further contemplate her situation. She would need to send someone home to retrieve her other kirtle, not knowing if she would be here for more than a few days. She must also contact her mother and father to let them know all was well.

Thoughts of the Laird's son, his white smile against the dark midnight of his hair and his sun-kissed skin, readily pushed all other concerns aside. *So verra striking,* she thought. *I understand why so many a lass would lose herself to him. But he knows that will no' happen wi' me, so why am I here?*

She went back to the window with its expansive view of the courtyard, full of spring flowers and people milling about. Noticing that the sun was high in the sky, she decided to venture downstairs to meet with Ewan. *And I will collect some flowers to brighten up this room.*

Ewan was speaking to one of the kitchen maids when Meg entered the great hall. His gaze caught sight of her when she first entered, nearly stopping him mid-sentence. She looked so natural entering the hall, searching for him, his heart skipped a beat. Unusual for him, he was uncertain of how to win her, afraid she would think his advances were for coupling only. He knew he had to restrain himself physically, so she would know that he was honest in his intentions, and mentally prepared himself for the comments he would encounter from kin and king once he made his intentions known. But he would worry about that when the time came. For now, he was content merely seeing her in his home.

He finished speaking with the kitchen maid and approached Meg. She raised an eyebrow at him, a gesture he found endearing, if not slightly irritating, as he perceived that she doubted him in some way.

"Were ye setting a date for later this eve?" she asked subtly, again amazed at the informality she assumed with him. Catching onto her joke, he allowed a roguish smile to adorn his face.

"Nay, for with ye present, your beauty blinds me, and I can see no other woman."

His flattery made her blush.

"Ye ken that your flattery is without reward, aye?" she tried to brush off his words, but they made her heart race all the same.

"'Tis no' flattery, but truth." He held his arm out for her. "Shall we?"

She grasped his elbow, allowing him to lead her from the hall. She saw him clutch a small covered basket as they left.

He led her first through the courtyard and the gardens. As they strolled through the foliage, Meg selected several varieties of blooms and stems to take to her room. When they happened upon a small clearing in the garden, Ewan pulled the cloth off the basket and spread it on the ground. In the basket was their midday meal, consisting of crusty bread and cheese. The basket even held a flagon of wine and two small wooden cups. To Meg, it was the most luxurious midday meal she'd ever eaten.

After they finished their meal, Ewan collected the remnants, placed them in the basket, and offered the remaining space in the basket for Meg's flowers. She placed them gently inside and covered them with the cloth. Ewan then guided her toward the stables.

They conversed lightly, with laughter and ease. Once in the stables, however, Meg's awe overtook her tongue. Ewan offered to teach her how to ride.

"I canna," she told him.

"And why not?"

"I'm afraid," she replied quietly. "Of the horses, I mean. They are so large. What if I fell off?" she lied. It was not the horses she feared but being near Ewan as he taught her. She could now understand why he was such a rogue. Try as she might, she found herself falling for his charms, and in truth, she was afraid of loving a man she couldn't keep.

"Then I would catch ye," Ewan promised, that soft smile on his face. He had no fear. It was too late for him - he was already smitten with her.

A quiet settled on them as they walked back to the hold late in the afternoon. Meg was pensive, knowing that she needed to address her two issues with him. Gathering her courage, she began slowly.

"How long am I to be here, sir?"

"Weel, until we catch the brigands who have been causing ye trouble. Why do ye ask?"

"Ye see, if it is to be longer than a few days, I will have to ask that someone be sent to retrieve my other kirtle."

She felt awkward asking him, with all of his responsibilities, for something so trivial and started rambling.

"It would no' be a problem, but I only have the one gown with me, and 'twill be quite dirty in a few days, and we left so quickly, but if 'tis too much trouble, I can make do . . ." she trailed off.

Ewan gave her another of his toothy smiles that made her heart skip. "'Tis already taken care of. Anything else?"

"Oh, weel, aye. There is one other thing. I have no' been away from home before and miss my family dearly. Would I be allowed to see them?"

He stopped her then, taking both of her hands in his. Gazing into her eyes, he saw her weariness, the insecurity of what was happening to her. He wanted to tell her all then but considered it unwise. Instead, he answered her question.

"What kind of monster do ye think I would be to keep ye from your family? We will make sure that your mother and father visit the keep at least once a fortnight, and I will personally escort ye to the cottage anytime ye wish."

Her eyes softened a bit, and she exhaled, not realizing that she had been holding her breath. She returned his smile with one that melted his heart. He released one hand and pulled her along with the other.

"Shall we go to sup?"

Meg didn't realize that sup with Ewan meant more than just his family. His father was not there; his illness, Ewan explained, forced the Laird to take his meals in bed. However, Ewan's brothers attended the table on the raised dais. Also present were several of the clan's high-ranking warriors, their families, the priest, and others in the MacLeod lands.

Ewan was guiding her towards the raised table, meaning to present her to society, Meg realized, and she paled. Dressed in nothing more than the common linen shift and kirtle she wore daily, and her hair haphazardly tied back with a nubby piece of cloth, she panicked. *I should no' be here. I am but a mere crofter's maid!* Ewan pulled a chair out for her, and she grasped his muscled forearm to stop him.

"Is there no' a more appropriate place for me to sup? In the kitchens perchance?" she asked, her voice full of fear.

"What?" Ewan responded incredulously.

"Ewan," she whispered sternly, aware that the noise in the hall had dropped off considerably. "I can no' eat with ye in the hall like this. 'Twould be unseemly."

"Unseemly?"

"Sir, I am naught but a crofter's maid, and my place is with the servants. Nay here in the hall with lords and ladies and officers. Please, direct me to the kitchen."

She dropped her eyes to the floor. Inflamed from the attention directed on her from everyone in the hall, she wanted to be anywhere else. She began to turn away and walk toward the kitchens herself. Ewan grabbed her arm and forced her to face him. The expression on his face was one of astonishment.

"Lords and Ladies? What do ye think *I* am, *mo annsachd*? Yet ye could be so informal wi' me in private? Ye are my guest, Meggie, and ye shall be treated as one. Now *sit down!*"

Meg was shocked to hear him speak with such force; he had been so soft spoken with her. Now she could see why the clan would follow him, how commanding he could be. She took a small step back, shying from him. Tearing his eyes away from hers, Ewan took a deep breath to compose himself.

"I did no' mean to shout. My apologies. Now, in my house, ye are a lady. Please, your seat, milady."

He gestured toward the padded, high back chair he held out for her. Meg looked at him, then around at the audience now focused on the head table. Moving her gaze to Ewan's brothers, she offered them a small smile to meet their amused look on their faces.

"My apologies," she told them. Returning her gaze to Ewan, she said, "My apologies," and swiftly sat down.

The fare was simple, but in more abundance than Meg usually saw at home. In her parents' croft, supper consisted of a small piece of mutton, rough brown bread, with water, tea, or some weak ale if it had been market day, to drink. Here, conversely, the amount of food presented could feed her family for near a month. Ewan commented that they would not slaughter a cow until later in the summer, so he apologized for the lack of beef.

Kitchen maids placed different cuts of lamb on the tables: rack of lamb, leg of lamb, and mutton chops. Fresh loaves of sweet bread sat on wooden blocks, slabs of butter melting atop each loaf, and they smelled heavenly. Small baskets held leeks and watercress and apples. To drink, the table offered a selection of wine (that went largely untouched), ale, whiskey, and goat milk.

Even with all the food placed before her, not to mention the hunger gnawing at her stomach, Meg barely tasted her food that night. She was too conscious of Ewan's presence next to her. She tried to keep up pleasant conversation with Hamish on her left while staring at those present in the hall, but she was all too aware of her dress, which was dirty and drab compared to the bright colors of the clan tartans and women's kirtles. Her nervous hand kept wandering to the ragged ribbon in her hair. Several times during dinner, Ewan's hand brushed hers, and for some reason, her skin tingled every time they touched.

The hall was so loud and so busy, Meg began to grow dizzy. It was a far cry from the quiet suppers at home, and she felt uncomfortable being waited on. She picked at her bread and sipped her ale. Ewan noticed she was not eating.

"Are ye finished wi' your meal?"

"Aye," she responded. "I'm no' very hungry."

"Oh, weel, if ye like, I could escort ye to your chambers if ye desire to rest. The piper is here, so we may have music later tonight."

"Aye. I think I would like to rest. 'Tis been a tiring day after all."

She spoke in a low voice, and Ewan sensed she was upset at the position he placed her in, and he was sorry for it. He stood and took her hand, helping her rise. They walked from the hall, Ewan pausing only to speak with his brother before escorting her to the stairs. The noise from the hall that had dimmed when they stood suddenly grew louder as they left. Meg knew that she was the cause of the suddenly loud conversation. Still strained and confused as to why she was there, she stopped Ewan as he mounted the stairs.

"Could ye have no' left me at home?" she asked, obviously pained at her situation.

Ewan weighed his options. He knew he was risking gossip by bringing her to the keep and was aware that the excuse of her safety was a weak one. He sighed heavily. Ewan wanted her, not as a petty indiscretion but as his wife. It was easier to woo her under his own roof, adjusting her to the lifestyle and to him, than it would be from her own home.

He wanted to tell her the truth right then but knew he would be in a better position once he was Laird. He decided to not lie to her.

"No, no I could not." He continued up the stairs with Meg in tow.

They arrived at her chamber door, and he stepped aside, allowing her to enter the room. She made to speak with him and froze midway, her eyes fixed on the bed.

Knowing she had few clothes, and even fewer belongings, Ewan had arranged for her to be attired in a manner suitable for the house. Recalling how she fingered the ribbon in her hair, he requested several of every color imaginable to be included with the clothing. A rainbow of color and fabric was draped on the bed.

"Ewan . . ." she breathed.

He leaned close and spoke softly into her ear. "Ye are too beautiful by far without the necessities, but I did no' think ye would believe so until ye were properly attired."

Meg stepped to the bed and gently brushed her hand over the garment that lay there. The kirtle was a forest green, trimmed and lined in ivory. Pale green beads adorned the low neckline and wrists. The panels of the skirt fell over a shimmering chemise of ivory linen. Ribbon flowed from the wrists, waist, and skirt panels. Meg had never seen, let alone wore, a dress of such beauty. All the green and light yellow reminded her of a soft summer day in the glen. Deep verdant slippers trimmed in ivory matched the gown. She marveled at the slippers, having never worn more than rough-shaped leather on her feet.

The snowy chemise peeked out of the gown's neckline. A fresh plaid was folded at the foot of the bed. Placed delicately on top of all that were ribbons of every color - colors such as she had never seen at market and saw only in her dreams. She held one up and felt its shiny softness before holding it to her hair, like a young child playing dress up.

"The ribbons pale in beauty next to your hair. They dinna do your locks justice."

Ewan had stepped into the room and gently touched her hair. She turned to face him, and worry strained her lovely face.

"But, I can no' pay ye for these. Ye will have to take them back."

Ewan barked out a laugh at how she so openly spoke her mind and expected naught.

"Take them back? But they are a gift to ye, it would no' be appropriate to return them, no?" He let a lock of her sunlight hair to fall from his fingers. "It would be your gift to me to permit me to see how stunning ye would look in such clothes."

He studied her intently. "I ask for no' other payment than that."

Meg glanced away, brushing her hand over the gown again, not believing that she could wear such garments.

"Will they suit ye?" Ewan asked, unsure if she cared for the dress. "'Twas the only gown to be fitted at such short notice. We shall obtain another for ye shortly, but will the green do for now?"

She smiled at him, humored that he would think she was in the position to object.

"Aye," she replied. "'Twill suit me. Thank ye, for giving me such beauty. Would ye like me to wear it now? For the music tonight?"

"Aye, I would." Ewan breathed more than answered. He moved toward the door, then caught eyes with his intense blue gaze again. "And Meggie? 'Tis ye who has given me such beauty."

He closed the door as he left.

She took a few deep breaths after he departed and dressed delicately in the new clothes, relishing the smooth fabric on her skin, so unlike the rough homespun she had worn all her life. With real slippers instead of rough shoes, she felt like quite a lady.

She selected ribbons for her hair, two pale green and one ivory. Pulling her tresses out of her face, she was finished, and felt like a princess. *A temporary princess, an imposter, for this will all be over once I go home.* She sighed. *Aye, a maid could get used to attire such as this.*

Fingering the fine fabric, she pulled the door open, and almost walked into Ewan. He was waiting right outside her door. He stared at her, as if he had never seen her before, his eyes burning – fire and ice. He had thought she was beautiful dressed as a crofter's maid, but in such finery, she looked a goddess, or a fairy come to steal his heart. He regained himself and offered her an arm.

"Milady, may I escort ye to the festivities?" From the hall, she could hear the piper had started playing, the high squealing notes of his bagpipes resounding softly in the passageway.

"While it may no' be appropriate for me to attend, at least now I look like I belong in your hall. Aye, sire, I would be honored."

And grasping his arm gently, Meg let him guide her down the stairs to the hall.

She spent the evening by his side. They listened to the piper together, and she smiled and clapped after each tune. Having been raised far afield, Meg never heard piper's music so closely and clearly as she did that eve. She had only heard echoes, for the pipe music traveled powerfully across the land, and not so very often, she and her family would stand in the grass and listen to the faint strains of the piper when he played in the Laird's field.

Here, up close, she could hear every note, and the music filled her head as it reverberated in the hall. 'Twas the music of the angels, and she closed her eyes to hear better. After a while of letting Meg indulge in the piper's music, Ewan took her by the hand and led her around the hall, introducing her to the clansmen attending. Ewan made her feel significant, as though she were someone much more important than a crofter's daughter, fulfilling every wish she'd ever had.

She fell hard into bed that night, asleep as her head touched the pillow. And when she dreamt, she dreamt of him.

The next morning, Ewan escorted Meg to meet his father. She became ashen at the prospect of meeting her Laird, but Ewan assured her that the Laird was just a man, a sick one at that, and that Ewan had held most of the Laird's responsibilities for the past two years.

"And ye are no' afraid of me, are ye?"

"Weel, a little, sometimes, if ye must ken the truth," she told him honestly. He grinned and led her to his father's chambers.

Ewan entered first, entreating her to wait in the passageway until he called her. Ewan approached his father's bed, noticing that the servant had already bathed him and removed his breakfast tray. The old Laird looked quite impressive, draped in the clan tartan, but the gaunt cheeks, labored breathing, and chronic cough gave away how sick he was. The Laird smiled at his son.

"Oh, but aren't ye the scheming one?" he teased his son.

"Aye, Father, but it worked, and she is now here, where she is safe," Ewan replied.

"And where ye can court her daily."

"Weel, aye, that too." Ewan's smile reflected that of his father's.

"While I can no' agree wi' what ye are doing, I have to give ye credit for your ballocks. Taking a crofter's maid and making her a lady? Seems I have heard a similar tale of an ugly duckling and a swan."

"No ugly duckling here, Father, but such a swan as ye have never seen. But 'tis more than that. She makes me feel *alive*, in a way I never have before. I can no' explain it."

"Mayhap ye do no' have to, my son. Mayhap your old father here understands quite well."

"I thought as much. Do ye want to meet her?"

MacLeod snorted. "I'm no' dead yet, Ewan. Ye'll still want my approval, aye?"

Ewan patted his father's hand before retrieving Meg, who walked into the room like a frightened kitten.

"He will no' bite ye," Ewan whispered into her ear.

He brought her near the bed where the Laird lay. Meg could see how ill he was, and while she still retained her fear of the Laird, she also felt pity for him, for all his sickness. Ewan placed a chair near the bed, and MacLeod gestured for Meg to sit. He then grasped her hand in his dry one and patted it.

"Weel, aren't ye the comely one," MacLeod rasped. Meg blushed, casting a sidelong glance at Ewan, who suddenly found the wall tapestry very interesting.

"Methinks I have heard that 'afore," she stated in a wavering voice. MacLeod's laugh turned into a cough.

"Aye, and a witty one too, my son!" MacLeod exclaimed.

Meg raised her eyebrows, trying to figure out what the Laird meant with that statement. MacLeod grew serious.

"Are ye intended, lass?" he asked her, a question the old Laird was sure Ewan didn't ask.

Meg drew back, holding her hand to her throat. Was the Laird upset that she had passed so many a summer with no husband, or even a handfast? Did the Laird have an intended in mind, and she was going to be married off to someone she did not like or even know? Panic filled her.

"Nay, my Laird. I have no intended as of late," her hurt voice told him. With her eyes downcast, she let her Laird of her clan, the man in control of her and her family's wellbeing, decide her future. Planning on marrying for love, she was afraid she now found her marriage being arranged. Her heart wept with sadness.

"A lass as pretty as yourself without an intended? Have ye had offers? Is there no one who has caught your heart?" he questioned. Meg did not see MacLeod glance at his son, and she thought the question odd.

"Aye, there have been offers, but none that I would have considered. My mother, be blessed, is permitting me to marry for love. My father, much to his despair methinks, has agreed."

MacLeod looked thoughtful. "Weel then, lass, we shall abide by the wishes of ye and your family and let ye marry a man ye love. Thank ye for visiting a sick old man. I hope your stay at the keep is a pleasant one."

MacLeod saw her glance at Ewan before she answered, and he smiled.

"Aye, milord, it has been quite pleasant thus far," she told him. MacLeod dismissed her, and Ewan had her wait in the passageway while bidding his father farewell.

"Ye have a good start, son," MacLeod said to Ewan. "Methinks she *likes* ye at the verra least. Ye dressed her well enough like a lady."

Ewan smiled heartily at his father. "Aye, Father, my lady. Ye may live to see me wed yet."

MacLeod rolled his eyes and coughed.

"If your mother was here, she would never believe it."

Ewan met Meg in the passage.

"Your father was verra kind. I thank ye for the introduction."

Ewan shrugged sheepishly. "He likes to meet all visitors to the keep. We have no' had any quite as lovely as ye visit as of late, so I am sure he enjoyed your company."

"If I may ask, has your father been sick long?"

Ewan nodded his head. "He is dying. He hopes to live long enough to see his son, the Laird apparent, wed."

"Oh," Meg replied, trying to hide the distress at the thought of Ewan betrothed to another, and not understanding why she felt that way. "When are ye to marry?"

"That is a bit difficult to answer. Ye see, I need to find a bride, first."

Meg's look of relief made Ewan's heart leap. Perchance he was already finding his way into her heart.

CHAPTER FIVE

Loving the Laird

ON THE EVE OF Beltane, Ewan came to her chambers.

For the three days prior, he had attended to his duties in the early morning, and before the evening meal, spent the majority of his time with her. His oldest friend and man-at arms, Gavin, was appalled at the attention Ewan gave this new young woman. He thought it would pass like previous infatuations, but Ewan's interest was still peaked after so many days. Ewan put off sword practice and left patrolling to others, something he had never done in the past. Gavin was furious. When he tried to discuss the English with him, Ewan brushed him off with little more than a shrug and that devil-may-care smile. Ewan did ask about *Sassenachs*, however, and when Hamish listed what they had seen, Ewan only nodded in response.

Gavin sighed his exasperation, then asked, "What shall we do now?"

Ewan flashed him a wicked smile. "I dinna ken about ye, but I am off to find the maid, Meggie, and see if she will join me for a promenade around the grounds."

Gavin shook his head in exasperation.

"What is it about this maid? Ye have pressing concerns wi' the clan and these English interlopers, yet ye pass your time wi' a crofter's daughter? Have ye gone daft?"

"I think I have, Gavin. Ye are my oldest, closest friend. More brother to me than no'. But wi' this maid, she is in my every thought. I canna get her out o' my head!"

"Ewan!" Gavin shouted at him. "Ye are like a green boy wi' his first crush! Smitten! What has this lass done to ye?"

Ewan shook his head, the smile still on his face. "I dinna ken, but God in Heaven, I am smitten wi' her, and I love it!"

With that, Ewan all but danced off, putting the clan concerns in the back of his head for the meantime, in search of the copper-haired lass who had entranced him.

As for Meg, she could not understand why he was with her so often, treating her like a lady. If she were highborn, she would think he was courting her. As it was, with Meg a mere crofter's maid, she decided that he must pity her being trapped within the keep and was trying to give her cheer. Unfortunately, this thought had the opposite effect and saddened her, for she had begun to care for the Laird's son, more than a crofter's maid of high morals should. She might not be a "petty indiscretion," but she knew that she would be nothing more than she was now once she left the keep.

Ewan had begun to teach her how to ride, and with the help of his youngest brother, Duncan, she was beginning to get the hang of it. She couldn't go much faster than a slow trot without fear, but her enthusiasm at her small accomplishments made both Ewan and Duncan laugh. Her first few attempts were pathetic, to say the least, with Meg groping the reins and the mane of her slow little pony, Bedbug. Meg had laughed heartily when she heard the poor pony's name and asked how it came about. Ewan told her.

"The night she was born, I leapt out o' bed to keep checking on her dam. It was like she was itching to keep me awake."

"It does make me feel better than had she been named Fire Foot," Meg commented, looking pointedly at Ewan's horse.

After a few laps around the gate on the comfortably named Bedbug, Meg felt more confident, and Meg, Ewan, and Duncan began to ride farther.

She didn't see Hamish as much as she did the other brothers. The reason, the house servants explained, was that he had his eye on the merchant's daughter, Isobel, and he spent as much free time with her as he could. While Ewan welcomed the company of his littlest brother, Meg noticed that he was much more reserved with Duncan present, lavishing her with compliments and flattery only when alone.

And he had not tried to kiss her since the day he saved her from the English, and she found herself also saddened but surprised by this. She tried to tell herself that respectable young lasses do not covet kisses from men who would only use them for the basest of pleasures, but she found herself hoping he would overstep that boundary every day. As much as she tried to deny it, she was falling in love with the Laird's son, a man she could never have, and this saddened her most of all.

The next morning, when he retrieved her from her chambers, she knew something was amiss. Ewan rapped on the heavy door as she was finishing with the ribbons in her hair. She twisted the front locks and pulled them back, fastening them with ribbon at the base of her head. Her sunlit tresses and ribbons cascaded down her back in a rainbow of color. Since Ewan supplied her with so many ribbons, she wore several of them, in several different colors, each day. She loved the way they hung in her hair, slipping through her tresses and hanging in the wind whenever there was a breeze. She often found herself catching the smooth strands, twining them in her fingers.

Ewan, who thought her lovely as a mere maid, was even more entranced when she was bedecked with ribbons and finery. It cast her in a glow, and this glow made her hair even brighter, like a fiery halo. He thought she rivaled the sun whenever she stepped into the hall.

He entered into the room when she answered, smiling hugely. He had not fully entered her chambers since he first brought her to the keep and was shocked at the difference in the room. The kitten curled up in a cloth covered basket near her bed. No longer a sparse room, Meg had flowers with ribbons on almost every flat surface, even on the window with the tapestry pulled back, and in the cat basket next to her bed. Hanging upside down on the walls were more flowers, in the process of drying, freshening the air with their different scents.

He recognized it immediately, as it was something his mother had done with fervor. Even after she died, her room smelled of lavender and heather for almost a year afterward. His father ordered it untouched, and only had the room cleaned once the scent of the flowers had dissipated.

Meg stood near the center of the room, a golden halo surrounded by the beauty and scents of the many flowers. Ewan was struck silent at the image of her, his blood pounding in his head and his chest. He wanted to take her in his arms then and there, kiss the silken glow of her hair, love her amidst the powerful scent of the heady flowers.

He caught himself, almost steeling himself, because he promised he would be a gentleman, and because he had a surprise for her that day that could not wait. Perchance he would ask for a small reward for the surprise, just as he had when he rescued her from the English. He stepped into the room and took her hands in his.

"I have a wonderful surprise for ye this morn, my darling lass. It is waiting in the hall for ye. Would ye like to see it?"

She raised an eyebrow at him with feigned contempt, bantering with him. He had hoped she would play with words with him this day. It made him feel full and alive to banter with her so easily.

"Aye, a surprise, eh?" She smiled at him. "It had better no' be Hamish in the barn in naught but his shirt again," she laughed recalling the day they first went riding, and the 'surprise' of horses he had intended turned out to be Hamish in a private tryst with the merchant's daughter.

"No lass, though that was a great surprise, even for me." He laughed with her. "Nay, tis no' my brother, but I think ye shall like it all the same."

He led her into the main hall where her parents awaited. Elspeth ran to her daughter, hugging her tightly. She whispered in Meg's ear at the same time.

"Is he mistreating ye, my daughter?" She could not hide the worry in her voice.

"Nay, Mother. He has been naught but a true gentleman," Meg whispered back. "I swear by my blood."

Elspeth looked much relieved and handed her daughter a basket as she asked Meg about her stay. The basket held flowers and spices not found near the manse. She squealed with delight. Elspeth, satisfied with her daughter's responses that she was content at the keep, then turned her attention to the Laird's son, letting Meg pay her respects to her father. Elspeth had noticed that Ewan's eyes had not left Meg from the moment they entered the hall. She curtsied to him.

"My wee Meggie says that ye have been a true gentleman to her while she has been here. Is that true?"

"I gave ye my word, mistress Lachlan, and I kept it. She has no' been hurt. Why look at her. See how she glows. 'Tis no' only the ribbons in her hair, methinks." Ewan patted Elspeth's hand in reassurance.

"Aye, she glows. I also meant her heart, ye rogue, when I asked for your word, ye ken."

Ewan looked at her, fire in his blue eyes, and at that moment, Elspeth knew what lay in his heart.

"Do ye no' think I knew that when I vowed?" he asked her softly.

Meg's father embraced her heartily, happy to see his daughter unscathed. While he was sickened at why he let his daughter out of his house and into the keep, seeing his daughter in finery, glowing like a candle, helped him come to terms with his decision. However, he still had to keep up the rest of his bargain to the English.

"So ye are well, my daughter?"

"Aye, Father," Meg responded. "I am treated well here."

"That is good, ye ken." Lachlan decided to be direct in trying to obtain information. "Have ye heard any word on the English who hurt ye?"

"Nay, Father. I ken that they have one man in the dungeon, but I ken naught if he still lives."

"What of the others that remain? Has the Laird or his son said what they are doing to remove the threat?"

"Aye. Ewan has told me that the *Sassenachs* are in league with John of Argyll, using MacLeod land as a direct route to the channel for communication. Since they still pose a threat to me, and to Scotland, Ewan has scouts searching each day for their presence. He sent a missive to King Robert yesterday last, to inform him of the events, but naught else has occurred. Why? Has something happened at home?" Meg suddenly sounded worried.

"Nay, lass. I wanted to be sure that the Laird and his son were being of service, and no' keeping ye here for, uh, entertainment." Lachlan paused, trying to find the right words. "I am happy to ken that they are trying to catch the English fiends, and that ye are treated well."

"Thank ye, Father, for your concern. Will I see ye and mother again soon?"

"Aye. I will bring your mother back in less than a fortnight, and the Laird's son has vowed to escort ye to the cottage soon."

Meg bade her parents farewell. Her mother told her that she was saying a prayer of hope for Meg. A pagan ritual of the old religion, true, but it relieved Meg, and she promised to say the prayer herself as well. Her mother then regarded her with a sage eye.

"Methinks 'tis more than your pretty ribbons that make ye glow such, and 'tis agreeable to me, ye ken. Keep my words close t' your heart, my lovey."

Meg gave her an "aye, Mother," but didn't understand what was agreeable. Perchance she realized how Meg felt about the young Laird to be, but then why would she remind Meg to keep her words of morality close to her heart?

Her parents were escorted from the keep, and she waved to them, sad to see her parents leave. She also had a terrible sense of foreboding, as though her simple life she had loved so much would drastically change, and part of her was very afraid.

On the Eve of Beltane, Meg stayed awake, wrapping flowers and twigs together, waiting until the moon reached its zenith. Then there would be enough dew on the grass to bathe her face. Unaccepted by the Church proper, the old ritual was taught to her by her mother. Like her mother, though she accepted the Church, Meg followed the old religious ways.

The ritual of a young girl bathing her face in the early morning dew of Beltane was to ensure youth and fertility. Elspeth still followed this ritual and taught all her daughters to do the same. As Elspeth had six children, Meg did not question its validity. Taking a candle from the mantle, she walked the darkened passageways to the kitchen, and out to the courtyard of the keep.

Ewan, not yet asleep, heard someone walk past his door. Afraid for Meg, he grabbed his plaid off a nearby chair, and not bothering with a shirt, he wrapped the plaid about him before grabbing his claymore and entering the passageway. As he turned toward Meg's chambers, he saw the incandescent glow of a single candle at the opposite end of the hall. His hand on the hilt of his sword, he trailed the candlelight.

Meg reached the door of the great hall, and turning, she went to the kitchen and crept out the servant's door to the side courtyard. If she been at home, her mother and sister would have gone with her near the forest and used the grass there.

Here at the keep, following a worn trail to the garden where the grasses and dew were the highest, she reached her hands out, gently pressing the flowers and grass, coaxing the dampness into her hands. She then touched her hands to her face and neck. She spoke to the ancient goddesses, asking them for blessings of fertility and the richness of nature in her life.

This year she had an additional request but knew it was inappropriate. *How do I ask for the Laird's son? 'Tis a petty request and one that would no' be answered.* She decided to ask instead that the goddesses bless her with a good and decent husband, which seemed a more likely request. The coolness of the dew was invigorating, and she closed her eyes to enjoy the heady summer scents of the flowers. She was rubbing the dew on her forearms when a voice startled her from her reverie.

"What are ye doing out here in the wee hours of the morn, fair maiden?" a half-joking, half-worried voice asked.

Meg spun around on her heels and caught sight of Ewan standing outside the night-shadow of the keep, watching her intently. Meg was at a loss for words.

The sight of him made Meg's breath catch in her throat. He wore nothing but his kilt and leather footwear and held his giant claymore with one hand. She could see every muscle in his chest and stomach, his arms both strong and thick. To her, he resembled an ancient god, and she thought he looked both wild and beautiful. But more unnerving than his appealing looks was his very presence. Embarrassed at being caught, Meg knew she could not admit to partaking in a pagan ritual. She feared Ewan would run to the priest. But how else could she explain what she was doing?

"Weel, I . . ." she started, then decided to take a different approach. "Why did ye follow me? Are ye suddenly my keeper?" Meg demanded.

"Of course, I'm your keeper!" Ewan exclaimed. "What if the English had found a way into the manor and took ye?"

Ewan stopped himself short of yelling. He was much relieved to find her safe and sound, still within the walls of the holding. He knew what she was doing once she took her hands from the flowers and brought them to her face.

"I apologize to ye then. I did no' mean to cause ye worry." She straightened up and started to walk back to the keep, but Ewan caught her by the arm. His closeness made her knees weak and she felt a rush in her up through her belly. If she desired, she could reach out and touch his strong chest and arms, and she cursed herself for acting like a smitten, empty-headed girl.

"So, shall I expect flowers at my door in the morn as well?" he asked her.

Shocked, Meg stared at his darkly handsome face, searching to find out if he would take her to the priest. He saw her concern and smiled to disarm her.

"My mother," he told her, "oft practiced the old ways. With Da's permission, she taught my brother's and I much as well." His smile softened with the memory. "Ye are already young and beautiful. Were ye asking for fertility for ye future husband?" he teased.

Relieved, she smirked at his teasing, and at his audacity to mention her fertility. She snatched her arm from his hand and started to dance away from him.

"Ye had best watch where ye step, my Laird-to-be, for I shall use thistles on your doorstep!" she called back to him.

Ewan chuckled and followed her back inside. It was a while before Meg fell asleep in her bed that night, and again when she dreamed, it was of the young, bare-chested Laird.

That same night, as Meg and Ewan frolicked in the night air, long after Connor Lachlan and Elspeth had returned home from the great house, Connor waited by a large aspen at the back of the stable near the sheep's grazing land. It was quiet and warm, a night of peace and a night for lovers, but it was not so for Lachlan. He heard a rustling and turned to Montgomery, who appeared like a ghost in the moonlight.

"Finally, old man. You have news?" Montgomery barked at Lachlan.

"I dinna ken if it will help ye, but they know of your plans to run the MacLeod's off their land. They ken of Argyll, and the young Laird has sent a missive to King Robert Himself."

"Anything more?"

"Nay. MacLeod has scouts looking for ye daily. I dinna ken anymore."

"Do they *ken* my name, or where we are?" The contempt in Montgomery's voice was unmistakable.

"Nay. My daughter did no' mention such to me."

"See your daughter again soon. Find out more. What is MacLeod's greatest weakness? Where can we hit hardest? Find out."

Montgomery turned abruptly and disappeared back into the moonlight, but Connor remained rooted to his spot. He did not need to see his daughter again to answer the English fool's question. Seeing Meg today answered them all. Connor Lachlan knew the Laird's greatest weakness, what could cause the most hurt. God save him, while Lachlan would give Montgomery almost any information to keep his family safe, he could never tell him of the young Laird's greatest weakness.

Lachlan had paled at the mere question, for he knew the answer in one word – Meggie.

CHAPTER SIX

The Valley of the Shadow of Death

COLIN MACLEOD, OLD LAIRD of the clan MacLeod, lay in bed on the eve of Beltane. His tray had been removed earlier, and he had lain in bed, almost motionless, since the serving girl departed.

He looked again at the letter in his left hand from none other than good King Robert the Bruce himself. The letter, masked in almost comic good humor, was one that he had waited days to receive, but in reality, he had been waiting years. Finally, there was an approval for the marriage of his oldest son. Colin loved all his sons dearly, but he held a special place in his heart for his oldest, as it was Ewan who most resembled his late wife.

From her, Ewan inherited his dark wavy hair, sparkling eyes, and carefree spirit. It was Ewan's spirit that had kept him alive these past years, since that carefree spirit had also kept Ewan from marriage. Colin's last living wish was to see his son wed to a woman he loved, and while Colin knew that he would not actually witness the wedding, Ewan was as good as wed.

Colin prayed that night, to the church's God, to the gods and goddesses that his wife had prayed to. He asked for strength in his coming journey, courage to make it through, and the good fortune to lay his eyes upon his wife once the ordeal was over.

Unlike most people, Colin welcomed death, for it would reunite him with his lost love. Caitir was passionate, loving, and the most wonderful mother and woman who ever lived, and Colin felt cursed in life from the moment he lost her. The only reason he lived after her death was for his sons, to make sure his eldest son would become an acceptable leader, and with marriage imminent, that goal was at hand. He also prayed that Ewan would have the daughter they never did, his granddaughter in Caitir's image. His only regret was that he would not see grandchildren in this life. The time was now.

The old Laird closed his eyes and saw Caitir. He saw her as she looked on their wedding day, scared, shy, radiant. As she looked full in pregnancy with each boy, and then nursing each son, holding him close, offering her love and protection. He envisioned her as she looked when he loved her, eyes glittering, breasts full, hair thick and dark on the bed. He then saw her after she was found in the glen, bloody, violated, her hands trying to hold in what was left of their unborn babe.

Colin saw himself as he lifted her from the ground, not letting anyone else near her, followed her to the kirk to receive a final blessing from the priest, and then to the far corner of the cemetery, where he dug her grave in the place she loved best, wrapped her in his own plaid for a shroud, and lay her in her coffin in the cold hard ground. He had cried as he poured the dirt on top of her, sealing her forever in death.

Since that moment, he had dreamt of her often. In his dreams, he stood at her grave and watched her rise up to heaven, holding her hand out to him. In his dreams, every time he reached out to her, she pulled her hand back and turned away. This time, his dream wife did not turn away from him. Instead, she held tight to his hand as she led him from life into the great beyond. With a smile on his lips, Colin MacLeod died.

⊰⊰⊰⊰⊱   ⊰⊱⊱⊱⊱

As Ewan stepped from his door that morning, the crunch under his boots told him that, indeed, Meg was already awake and had left flowers at his door. He bent to retrieve them and saw that she had used thistles in his bundle. He placed the bundle on his bed, grateful for the small gift from her, and went down to the great hall. He noticed all the doors in the passageway had flower bundles before them. He began to wonder if she would have a maypole erected in the meadow outside the walls of the keep.

He found her downstairs finishing her porridge. She smiled at him and his heart melted. Ewan understood the smile was only because she no longer had to fear the discovery of her, or her mother's, beliefs, but he hoped as well that the smile was because she was happy to see him.

After his fear of the thought of losing her the night before, Ewan came to realize how much he loved her, and how little she knew of it. He also realized he would have to start making some more obvious gestures to show her how much he cared and find out if she cared for him at all. As much as he loved her, he could never vow to spend the rest of his life with someone who did not care for him. Perchance it was unfair to use his parent's deeply loving relationship as a comparison, but it was all he knew. He wanted love as deep as that his parents had shared.

"May I ask a favor of ye, milord?" she asked as she approached him.

"Only if ye call me Ewan, my sweet," he responded, making her blush.

She is so beautiful, he thought to himself, and his heart ached. She wore her hair pulled back simply, but draped in the ribbons he bestowed upon her, knowing they made her happy. The ribbons twined in her hair, as colorful jewels set in deep gold.

"Today is as fine a day as any..." she rambled trying to speak her request.

"And the favor is?" Ewan got right to the point.

"Would ye ride with me this day?" she ventured.

She was becoming comfortable enough to enjoy riding the plodding little Bedbug and wanted more practice to improve. This was the first request that she had made to him outright, and she was nervous to be so brash as to ask. His eyes twinkled with delight at her request, hoping to turn her on to riding, on a minor scale of course. He grasped both her hands in his, kissing them.

"It would be my greatest pleasure, my sweet. Let us get ye ready."

Ewan spent the greater part of the morning showing her the basics of trotting at a good clip. Once she was comfortable with the finer aspects of riding, Ewan suggested a short, faster ride around the keep. Excited over her accomplishment in riding thus far, Meg was more than agreeable to a short ride.

They conversed lightly as they rode, Meg having to concentrate more on staying on the horse than she could dedicate to conversation. Once she grew accustomed to the faster pace, she broached the subject of her midnight stroll the evening before.

"Thank ye, for understanding about Beltane, and what I was doing in the garden," she looked at him earnestly.

"Tell me of your parents, Meggie."

"There is naught much to tell. My father is a Lachlan, but the youngest of many brothers. He came here wi' a cousin and brother for market day in town, passing through, ye ken? And they wanted some food and drink for their travels."

"And where was your mother on that market day?" Ewan asked

"Oddly enough, right next to him, speaking to the tanner's very heft wife. The wife was close to her time wi' her second, and my mother was offerin' to help ease her sore back." Meg paused for a moment, smiling as if to herself. "I always thought 'twould be like that for me. I would meet my intended at market day."

She stopped abruptly, shaking her head and waving her hand at Ewan. He regarded her softly, entranced by her story of serendipity with her parents, and how it thusly affected Meg's expectations in life, in much the same way as Ewan's parents affected his.

"Anyhow," she continued, "My father stopped amidst his purchases and touched my mother's hair. It used to be much like mine, ye ken. And she keeps it covered now. My father asked for an introduction and received it. He stayed with some distant relatives 'til they wed. My mother's only request was that, since she was t'only midwife in the clan, he would stay here wi' her. Of course, he agreed. How could he not?"

"Of course," Ewan repeated. "How could he not?"

"'Tis good to ken that there is another who is at least sympathetic to my mother's ways." She offered him a thin smile of gratitude. "Your mother sounds like a wonderful lady, to be so concerned that ye learn her ways as well. And ye father too, for allowing it."

"Aye, my mother was a grand lady." Ewan's eyes lit up when he spoke about her. "She could indulge my brothers and I without spoiling us. She and my da were so much in love wi' each other. It devastated him when she died."

"And ye, as well?" Meg asked.

Ewan nodded his head. They rode silently for a moment, then Meg spoke again.

"May I ask what happened t'her? I was naught but a young child when she passed on."

Ewan was quiet, then spoke softly.

"There was a reason I was so enraged with the men who were mistreating ye. Not only because of what they were trying, but I hate all English." Ewan paused, then spoke again, a bit more forcefully.

"She was pregnant wi' what she and my da hoped would be a daughter. I was ten and five years, so they had waited many years for another child. 'Twas near Beltane, and she went out to collect blooms, just like ye do, only she did no' return. My da went out to find her, but she was gone from the keep. A search party found her within t' wood. She ha' been beaten and . . ." here he paused.

"Beaten and killed, Ewan?"

"Aye."

Then he exploded.

"Nay! 'Tis no' all!" He grasped her by the arms, frantic, angry and dark, as though hatred had clouded over him.

"She was beaten and tied to a tree and violated," he shouted. "And when they couldn't do anything more than kill her, they tried to cut her bairn out of her, out of her body, and she and the babe bled to death out there, all alone!"

He then pulled her to him roughly and kissed her hard. Not brash, as the first time he tried, but wanton, fervent, as if he were trying to find solace from the horror of his mother's death in her.

Meg let him kiss her. She didn't fight but let him take what he needed in that kiss, and she found herself responding. She pulled him closer to her, let his mouth ravage hers, and did not pull away when she felt his tongue press into her mouth. His tongue probed hers, and she welcomed it, kissing him back with equal passion. When he pulled away, she felt disappointed and elated at the same time. It was also difficult to breathe.

"I apologize. That was no' verra gentlemanly."

"'Twas quite alright."

"That is why I was so upset t' find ye gone on the Eve of Beltane," he offered as an excuse.

She warmed to know he was concerned about her, and Ewan reached out and took a reddish-gold lock of her hair between his fingers, stroking its softness. She held her breath. Her insides had melted at his kiss and her head was spinning so much she feared she may fall from her pony.

This is what her mother had warned her about. These feelings were so powerful, it was no wonder the Laird's son had women fawning all over him.

"Do ye see, Meggie?" he asked her. "I –"

They were interrupted by Hamish bursting through the trees. His hair and clothes were in disarray, and his earthy hair stood on end in a state of panic.

"Ewan!" he yelled. "Ye must come now! 'Tis Father - he is dead!"

With that, in one fluid move, Ewan hefted Meg from her mount onto his lap, threw her reins to Hamish, and rode like a fury back to the keep.

Ewan leapt off his horse in the courtyard, racing up the stairs to his father's chambers. There, amid many a crying servant girl and teary-eyed faithful soldier, lay his father on his bed. No one had touched the old man. In MacLeod custom the oldest son buried his father, and they knew Ewan would want it that way.

Meg had followed Ewan up the steps and finally caught him in Colin's bedchamber as he knelt on the ground beside his father's bed. She watched him take Colin's hand, remove a parchment clutched there, and bring the hand to his lips. Ewan quietly said goodbye to his father and bid him Godspeed on this journey to his mother. He stood, wrapped his father in the MacLeod plaid that covered the bed, then lifted his father's frail, lifeless body into his arms. A priest was already waiting by the door to bless Colin before they buried him.

Meg hung back, trying to hide amongst the throng who cluttered the chamber. She did not know what to do or say -- Ewan looked too distraught to even try to approach. It suddenly occurred to her that she was no longer under the care of the Laird's son, but of the Laird himself. Ewan would most likely accept leadership within a few days, followed by a clan gathering for all to swear alliance to the new Laird, just as the clan had to Ewan's father.

Meg realized that with the death of his father, his imminent ascension to the position of Laird, and all his newfound responsibilities, Ewan would no longer bide his time with her. She was no longer of consequence. Comprehending this with a sad heart, she quietly slipped away to her room to prepare to leave.

Little did Meg realize that Ewan had been in the position of Laird since the moment his father fell sick, if not yet in title. The English interest in Meg concerned him greatly, not only with regards to the safety of the clan, but also with Meg herself.

In Ewan's mind, Meg was the furthest thing from inconsequence and planned to let her know that as soon as he took care of this father.

A great audience awaited as Ewan lay his father to rest in the cemetery next to his mother. Ewan spoke extensively in Gaelic, asking for swiftness and security in his father's journey into death. He then took his father's claymore, raised it high above his head, and with a mighty heave, thrust it into the ground at the head of the grave.

Squatting low to the ground to give one final blessing to his father, he whispered, "May ye finally find solace in mother's arms once again."

Ewan rose quickly and left the gravesite before anyone realized he was missing. The large group, wiping tears aside, slowly said their farewells and departed. Eventually, Meg stood alone in the garden at the foot of the two graves, her heart filled with pity for the woman and her lost babe, for the nice old man forced to live so long without her, and for the son who had now lost them both.

Grasping a handful of creamy white heather, she lay the stems on both graves, offering an ancient prayer for the dead that her mother taught her when Meg's own grandmother had passed. Meg turned and walked toward her chamber to begin collecting her belongings. She was certain she would be asked to leave soon.

After leaving the cemetery, Ewan set about preparing the keep for the events to come, specifically the naming ceremony, in which Ewan would officially be named Laird of the clan MacLeod, and the clan gathering. While the naming ceremony was a small, intimate affair that would take place the next day, messengers needed to be dispatched for the clan gathering to allow those on the outskirts of the MacLeod land, and other clans who aligned with MacLeod, time to arrive at the gathering.

After sending Hamish and another warrior as messengers, Ewan strode up the staircase in search of Meg. He found her in her chamber, assembling her belongings in the center of a plaid on the bed.

"Meg," Ewan approached, not sure of what she was doing, "are ye rearranging your chambers?"

She noticed he was eyeing her belongings as he spoke. The kitten, growing steadily with a diet of milk and fish from the kitchen, curled up on the plaid next to her belongings. She opened one lazy green eye at Ewan, then yawned hugely and tucked her face back into her paws.

How quiet his voice, Meg thought, but Meg herself also felt reserved. Death always brought sadness. On top of the gray pallor of death over the day, as much as she tried to deny it, she had enjoyed her time at the keep and reveled in the little luxuries he had given her. She already changed back into what she wore when he brought her to the keep, the coarse, colorless linen shift and woolen kirtle. She was tying a strip of linen in her hair to replace the beautiful rainbow of ribbons that previously adorned her copper tresses.

However, more than that, Meg was saddened to be leaving and tried to keep it from him. *The rogue 'twould be happy to see me cry, knowing he had captured the heart of yet another maid.* She sighed and looked at him.

His eyes were red and swollen, his hair and clothing altogether tired and disheveled. Even his broad shoulders slumped a bit as he stood in the doorway of the chamber, most of his cocky stance replaced by the weight of his father's death and his responsibilities as Laird. Her heart went out to him, though she willed it hard against him. He no longer needed to concern himself with her welfare. She had been a little game to occupy his time until he had responsibility, and now that time was here. She steeled herself against him and answered.

"Me thinks I have overstayed my welcome, milord. 'Tis time for me to return home." Her voice was barely above a whisper.

She turned her saddened gaze away from his stricken face and resumed her packing. It did not feel proper to take his gifts with her. She looked with longing at the beautiful ribbons lying on the chest at the end of the bed, then tied all her belongings together in the plaid.

When she reached up to pull the ribbons from her hair and place them with the rest, she felt his hand stay hers, and his fingers caress her hair. She hadn't realized he had moved away from the door.

"Nay," he whispered, his eyes on her hair. "*A leannan*, I want ye to stay."

Meg was appalled by his statement. With his father dead, even with the keep's servants, there was no proper chaperone, and her mother would die where she stood to learn her daughter was sleeping in a man's house unchaperoned.

"I can no' do that, milord," she stated firmly. "With appearances, and your new duties as Laird, I would be an inconvenience, and 'twould be unseemly. I should no' be here. 'Tis no' my place."

His hand gripped her hair and his face took on a bewildered look.

"No' your place? Pray tell, what the devil are ye talking about?"

His low tones had a harshness that made Meg want to cower with fear. Though she had spent the past days with him, she had not truly taken in his size, his power. She looked at him anew, seeing how immense he was, how muscular, and how all those muscles seemed strained. He spent hours daily training with the soldiers, now *his* soldiers, and she was a mere crofter's maid who, at the moment, seemed to be angering her lord.

But the heat in his eyes made it impossible for her to look away, and his hand grasping her hair would not have allowed for her to turn. Her heart beat a fevered flutter in her chest and her blood pounded in her ears. She was awed at the power in him, power that he seemed to keep at bay when they were together riding or joking.

Now that power seemed real and raw and immediate, and she wondered how she loved him but also feared him as well. She spoke in a low voice.

"Ye have duties, milord. Duties that are far more important than a mere maid who occupies a space well above her station in her Laird's home. 'Tis time for me to go home and accept my place."

"Accept your place? By God, Meg, *this* is your place! I will no' let ye leave. *This* is your new home and your new place is here with me!"

Then, before she could breathe, he swept her towards him, crushing her against his solid, unyielding frame, kissing her raggedly. He clung to her and she could not push herself away. His mouth possessed hers repeatedly, hungry for her. She felt the hardness of his body, his strength, and his power, that power she had only seen before, and she could not think, could not move, could not breathe. She weakened against him as his mouth continually sought hers, and she grasped onto his tunic for purchase. One hand was in her hair and his other slid down her backside, and she stiffened with the intimacy of his touch.

Suddenly, he thrust her away from him. She stared at his ragged frame, stunned by his actions and her response to him, her lips aching from his attack, her skin sore from his stubbled growth of beard.

"Ye will stay here wi' me as is your place," he commanded, then stormed from her chambers.

Meg blinked, trying to regain her composure, then went back to her plaid. She did not know what to make of his statement. How could the keep be her place? It had been a temporary solution to an insignificant problem.

The mood of the keep was solemn that day. While servants remained busy preparing for the naming ceremony and guests to arrive, they were not jovial or laughing as usual. Meg kept to her chambers, as saddened as the rest, but also introspective. Her heart was heavy at the death of the Laird but also concerned as she went from being a guest at the keep for her safety to, apparently, a prisoner.

And Ewan's odd behavior left her confused. On any other day, she would have felt joyous, all things considered, that he wanted her to stay with him. The inevitable had happened, and she was smitten with the new Laird.

She knew her feelings were for naught. As a crofter's daughter, she lacked noble blood, lacking importance. Though she was but a crofter's maid, she would only give herself in marriage, and leaders of the clan did not wed low-born crofters. Leaders of the clan dallied with the lowborn, but wedded women of import -- ladies of more noble birth.

Meg sighed heavily, resigning herself to pining for a man she would never have a claim on. She felt no better than other girls who had been in her position, though he had not bedded her, and she realized how easily and quickly Ewan had made his way into her heart.

I love him, she thought with an air of sadness, knowing nothing could come of such senseless emotion. Putting that silly thought to the back of her mind, she left her chambers.

She went to the evening meal dressed as she was, feeling it appropriate for a funeral meal, only adding ribbons to her hair. *Best no' let them go to waste. How vain am I!* As she walked down the hall to the stairs, she heard some women speaking as they cleaned the chambers. She heard her name and halted her step.

"That Meg, I wonder will the Laird send her home now?" an older voice commented.

"Why would she have to leave?" a younger voice responded. "I think the Laird fancies her."

"Aye, that is all well and good, but 'tis only Meggie Lachlan and when the Laird is finished with her, she will ha' to go home. The Laird must wed a lady of respect; perhaps 'twill be Elayne MacNally. Her father's lands are no' too far south, I've heard, so 'twill be a good ally for the clan."

"Where will she go, that Meggie?" the younger voice inquired.

"Home, mayhap with a bairn in her belly. Many think 'twould serve her right, prancing 'round the keep like a lady of the manor."

That was all Meg heard. Blinking back tears, she stepped lithely past the chamber to the stairwell.

Ewan was already seated, speaking to the man who would become second in command, Gavin MacLeod. Second only to Ewan, Gavin was one of the most sought-after bachelors in the MacLeod lands. Both Ewan and Gavin's eyes flicked to her when she took her seat by herself near the end of the hall. Meg was well aware that Gavin did not care for her.

He thinks the new Laird is flitting below his station as well. Either that or he resents the time Ewan has spent wi' me. These thoughts made Meg feel even more unwelcome, and she wondered if those in the keep believed as the chamber women and Gavin did.

All the wonderful time she had spent here the past few days seem to crumble under the weight of what everyone else was thinking. Had she been living in a bubble? How could she have missed what others were saying about her and the new Laird? How could she not have realized what people would think of her presence at the Laird's house? Meg shook her head at her naiveté.

Ewan's conversation at the head table was heated, for Ewan's yell could be heard throughout the hall.

"I dinna care what ye think!"

Both men's heads sprang up, and Ewan's heavy blue eyes lifted to her, then moved back to Gavin. They resumed their discussion until the food was served.

CHAPTER SEVEN

And Then a Wedding

UNABLE TO SLEEP, MEG stood near the window, feeling the warm, late spring breeze. When she had retired to her chamber after supper, she noticed that the chambers of Ewan's father being cleaned and aired. Many of the personal items were removed, and new bedding and rushes brought in.

Meg knew in her heart what these changes meant. Ewan already had plans to bring his wife to the keep. *Would she arrive tomorrow for the gathering? Will she be upset that I am here? A strange, lowborn woman in her husband's house? Oh, what will she think?* Meg felt alone, unwanted, and out of place. She suddenly wanted her mother. *At the verra least, when I go home, 'twill no' be with a bairn in my belly.* She sighed.

As the breezes swept through the window, the smell of the light, calming heather clung to the air. A burst of laughter below broke her from her thoughts. Noise and laughter rang from the great hall all evening. Throughout the evening meal, Ewan's men seemed to encourage him to drink, to share stories of the old Laird as they drowned his sorrows most likely, and he was well in his cups when she left. Were they trying to drink away his sadness at his father's death? Or was the drink for another reason? One-upmanship?

Suddenly there was a loud cheer, then a thump, and the raucous noise quieted to a low murmur. She contemplated returning to bed, for morning came all too soon, when there was a thump at her chamber door. She whirled around and lifted the latch. Ewan all but fell into her.

"Milord!" she exclaimed, catching his stumble with one arm. "What has happened to ye?"

Ewan reeked of ale, but his stupefied look turned serious at the sight of her.

"Och, lass. I had to get away from the likes o'them." He straightened up, not as drunk as she thought.

"Did they mean to drink ye into death then?" she asked. He grinned at her.

"Nay. 'Tis nothing as serious as that. My men mean to make sure that their new Laird can drink wi' the best o' them and no' lose his senses." He paused. "A show of trust and strength, ye ken?"

Meg was contemplative. She dreaded drawing attention to herself, especially when she knew the conversation regarded her residence at the manse. Meg inhaled deeply, trying to act proud, and opened her mouth to speak, and Ewan was there. He rested his hand on her side, and with the other, held her face gently.

"Do ye ken how beautiful ye are in the moonlight? Like a fairy, e'er small as one, the ribbons sparkle like their dust."

Then his mouth was on hers, not rough or powerful like earlier but lightly and passionately, and she melted into his chest.

She opened her mouth slightly, to gasp some air, and instead his tongue touched hers, again shocking her, sending nervous shivers throughout her body. Never had anyone been so intimate with her, and she pulled back slightly. He moved his hand to the back of her head to keep her close, and as his kisses grew more bold, more fervent, she felt his arm clasp her close to him. He smelled of ale and heather, sweat and maleness, and her head spun once more.

What is this, she thought, *that should make me feel so heady, so wanton, and so frightened all at once? Can he feel the power in this? The power he has over me?*

Her knees weakened as the fierceness of his kisses grew, and then his tongue was on her neck, her throat, and she heard her mother's voice in her head, whirling with all the other thoughts, yet she could not turn Ewan away. He felt like fire, and she burned where he kissed her.

He lifted her and crossed quickly to the bed, but with his heat, his lips, and the burning she felt for him, Meg didn't notice. He sat on the bed with Meg on his lap, and his lips and tongue continued his burning caress to her shoulder. When his hand rested on her breast, she didn't flinch. She couldn't regain her mind as his hands and lips touched her in ways she had never experienced.

Before she knew what she was doing, her hands were on him, her fingers twining in his hair, her other hand on his chest, hot through the fabric of his tunic. She felt his strength in the movements of his chest, that fierce power of his muscles as he kissed her, and that sensation made her burn even more.

His fingers played with her nipple through the gown, and she gave a gasping moan at the thrills he caused. Ewan moaned in return, his lips moving to her breast, down the swell. He had pulled her breast free of the confines of the rough gown and kissed her nipple. He gingerly touched with his tongue, and then suckled softly.

Meg was in agony and ecstasy. No one had ever dared touched where he touched, kissed where he kissed, and the rush of emotions and sensations made her dizzy and hot and wanton. Her head was swimming, and she was letting him go on, and by God, the sensation was glorious.

It was only when his hand went under her gown and trailed her thigh did she come to her senses. She stiffened and caught his hand in hers.

Ewan did not fight her. He lifted his head and looked into her eyes, still glazed with the novelty of passion. Blue eyes regarded green as he discretely adjusted her gown. Meg couldn't speak as she feared her voice would betray her with emotion. Her hand rose to clasp her shoulder in a nervous gesture as she tore her gaze for his.

Ewan took a deep breath, gathering his wits.

"My apologies, lass. I did no' mean for it to be this way," he whispered hoarsely. Her head snapped up, her eyes pinched in confusion.

"This way? This way? What, wi' me as your mistress and your wife across the hall?" He could hear the anger in her voice, but when he tried to speak, she cut him off. "Ye forbade me to leave, kept me here for what? This? I may be lowborn, milord, but mindful of what ye have found elsewhere, I am no whore!"

Ewan's face reflected his shock. "Whore? Ye think I mean for ye to be my whore?" He barked out a laugh that made her jump. "By Christ, Meg, ye have it all wrong. I want to bed ye, aye, but do ye ken why I stopped?"

Meg shook her head, copper hair and bright ribbons settling around her. Ewan took her hand and moved forward, close enough for her to feel his breath on her face.

"Aye, I want to bed ye, but I will wed ye first."

This time, she barked out a laugh. She leapt off the bed and spun, glaring at him.

"Och, so that is how ye do it!" she exclaimed. Ewan sat utterly confused.

"Do what?"

"I oft wondered how ye could bed so many lasses, wi' nary one none the wiser. Ye may be quite the rogue for certain, but I would think that some women ha' the will to resist ye! But that is no' the way of it. Do ye promise all the lassies marriage before ye bed them, or just the ones who do no' quickly fall for your charms?"

Ewan stood then, his face dark, and she was afraid. That fearsome power had returned. She had forgotten her place, living at the keep, and while she would like to think herself high enough to speak to him as such, he was still the Laird of her clan. She was naught but his servant, and she haughtily insulted him. He could justifiably beat her or punish her as was his right. Meg paled, wanting to throw herself at his mercy, but the deed was done, so she stood her ground, her chin raised in defiance. Ewan walked to the fire and leaned on one arm against the stone. He ran his hand through his black hair in aggravation, making it stand up. He looked wild but spoke softly.

"Do ye think me a liar, Meg?"

"Nay, milord." Her voice was barely a whisper.

"In the time ye have been here, have I shown ye that I am a crude man? One who uses others for his own gain?"

"Nay, milord."

"Do ye always believe idle talk of jealous mouths, wee Meggie?"

"I try no' to, milord."

"Do ye think me the cruel rogue that ye have named me?" With his thumb, he rubbed the nightly growth of beard that had begun to spurt, and Meg recalled the feel of it on her face. She sighed heavily.

"Nay, milord. Ye have shown me naught but the utmost respect."

"Then why, Meg, would ye insult me so?"

She froze, realizing that he knew her words to be the curse she intended. She was quiet for a long moment, thinking. Seeing this dark, almost vulnerable side of him frightened her. He seemed the wounded animal, one that she wanted to console but hesitated for fear of its bite. He was showing her honesty, and she felt obliged to do the same.

"Milord..." she began.

"Can ye no' call me Ewan? 'Tis my given name," he interrupted.

"Aye, weel, Ewan. Oft it seems easier to believe the bad of a person than to admit that ye care for him."

She thought her voice was barely audible, but he heard her all the same. He shifted his eyes to look at her with his wounded gaze, then paced away from the wall.

"Do ye, then?" he asked

"Aye," she whispered.

He moved to her, wrapped her in his arms and placed a kiss on her forehead, only to be pushed away.

"Meg!"

"Aye, I care for ye!" she exclaimed, tears shining in her eyes, confounding Ewan completely. He wanted to wed her, and now she was upset that she cared for him?

"I care," she yelled again," but 'tis all for naught! I can pine from afar but for what? To see ye wed to another? To the daughter of a neighboring Laird? I canna do it, milord! But ye have kept me here, and treated me so fine, that I have begun to think myself above my station, when I am only the daughter of a crofter! My da doesna even have any land to call his own! Ye canna wed me, so why can ye no' let me return home?"

"Canna wed ye?" Ewan's dark mood was gone, replaced by pure shock. Surely the lass did not consider herself so low that to wed her would be impossible? "I can wed ye if I like and wed ye I will!"

He grabbed her arms, wanting to shake her senseless and crush her to him at the same time.

"Do ye think by virtue of your mother's womb ye are so much less than another? Do ye think that God would breathe life into a worthless creature?" The shock never left his face.

"That is the way of it, right, milord?"

She stared him in the eyes as he pulled himself up to his full height, his frame dwarfing the entire room.

"Who has said such things to ye?" The darkness returned, and he looked ready to kill.

"'Twas only words, milord. They did no harm."

"Only words, yet ye think yourself a lowborn wench who canna have the right to wed the man she loves 'acause of his station?"

Meg had no answer to his question. She could not even deny the word *love* for she would be lying. Sometime, between their first encounter in the glen and this very night, she had fallen in love with her Laird.

"Let me show ye something." He reached into his sporran and removed a parchment, similar to the one clutched in the old Laird's dead hands.

"My father," he told her as he unfurled the scroll, "waited long for me to select a bride. Now, I am no' verra drunk or daft this eve, so listen well. My mother and da were passionately in love, and when mother died, father wanted to join her, but remained to see me wed. Methinks he would have liked some grandchildren as well before he passed. But though I searched, I found naught but lasses wi' no spine, no will, nary a thought in their heads, until I found ye. When ye rejected me, I saw ye had passion, ideas, and I wanted ye. Yes! I wanted a lowborn maid! For she stirred me like no other. My father worried about stations, alliances, and neighboring lands, but I had little selection in those respects. My father then wrote a missive to King Robert the Bruce Himself, asking his permission to allow me the bride of my choosing, regardless of common practice. Here."

Ewan thrust the parchment at her, and she took it with a shaking hand. "This was the scroll my father held as he passed into death. Go ahead, read it!"

Meg held the parchment lightly, barely glancing at it. She dropped her eyes from Ewan's intense gaze and handed the paper back.

"I canna read," she told him.

Ewan paused at this, taking the parchment back. He stared at the message for a moment, lost in deep thought.

He then raised his head and stared past her out the window to the starry night that marked the end of the day that his father died. Had it only been one day? It seemed longer than a fortnight and Ewan suddenly felt very, very tired. He was thinking of his mother as well, and in a daze, it was of her that Ewan spoke.

"My mother could read. Not many women could - fewer than even now." A tightness pulled at this mouth at his memories. "My mother and father would read treatises and contracts, and then discuss the works together, often arguing over finer points. Mother, with her more ancient wisdoms, and father, with his 'male surety,' as Mother called it, would argue about a piece of work for days on end."

The memory suddenly ended, and Ewan's attention snapped back to Meg who had remained silent during his reverie.

"Och," he grunted, grasping the letter in his hand. "I shall read it to ye."

Most Respectful Laird MacLeod,

"My father," Ewan inserted for clarification.

I have received your Missive, and I admit, while it is one of the Lesser Concerns I have, it is one of the most Intriguing. Your son Desires to wed a Lady of his Choosing, yet you fear the Retributions of his Binding to a Lesser Maid. Let me Answer with this.

Is Love such a Common Thing that we, mere men in this God's World, should deign to turn our Backs to it when it appears before us? We have only just relieved our country of years of English Tyranny. Think you I would follow the Lead of Longshanks and his Predecessors and Command where the Heart should Lead? Has he yet shown you, in acting as Laird of the Clan MacLeod, that he oft does what is Right and Just?

If your Son be strong in his Love for this maid, as you were strong in your Love for your Wife, then let him follow the Dictates of his Heart. Let us, as men, try to be as little like the Dreaded English as possible.

Your Most Honored King Robert the Eighth Earl of Bruce

Meg was silent as Ewan finished reading. She held her hand out to take the parchment, and again, Ewan gave it to her. She bowed her head to the letter, tracing her fingers over the strange lettering she could not understand.

"Ye taught me to ride, milord, would ye teach me to read as well?"

"Aye, Meggie. I would."

A small smile played at the edge of her lips as she handed the missive back.

"Good, for I shall one day wish to read the words o' a King about my future husband."

Ewan let out a laugh and swung her up into his arms. Placing her back on her feet, he kissed her, hot, needing, and full of love.

"I promise ye, Meggie Lachlan, that ye shall be happy for all o' your days."

Though his father had passed away that very day, Ewan slept easy. He felt that his father would be pleased he had finally found a bride, one he loved. Ewan had seen the passionate love between his mother and father and wanted nothing less for himself.

It was only the next morning, when he realized others may not take too kindly to his choice of a bride, that the reality of his actions confronted him. Gavin, for certain, would be most appalled. He would have hoped for his Laird to select a lass from a nearby clan, probably the horrid daughter of Laird MacNally, to form alliances.

As nice as those fantasies might be, Ewan knew his clan and its demesne were small and forming alliances was not a priority. His father had established strong ties to several surrounding clans, and Ewan had spent the past few years fostering those ties, but feeding his clan and making sure his people were happy were Ewan's priorities now.

He was not surprised to find Gavin waiting for him in the hall. Seeing the look on Ewan's face, Gavin paled.

"Tell me," he said harshly. "Tell me ye didna ask the maid t' wed ye."

"I canna do that, Gavin. We shall be wed this aft noon."

"Christ, man! Can ye no' see what this will do? With the problems wi' the English, and the size of your lands, ye should welcome a match wi' a respectable lass who can bring ye land and followers. No' a crofter maid who will bring ye and your sons naught but ridicule! Can ye no' see that?"

Ewan's demeanor shadowed, but he held his anger in check as he spoke to his best man and second in command.

"Gavin, do ye wish me to release ye from your duties, so as ye dinna have to serve the likes o' a man who takes a bride of his choosing? For if ye dinna abide by my choice, if ye insult my wife to be, I dinna think I need ye. Ye have been my closest friend and advisor my whole life, but I will no' stand by and be insulted, nor will I let my wife or children as well."

Ewan fell silent as he let Gavin digest his words.

"So, what shall it be, man? Shall ye stand wi' me, and your Laird and your friend? Or shall ye turn over your sword?"

Gavin sighed heavily. He had stood by his Laird as a childhood friend, as a warrior in training, and now in the honor as second in command. Ewan MacLeod lived a charmed life in Gavin's eyes - even as children, the most absurd of ideas turned into great adventures, a simple thought into a brilliant plan.

Gavin was much more serious than his lighthearted friend, looking at the larger picture, the more serious ramifications. Gavin acted precisely, diligently, and usually with extreme caution. With Gavin's light hair, Ewan often called him a guardian angel, always watching out for Ewan.

And presently, Ewan could not truly fault his friend for his words. Wasn't that what Gavin was doing now – watching out for him? Gavin wondered if he could walk away from his old friend and new Laird, after all they had been through, over a mere lass. Gavin sighed heavily again, his habit when he believed Ewan was acting recklessly.

"We havena let a lass come betwixt 'afore, Ewan, why should now be any different? Aye, I will stand by ye, man."

Ewan smiled at Gavin's choice of words. Rakes that they both were, Gavin was right; never had a lass caused strife between them before. Ewan held out his hand to his second in command, who grasped it heartily.

"To warn ye, MacLeod," Gavin cautioned, "I am no' the only one wi' an opinion on this matter. Surely ye can see how this may affect people's regard for ye." Gavin paused, then spoke more gravely. "I ken wi' the death o' your father that ye may feel the pressure o' the clan, and I will welcome this lass as your bride. But I feel I must speak plainly. I fear that your new wife may come under scrutiny more than ye will. Is she ready to be subject to the cruel whims of others? Already there is talk of her as ye whore."

Ewan smiled at this, surprising Gavin to the core. "Well, after we wed, there will naught be talk of her as my whore, aye?" Gavin snorted in response.

"And," Ewan continued, "I will command respect for her as my wife. Those who do no' follow in suit will answer to me."

Ewan turned to find a place to eat, and instead found Meg standing right behind him. She had been hiding and heard most of the exchange. Gavin looked to Ewan, then fell to his knees before Meg.

"Lady, I apologize for the coarse words that ye may have heard, from my mouth or the mouths of those whom I command. I swear I shall serve ye as I serve him, as the bride and wife of my Laird."

Meg was flattered and obviously embarrassed by Gavin's show of affection, and she tugged on his arm to have him rise.

"Please stand, Gavin. Ye need no' kneel before me. And dinna call me lady, for I am no' one."

"Oh, but ye are," contradicted Gavin, grinning at her humility. "Ye became one when MacLeod asked ye to wed."

"Oh, aye," she agreed, smiling in return, "then let us keep this lady title betwixt we three. Shall we?"

Her eyes twinkling to match her smile, she offered her arm to Gavin, and he and Ewan escorted her to the table. Seeing Meg act such, and hearing her speak, Gavin could understand why Ewan fell so hard for this scrap of a lass. She was stunning, no doubt, but also lively and, had she been more than a crofter's maid, perfect for Ewan. Gavin leaned toward Ewan, and in a whisper, said,

"Och, I ken now why ye wanted to wed this one. Ye are lucky to have found her before I, or ye would be attending my wedding this aft noon."

Ewan made the announcement of the upcoming nuptials to the manor and those in attendance that morning. Cheers lauded the couple, but Meg still noticed the hard looks that several people gave her. She tried to focus on the floor as Ewan spoke.

After they broke the fast, Ewan stood and offered Meg his hand, intending to introduce her to the guests who had arrived that morning. Since the death of his father the morning before, messengers had ridden long and hard to bring news to tenants, clan landowners, and fellow Lairds about the gathering to name Ewan as the new Laird of Clan MacLeod, which was to be held the next day. Having the wedding the day before would ensure witnesses for the event, but also leave him and his new bride with energy for the wedding feast and night to follow.

Meg, however, seemed hesitant and preoccupied. Bending low, Ewan questioned her.

"What ails ye, my love?"

"Well, 'tis the wedding, milord."

"We are to be wed, Meggie. Can ye no' call me Ewan as your husband to be?" He gave her a wide smile, which she returned half-heartedly.

"Aye, weel, Ewan then. I have a concern."

Ewan strived to hide his worry. "A concern? About the wedding?"

"Weel, aye, ye see, I ... weel..." Meg was horrified at how she stammered. *He is to be my husband and I canna even ask him this one simple thing!* She took a deep breath and started over.

"I ken that tenants and landowners come to the gathering, and some tenant farmers if they have the time or energy, but, wi' the wedding, does my mother even ken that I am to be wed?" A note of desperation hung in her voice.

"I dinna ken if she has yet been told. Shall ye want her here, your whole family? I will send Gavin now to bring them to ye." Relief washed over her at Ewan's words. She rewarded him with a true smile.

"I think 'tis important for a maid to have her mother wi' her on her wedding day, aye?" she commented, and Ewan nodded in agreement. "And thank ye, Ewan."

He leaned forward and kissed her hand before turning to Gavin.

Elspeth found her daughter a few hours later, in her room, pacing. On the bed lay her one gown that Ewan had given her and some ribbon.

"What are ye doing, my lass? Ye are to be wed shortly!" Elspeth told her.

"Aye, I ken! But Mother," Meg cried, rushing to Elspeth, closing her in a warm hug. "I dinna have a gown, or yet a gift for him!" She gestured to the bed. "'Tis the only finery I have in all the world!"

Elspeth smiled at her daughter's ranting. When the news had arrived of her daughter's wedding to the Laird, from his second in command's very own lips no less, Elspeth had been surprised and pleased, but not shocked. She had seen how the Laird's son looked at her daughter, and how Meg spoke of him, and knew that only good could come from it. Wee Meggie was to be the bride of the Laird!

Part of her saddened at the prospect of losing her daughter. Such was the lot of a mother - to carry and guard this tiny life, to go through the seemingly unbearable pain to bring that wee life into this world, then love and protect that child even when grown, only to have that child tear itself away and bind to another. Elspeth wanted to weep, with sadness, with joy, until she had glanced at Connor.

Her husband did not appear pleased with the news that his daughter, a crofter's maid, had enamored herself to the Laird and was to wed him. His face pale, he scarcely breathed. It looked as though he had been told of his daughter's death instead of her wedding.

"'Tis why I brought ye this," Elspeth said, as she reached into her sack and removed a plain white chemise. It had no trimmings at all, but made of a fine linen, and would help make the most suitable wedding gown.

"Oh, Mother," Meg breathed, fingering the dress. Her mother, who had so vigilantly decried vanity, had worked to make her wedding attire.

"I think wi' some of those ribbons ye have there, we could make this into a fine gown."

Meg could only nod at her mother's words. Already overwhelmed with emotions, her mother's presence and the gesture of the dress nearly made her weep. She blinked back the tears.

"But ye must have something over it," Elspeth continued, "and your husband-to-be gave ye this." She lifted the plain white kirtle to reveal a wonderful gown, the color of new heather, creamy white, made of a soft material Meg had never felt before.

"It must have cost him a fine penny to be sure."

The kirtle was trimmed in a gold braid, with fine beading on the neckline and hem. The back was a bit longer than the front, making a train to trail behind Meg. The beading on the back was layered up the dress and shimmered as the gown moved. The material itself shimmered as well. To Elspeth, Meg would look like an angel in it. To Meg, it looked too beautiful to wear.

"Methinks 'twill wear well over the white chemise," Elspeth said, and Meg nodded in agreement. She was too entranced with the material to speak a word.

"Since ye are no' brooding over this wedding, am I to assume that ye care for the man?" Elspeth asked her daughter. Meg smiled, causing a single tear to escape her eyes.

"Oh, aye, Mother. I do care for him." She sat on the bed and motioned for her mother to join her. Elspeth sat and brushed at Meg's hair as she listened.

"I did no' want to care for him. He seemed so rude, and ye heard the tales of him being a rogue. Yet when he protected me from the English, then took me to the manse for safety, I felt that nothing could happen to me. He wouldn't let it. Then he was so pleasant to me, as if he truly liked me as a person, not just as a ward." Meg paused and glanced sidelong at her mother. "Then he kissed me and made me like to faint. I think then. That was when I kent I cared for the man."

Elspeth hugged her daughter close. She had hoped Meg would wed a man she cared for, a man who would love her for herself, and now it looked as though it would happen.

"I am so pleased for ye, my daughter. Your whole family is."

"How is father?" Meg asked suddenly. Elspeth frowned.

"I dinna ken about your father," she said, folding her hands on her lap. "I would think he would be pleased at this match, his own daughter marrying the Laird, ye ken. But he looked stricken." She paused and looked directly at her daughter. "In truth, Meggie, I am afeared. Your father has no' been the same man these past few weeks. He leaves, late in the night, and always looks scared. I fear he may be hiding too great a secret for him to bear."

This news worried Meg, for she could not be there to assist her family.

"Will I see him today? Will he take me down the aisle?"

Elspeth smiled to reassure her daughter. "Aye, lass. He will be there. Mayhap his fears will be allayed once ye are wed. Mayhap 'twas ye he was afeard for." She took Meg's face between her hands and kissed her forehead.

"Now, wee Meggie, let us dress ye fit to wed the Laird of the clan."

Several hours later, Meg was ready to enter the kirk. Her father stood at her side, and she faced the doors that would lead her inside. Her mother had quickly sewn several ribbons to the waist and sleeves of the dress, and put several more in her hair, so Meg almost floated when she walked. Her mother had also made a coronet of flowers, heather, thistle leaves, and thyme, to wear on her head, for happiness and fertility.

She handed Meg the linen she had been working on before she left home, plain ivory with an embroidered edge, one of the few truly pretty things she had ever sewn. *For your husband,* her mother had said, handing it to her. Meg was touched that her mother remembered the pretty cloth.

Meg stood ramrod straight, next to her father. He hesitatingly escorted her to the arms of her new husband, and as he did, he leaned over to her and whispered in her ear, "I love ye dearly, my Meggie. Please ken that all I do was done for ye." Then he kissed her on the lips and gave her arm to Ewan.

The wedding seemed to pass in no time, and Meg felt as though she was not in her body for its entirety, as if she was watching herself get married to the tall, dark man next to her. He was freshly washed, and his black hair shone. He had rebraided the plaits near his temple but let the rest of his hair flow by his shoulders. His linen tunic was clean, and an ivory that matched her gown. In fresh plaid and tunic, with his sword in the scabbard at his side, he seemed even larger than the everyday Ewan she was used to seeing.

The moments passed by too quickly for her to grasp. Suddenly she was kneeling before the priest, saying "I do" before man and God. She was barely aware when Ewan placed his clan tartan over her shoulder and a gold ring on her finger. She handed him the small square of cream linen. Taking both it and her hand in his, Ewan knelt before her, and grasping his sword with his other hand, he held it in front of her as he swore himself to her before the congregation.

"I do solemnly vow that I shall take thee this day, protect thee with this sword and this body, and love thee all the days of my life, 'til I pass unto death."

He stood, and Father MacBain cut the palm of each of their hands, pressed them together, and bound them with another strip of MacLeod plaid. She then heard the priest say the words, "Man and wife." Ewan crushed her to him, kissing her passionately as cheers went up from the witnesses.

CHAPTER EIGHT

A Rose by Any Other Name

MEG WAITED IN HIS chambers for Ewan to arrive. A small feast had been planned following the wedding, and all those in attendance celebrated the nuptials. Meg was honored that Ewan had her family sit near their table, so she could share her good fortune with those closest to her. When her parents finally took their leave, Meg decided that she, too, could find a use for a brief rest, and bade the well-wishers good night. Ewan had pulled her close, telling her to await him in his chambers.

She had lit some candles in the room, giving it a soft glow. She removed her coronet, but uncertain how to present herself to her new husband, she kept the gown on. Gathering up a few of the remaining flowers from her wedding bouquet, she reclined in a plush chair near the hearth, and wove the blooms together. Once she was satisfied with her work, she tied the flowers off with a ribbon, then placed the small floral piece under her pillow - another fertility rite she had seen her mother do a year or so after the birth of a third daughter. It must have worked, or at least helped, for Abel was born not nine months later. Ewan walked into the chamber as she was straightening the coverlet.

He bolted the door and walked over to her, holding her close to him. He could smell the freshness of her hair, tainted by only a slight sense of fear. A virgin bride on her wedding night, and he vowed to himself to be as gentle as possible. She was not a local wench to use for biding time; she was his wife, a beautiful, tiny, and virgin one at that. He bent low and kissed her fully on the lips, enjoying how she responded, as though she was testing the water in a pool before submerging herself. He pulled away slightly and gazed at his new wife, a vision of golden red in a pristine gown. A small smile tugged at his lips.

"Do ye ken, Meggie, what passes betwixt a man and his wife?" he questioned softly. She nodded.

"Mother explained, albeit in brief, what happens on the wedding night."

"Are ye frightened, lass?"

"Nay, a wee bit nervous. Is there something I should be frightened of?"

She searched his eyes, looking for any indication that there was something more than her mother told her, something she should fear, and while his intense blue eyes were warm and dark, there was no sense of anything to fear. Her new husband seemed the mighty warrior, but in the intimate solitude of their bed chamber, he was her gentle lord. He pulled her close again.

"Nay, lass. Ye shall never fear wi' me."

He then caught her lips again, sucking on them, pressing forward gently with his tongue. She opened her mouth to accept his tongue, tasting and testing the newness of the sensation. His mere kisses caused her body to burn, and his hands on her breasts and backside burst into flames. This time, there was no feeling of impropriety as before. As his wife, her body was his to touch and take as he liked. She tried to dispel the nervousness and enjoy the feelings he gave her.

Ewan was anxious to take her to bed but knew that, for the first time at least, he would have to move slowly. Feeling her acceptance of his tongue on her lips and hands on her body, he pressed forward and began unlacing her gown.

The simple white dress fell to her feet, and she was clad only in her chemise. Her skin glowed in the incandescent light of the candles. Her nervousness seemed to return as he gazed at her. He ran his hand through her hair then reached for the laces of her chemise. Meg stopped his hand with hers and stepped away. A quick flash of anger and desperation rushed through him, then he watched her reach for the laces herself.

Hiding her face in her hair so he could not see her embarrassment, she tugged at the laces and the chemise fell to her feet. Meg stood before him as she had never stood before anyone. She was anxious and breathless as well.

As Ewan's eyes roamed over her body, she prayed that his fearsome power that she had beheld and felt before would be held in check, at least this night. She was more than a bit afraid of how he made her feel of what was to come in their marriage bed.

To Ewan, Meg seemed a vision of a goddess on earth. He too was breathless. Her hair had fallen partly over one breast, and he followed that line to the swell of her hips and the reddish gold treasure between her legs. He had lain with women before, but none that he had loved, none that he had waited for, and none that were his. She stood silently, as if waiting for approval, and Ewan struggled to speak.

"Ye are perfection," he rasped. "Ye are my own goddess and I shall worship your body." He stepped forward and reached to touch her when she took another step back.

"Nay, milord. 'Tis my turn to worship yours." She took a hesitant step forward, reaching for his plaid. She raised her eyes, seeking a response to her invitation, and Ewan stood stock still.

"Aye," he whispered, and let her undress him. The whispery touch of her fingertips as she removed the plaid from his shoulder was agony. He knew she had no idea of the torture she was putting him through, and when she began to remove his kilt, it took every ounce of his strength not to take her to bed then. The mere fact that she wanted to undress him, had the courage to want to see him fully, made him want her even more. Rare was the woman, the wife, who desired her man's body as the man wanted hers.

She unfastened his kilt and put it to the side on the stool. Ewan stepped to her, taking a breast in one hand and covering her lips with his. He swept her into his arms and moved to the bed. He lay next to her, taking in every inch of her body, letting his hands trail over her beautifully rounded breasts, down to her belly. He leaned over her, and as his fingers found her red-gold curls, he took a rosy nipple into his mouth. Meg gasped, grabbing at his shoulder.

"Milord!" Her breath caught.

Ewan lifted his head slightly and trailed his tongue across her chest to the other breast, sucking gently on that nipple. She gasped again. She could feel Ewan chuckle to himself.

"I guess your mother forgot to tell ye about that?" He lowered his head back to her pink peak, touching his tongue to it again.

"I wouldna have believed her. Oh, milord, what are ye doing to me?"

"Are ye enjoying it?" He began to trail his tongue down her body to her belly, then lower.

"'Tis frightening and wonderful at the same time, milord," she panted.

He flicked his tongue over her stomach, then rubbed her golden curls with his fingers. Her breath caught again, and when he placed his mouth between her legs, she gasped out,

"Nay!" and tried to withdraw. Ewan pulled up and placed a hand on her hip to stop her. He gave her a guarded look, and Meg thought she had angered him.

"My apologies, milord," she whispered, immediately contrite. "I ken ye are my husband, and my body is now yours to do with as ye like, but isn't that, well, unnatural?"

Ewan's smile broke the dark look on his face and Meg relaxed slightly.

"Meggie, I said I would worship your body, and I am. Is it unnatural for me to want to kiss ye all over? Your fingers. Your toes. Your knees." He brushed each spot as he spoke it. "Is it unnatural for me to want to kiss those?"

"Nay, milord," she breathed, her pulse quickening again under his soft touch.

"Then it is no more unnatural to want to kiss ye here," he responded, brushing his fingers over the tangle of reddish-golden curls again. She gave him a virgin's look, one of excitement, edginess, and fear over her body's response to him. He parted her folds and touched her warmth, and Meg gasped again.

"As your husband, I want only to bring ye joy. Will ye trust me to do that?"

Meg could not speak, only nod briefly as his fingers continued to stroke her into flames. She moaned softly, giving into his touch. Ewan then leaned forward, pressing his lips to her warmth, stroking gently with his tongue.

At the touch of his tongue, Meg thrust her head into the pillows and arched her back. Never had she thought it could be like this between a man and wife, these intimacies. The fire in her built, becoming hotter with the knowledge that her husband was touching her, making her feel this burning. She felt the power, the raw power between herself and Ewan, and after clawing at the furs and finding no purchase, she grabbed for her husband, entwining her fingers into his hair.

Ewan was close to bursting, tasting his new wife where no one had before, giving her pleasure she had never before experienced, knowing what was to come. Her fingers in his hair, further urging him, made his blood beat even faster in his body, and he held himself in check until he was certain she was ready.

He pressed into her with his finger, and touching the wetness, he lifted himself over her. She opened her eyes at his movement and gazed at him. His hardness pressed between her legs, and he saw the nervousness creep back into her eyes. He kissed her, then spoke softly.

"I have yet more pleasure to give ye."

He then pressed his full manhood into her warmth, breaking past her maidenhead and trying to stop himself from ravaging her right then. Had it ever been so hot for him? So consuming? This maid, this lass, his wife, and he felt his control flee as though it was his first time as well.

Meg cried out as he pressed into her deeply. She had never known a pain like this, quickly sharp, then a dull, pulling sensation. There were tears in her eyes as she tried to push him away.

"Nay, my love," Ewan whispered into her ear. He was still, not moving inside of her, allowing her body to adjust to the invasion of him inside her. "'Tis the pain of first love, a gift to me. 'Twill subside, and ye will find most blessed heaven with me then."

He stroked her face and hair as he spoke, calming her, and only when she stilled did he begin to move. She gasped at first from the sensation of him moving inside her, from surprise or pain, he did not know. He was as slow and gentle as he could muster, but the feel of her, the tightness, her velvet warmth, made his thrusting more urgent, and he could barely control himself.

The pain lessened as Meg adjusted to the stroke of him, and then the burning returned. Not the pain for first love, but the flames that kissed her as Ewan had. Heat and fire burned her from inside, and as she started to moan and cling to Ewan, he pressed harder and faster, matching her passion.

Suddenly, the fire was too much, consuming her completely, and she cried out his name as she felt herself explode. Ewan reached his peak with her then. His whole body stiffened, and he groaned loudly, spilling his seed into her. He dropped his head low to her shoulder, his dark hair blending with her gold, and breathed heavily, spent and satisfied with the knowledge that she was now his. *Truly my wife now.*

Meg opened her eyes and gazed at her husband lying atop her. She suddenly felt awkward, realizing she was nude, legs spread, with an equally nude man covering her. She averted her eyes, but he caught the movement.

"What ails ye, my wife?" He breathed into her ear, kissing her neck. His simple gesture made her stir with desire again, and she was shocked at her body's ready response for him.

"'Tis naught," she whispered, eyes still cast away. Ewan gently held her chin and drew her face to his, kissing her fully on the lips.

"Methinks ye do not speak the truth," he whispered back. "Tell me. I am your husband, and I will ken all that occurs in our marriage bed."

Tears formed in her eyes, from both embarrassment and shame. She averted her eyes again and spoke.

"I am sorry. Ye are, well, ye ken," she stammered, "but I didna ken what to do!" she cried. He chuckled softly, kissing her on the forehead, cheeks, and nose.

"Well, I would hope ye wouldn't. 'Twould have been quite a surprise, and I would have been disappointed if ye had, my love." He grasped her hand and held it to his lips. "Ye were perfect, wife. Ye gave me the most valuable gift of your first love, and I wouldna have had it any other way."

Meg smiled back at him and used her hand to pull his face close enough to kiss. She flicked her tongue to his, as he had done with her, and his breath became heavy.

"Nay, lass. 'Tis too soon for ye," he rasped.

She ran her tongue over his, and slid her hand down Ewan's backside, pulling him closer again.

"'Tis no' too soon, for my body tells me I want ye again, my husband."

His control faltered, and he rolled onto her again. She stiffened a bit as he entered her, but then moved with his body, encouraging him, making Ewan want her even more. He loved her again, and it was early morning before they rested.

As she drifted off to sleep, Ewan pull her close to him, her back rounded to his chest. He radiated heat, and his breath was warm on her cheek.

"Ye have made your mark on my heart, wee Meggie. Strong and deep," he whispered in her ear, right before he fell asleep.

More kinsmen and friends arrived throughout the following day. The courtyard was filled with men competing in games to test their strength. The view was a wash of vibrance, for not only were the men and women present wearing their own MacLeod plaid, but the colors of the MacDonnells to the east as well, then of the MacNallys to the south as their entourage strode into the mix.

Ewan did not demand that Meg rise early to greet the coming guests. He thought she was still asleep as he left their bed. She was not, however, and while he dressed, she peeked with one eye and took pleasure in watching his body move about the chamber, naked as the day. He moved lightly for a man so big, and she saw how his muscles bunched and flexed as he donned his plaid.

Once dressed, he reached for her, running his hand over her copper hair and her cheek flushed with sleep. As he cupped her jaw, she reached her hand up to grasp his.

"So ye are awake, wife."

"Aye," she responded with a yawn. "That I am." She sat up, forgetting she was as indecent as he, and yawned again. Ewan took in the view of her hair tumbling over her breasts and wanted very much to press her back into the covers and be late tending his guests. His passion burned in his eyes and in his loins, and he couldn't resist the urge to take her breast in his hand. He held it gently, letting its weight fill his palm. She gasped slightly at his touch.

"Did I hurt ye badly, then?" he asked quietly.

"Nay, my husband. Ye were most gentle." She reached up her hand and touched his cheek, his morning beard scratching her. "But did I please ye? 'Twas but my first time, and . . ." her words drifted off, and Ewan finished her thought for her.

"Ye were afraid ye weren't good enough in our bed?" He chuckled lightly. "Oh, Meg, I dinna think I could ask for a wife more satisfying. Ye have passion in ye. I am glad that ye bring that passion to our chamber."

"Will ye want me again tonight, my husband?"

Ewan pondered that. She was a virgin, come to his bed. He did not want to hurt her more than he did last night. He told her so.

"I dinna want to hurt ye, wife, and ye may still be sore." He saw her eyes drop a bit and smiled at her disappointment. "But if ye think ye could, I would love to taste your passion again."

At that, she flung herself to him, kissing him fiercely. He groaned at the feel of her, and then as quickly as she moved to him, she moved away.

"I shall await ye tonight," she told him, pulling her body out of his hands, and covering herself with a linen sheet. Ewan rose to leave, and as he reached the door, she spoke.

"I think ye have made a mark on my heart as well, husband."

She dressed quickly, wearing her creamy wedding gown, the only nice item she owned since her green kirtle was starting to look a little worn. She decided that after the festivities concluded, she would make a brief foray to her secluded glen for a thorough washing. As warm as tub baths were, she didn't feel as clean as after a swim in her loch.

Not to mention that the clear water would do her gown some good as well. Not dwelling on vanity, she twined some ribbon in her hair to pull the strands out of her eyes and left to join her new husband below.

Near chaos greeted her downstairs. The MacNallys had arrived, and while Laird Mac-Nally was respectable and genteel enough, his kinsmen were loud and his daughter a dictator. Meg presented herself at the base of the steps, unsure how to proceed. Did Ewan want to make introductions? Or was she to introduce herself? Since Ewan was occupied with the Laird of the MacNallys, Meg decided to join Ewan at his side, and let him take the lead.

She had barely stepped towards him when she heard a woman's loud voice making demands of the househelp. Meg noticed one of the kitchen maids, Jenny, taking instructions from this woman with much disdain. Flicking her eyes from the woman to Laird MacNally, she noticed similarities -- the same dark brown hair, pale grey eyes, and deeply slanted eyebrows.

The greatest similarity, however, was height. The Laird was tall for a man, taller than Ewan, though that seemed impossible. The young woman was tall as well, almost as tall as Ewan, and that was daunting to Meg. *MacNally's daughter*, Meg deduced. *The supposed fiancée. Elayne.*

Seeing how Elayne found it necessary to command the servants, Meg decided to approach her first and make introductions. Maybe she could help Elayne with whatever it was she needed.

As she approached, she heard Elayne bellow, "I dinna *care* how many people are here for supper! I need a bath! Ye will get me hot water. This is why Ewan needs a woman in his house, ye servants dinna ken *anything.*"

Suddenly, Elayne grabbed at Meg's sleeve.

"Ye. Are ye a chambermaid? I need a bath and the kitchen maid here does no' want to assist me. Get ye a tub and some water to bring to my chamber."

Meg found herself without a voice. She gawked at the young woman, craning her neck to look her in the eyes. Humiliation burning behind her eyes, she thought to herself, *See husband? I am no' worthy of being your wife. I canna carry myself like the lady of the manor, and even your guests can easily guess my place.*

"My apologies, milady, but ye are misinformed. Ye see, I am no' a chambermaid . . ." Meg was unable to continue as Elayne cut her short.

"Ye are a kitchen maid, too? Bah! Get ye from my sight!" And with that, Elayne shoved Meg away. Jenny tried to grab her as she stumbled back, but only touched the wisp of her sleeve. It was Ewan who caught her, his attention diverted from Laird MacNally the minute Meg left the steps.

"Meg?" he asked, implying more to the question than merely her name. Meg regained her feet but held Ewan's hand firmly in her grasp.

"'Tis fine. I am well," she responded, and then Elayne was there, braying like a donkey.

As much as her mother taught her to love all of nature's creatures, Elayne and her voice were truly trying her patience. Meg tried once more to explain her position to Elayne, only to be cut short again.

"Ewan, really. Ye need better servants. Ye treat them too well. They have their place ye ken," Elayne lectured. This time, Ewan interceded.

"Nay, Elayne, the lass is correct. If ye listen for a moment –" Ewan didn't finish as Elayne gushed forth again.

"Ewan, once ye and I are wed, we must replace these servants. They speak to their betters most indignantly—" This time Ewan stopped Elayne short.

"When *we* are wed? What in the name of God ever gave ye the idea we would wed?" Ewan's voice thundered in the room, and even the raucous noise from MacNally's kinsmen ceased.

"*Ewan*," Elayne brayed, darting her eyes around the room. "I dinna think that we should have these words here."

Meg was impressed. The woman almost sounded embarrassed. Meg stood next to her husband with a bit more pride and put a dazzling smile on her face.

"I think we must have these words here. Otherwise, I fear, ye may insult my *wife*," he emphasized the last word, and Elayne answered him with a gasp.

He gently pushed Meg forward, and she clasped Elayne's hand between both of hers in a gesture of greeting.

"Welcome to our home, Elayne," and Meg nodded to her father, "and Laird MacNally. We are pleased ye could be present for my husband's gathering." Elayne yanked her hand back as though it had been burned. She glared at Meg like a snake had wed Ewan.

Now a circle of curious people appeared around the trio, with the household servants on one side, silently applauding Meg, and Laird MacNally and his kinsmen on the other. Ewan stood in the middle and smiled heartily. Elayne was so rude, but Meg came through with colors flying. *Clever and spry. Words that describe my wife best - clever and spry.*

Elayne's dominating visage was replaced with repulsion.

"Ye married this lowly whore?" she cried. "Did she trick ye? Are ye sure ye are truly married?" Elayne's words enraged Ewan.

"Ye dare call my wife a whore?"

"Are ye sure ye are married?" Elayne continued, "Ye can have it annulled –"

"I am certain," Ewan glared at Elayne, "that this marriage could no' be annulled. God willing, there is a bairn growing in her belly as we speak." Meg went utterly pink at the discourse on her wedding night and nearly fainted at Elayne's next comment.

"Then are ye sure it is yours? The whore that she is, it could be any man's . . ." But Ewan did not let her finish.

With a roar, he grabbed Elayne, ready to strike her - strike a woman for the first time in his life over mere words, when he felt his wife's hand on his arm. MacNally stepped forward, partially blocking his daughter.

"MacNally," Ewan spoke in measured tones, "I advise ye to teach your daughter to curb her tongue." Then, turning to Elayne, he hissed, "I think I would ken if my wife had been with another man before our wedding night, but that is my business, no' yours."

Turning back to MacNally, Ewan started to speak when Elayne began screaming and clawing at Meg.

"She's witched ye!" Elayne shouted. "She's a witch and she cast a spell on ye! That is how ye can defend this whore! Call her out! Call her out for the witch she is!"

Elayne pulled at Meg's hair, tearing at the ribbons. Meg slapped at Elayne's hands, and one of Elayne's fingernails caught the skin of her hand, scratching it.

"Cease!" Ewan roared at her. Grabbing Elayne's hands, he held her still. "MacNally, ye will control your daughter, or I will have her escorted home!"

Jenny, overcoming the shock of these events a bit more quickly than anyone else, had stepped forward with a cloth to blot at Meg's hand. The gouge was not long, but fairly deep, and was quite bloody. While Jenny applied these ministrations, Ewan dragged Elayne to a chair and threw her into it and spoke harshly with Laird MacNally.

Meg's head was bent low to Jenny's, and she spoke softly. "I did no' intend to make such a scene." Jenny giggled.

"Weel, I think 'twas Elayne's scene, no' yours. Have ye ever met such a woman?" Meg shook her head. Jenny took Meg by her good hand.

"Come. While your husband has words with the MacNallys, we will tend to your hand in your chamber."

Jenny led her to the chamber that had been Meg's until last night. Nothing had yet been moved, and the scent of the dried lavender and sage was soothing on Meg's nerves.

"I can do this. Ye dinna have to wait on me like some spineless old woman," Meg told her. Jenny shrugged.

"I ken ye could care for your hand, but I dinna mind, and ye are the lady of the house now. We would like to help keep ye well. And truly, I dinna want to be down there any longer. I can no' stand the likes of Elayne."

"Was Ewan betrothed to that woman?" Meg ventured as Jenny bathed her hand in warm water, scrubbing lightly at the wound.

"Ah, nay. No' really. But her father kept trying to bribe Ewan's da. I think he's trying to sell her off. Would ye like to be burdened wi' the likes o' her?" Jenny asked with a flick of her head towards the door. Meg laughed.

"Nay. This one encounter was enough."

"Aye, weel, we didna want the likes of her, either." Jenny was quiet for a moment, patting at Meg's hand absently. "We are glad that he chose ye."

Meg's eyes widened in surprise. "Ye are? Why?"

"I have been in his house for nigh three years. My mam worked the kitchens until she died over two years past, and my da died many years ago. Instead of charity, the old Laird took my mam in to work to feed her family. The old Laird and his sons let us take pride in our work. They dinna beat us, or threaten us, and the work is good. My mam felt good working here. Ewan and his da and brothers were never better than us, ye ken?"

Meg nodded. She did understand. Jenny's words brought back the night Ewan had told her they would marry. *Are ye so much less than another? Do ye think that God would breathe life into a worthless creature?* What manner of man, a Laird, and his noble wife, would raise children, sons, with such beliefs? She looked back at Jenny, who continued.

"We feared that Ewan would take a wife who thought much of betters, and less of us. Someone like Elayne. So, when he fell in love wi' ye, and wed ye no less, we were relieved. The whole of the clan was relieved, methinks."

Meg was pleased. She had worried that she would be set apart, or seen as trying to rise above her station, but her fears were for naught. She smiled at Jenny, and with that, the bonds of friendship had been forged. For the first time in her life, Meg felt that she had a friend.

"I heard talk, the day afore last, about Elayne and my prospects wi' the Laird. 'Twould seem she was no' the only one to think he dallied wi' me afore he wed her." Jenny's head came up and she smiled at Meg.

"Aye, wi' the Laird's history, 'twas what many of us thought, sorry to speak so plain. But in truth, to look at him, any could see that he is smitten wi' ye." Jenny wrapped some linen around Meg's hand and tied the ends in a tight knot. Meg had glanced at the door.

"Smitten wi' me, aye? Do ye truly believe so?" Meg dared to ask, and as if she called him to her with those words, Ewan flung open the chamber door.

"There ye are!" he exclaimed. "Why did ye no' go to our chamber to care for your hand?"

Jenny spoke first.

"My fault, Laird. I ken she likes the flowers and thought their scents would soothe her after the ordeal wi' Elayne." Ewan nodded in agreement.

"Aye. Jenny, would ye see that my wife's things are moved to our chamber. 'Twould be nice if she could feel soothed there." Jenny nodded to him, and smiling at Meg, stepped lightly out the door.

It was then that Meg began to understand what Jenny had meant about Ewan and his family. He didn't command her or order her; he asked her for assistance, unlike the awful Elayne who bellowed her orders to others. Meg found herself watching Jenny leave and thought that she had certainly made a friend here.

Ewan knelt beside her chair and took her in his arms.

"I apologize for her behavior," Ewan started to explain. "I was telling MacNally that I was already wed when Elayne turned int'a banshee. Christ, what a morning, and we have yet to break the fast!" Meg giggled into his arm.

"I think, husband, that your charms ken no end if ye can command women to wed ye without a word."

"Ahh, ye think this funny?" Ewan didn't know if he should be angry or relieved. "I would give all my charms t' the devil should he rid me of Elayne." Then he leaned forward and caught her lips in a kiss, soft at first, then turning passionate, his hands roaming over her breast, her hips. "But I have no need o' that, since I have ye. Unless ye would prefer me wi' out my charms?"

She leaned back in her seat and eyed him, seeming to contemplate.

"Well, since I can no' see ye wi' out them, methinks ye should keep your charms. Better than dealing wi' the devil, aye?" He heard the laughter in her voice and was relieved that Elayne did not get the best of her. Clever and spry, and Elayne was no match.

"Did the woman hurt ye overmuch?" Ewan asked, concern for her creeping back into his voice. He regarded her hand.

"Nay. Jenny cared for it well, and it should heal quickly. Are they still in the hall?" Meg referred to the MacNallys.

"I sent Elayne and her father to the chamber below, and her kinsmen will camp out o' doors. They will leave after first light tomorrow, so ye need no' be near Elayne for too long. Come," he took her hand, helping her rise, "I am hungry, and we should break our fast and join in the festivities."

They went downstairs to try and begin their day again

Meg's mother was in the hall when they returned below, looking uncomfortable amongst all the guests. Elspeth located her daughter, and Meg gestured to the chair next to her. Elspeth sat but felt even more uncomfortable claiming a seat of prestige at the table. Elspeth was used to a simple life, such as the one she had led from childhood into adulthood. Having her eldest daughter wed to the Laird, while a blessing in one circumstance, was disruptive in another. Elspeth perched on the edge of the chair and spoke to her daughter in low tones.

"Are ye well, my Meggie?" Elspeth asked cautiously. She regarded her daughter's injured hand briefly, but as a midwife, her attention focused on her daughter's wedding night.

"Aye, Mother, verra well." Meg leaned toward her mother. "He was verra gentle wi' me." She gave Elspeth a smile that melted Elspeth's heart.

"Oh, my daughter, it does my heart good to hear such and to see the truth in ye. But tell me, are ye sore?" Elspeth reached into the folds of her rough woolen skirts and pulled out a small satchel tied with string. "Take this. 'Tis herbal, and if ye soak it in warm water, then wash wi' a cloth, 'twill help."

Meg took the satchel from her mother, patting her hand.

"I thank ye, mother. Will ye stay for a bit? There are festivities out o' doors, some games near the woods, and tonight is the oath-taking. Will ye and father be there?"

Elspeth was quiet, and Meg nudged her softly.

"Ye father left afore daybreak, and I dinna ken where. I have to be going back soon. I was wanting to see ye, my Meggie. 'Tis all." Elspeth hugged her daughter tightly, then fingering one of the ribbons in her daughter's hair, shook her head and withdrew.

Meg watched her leave, but she was not the only one. Ewan leaned to her and asked, "She is worried about your father?"

Meg shook her head.

"I dinna ken myself. Da leaves to tend to the stock in the morn. I dinna ken why she frets."

Ewan looked back to where Elspeth had left. He fingered the satchel Meg had placed on the table, winking at Meg as he excused himself.

Various guests came and went from Meg's table, some faces from the previous day, and some new faces introduced to her. Laird MacNally strode by to offer an apology for the behavior of his daughter. Meg waved it off, telling him not to concern himself. She decided to take her mother's advice and wash with the herbal remedy Elspeth had left, but when she turned to retrieve it from the table, the satchel was gone.

➤➤➤➤ ◀◀◀◀

Meg enjoyed the rest of the day, much of it spent with Ewan. She cheered him on as he competed in a few games, and worried as he sparred with other warriors. He wore no tunic under his plaid, for the day was warm, and she watched as sweat began to form and glisten on him. He thrusted and heaved his claymore as if it were a child's wooden sword, and only the bunching of the muscles on his back gave testament to the work he was doing.

His face was stern and dark, a look Meg had seen before – she had seen it in the garden at Beltane, and the night he showed her the letter from Robert the Bruce -- his look of determination and power. Meg was in awe of it when he was inside and unarmed; she did not comprehend how these men could try to face Ewan when he exuded such power and wielded a weapon nearly taller than she.

However, when she saw him compete and win a target competition with a bow and arrow did she realize how accomplished a marksman he was. She recalled the day in the glen when he saved her from the English and that evening in the garden when she saw him bare-chested for the first time. Meg thought he was beautiful. *And he is mine. Thank ye, Dear Lord, for such a fine man.*

She approached him when he was finished and used the edge of his plaid to wipe moisture from his neck. Ewan smiled at the intimacy of the act and wondered if she realized how she touched him.

"'Twas a great show, milord," Meg said quietly. "'Tis a good thing, I think, that ye yield the arrow so well, or we might not have found the same path together, aye?" She looked up at him, eyes twinkling.

"Och, and I thought 'twas the rock ye wielded that saved the day," he teased.

With a sudden urge, she pressed her face to his and kissed him. Startled by the boldness of her act, he wrapped an arm around her waist, pressing her to him. He smelled of sweat and work and so *male*. He was hot, and she could feel his erection rise to her. His lips took on the passion of her kiss, then he broke away suddenly.

"Again, ye make me want to leave my duties," he growled, nuzzling her hair.

"Aye," she responded, letting her fingertips trail over his bare chest. "Is that so wrong, milord?" He tilted his head toward the audience that was gathering about their intimate moment.

"'Tis wi' a crowd." He lifted her hand from his neck and kissed the palm.

"Tonight," he promised, then took her hand in his and led her toward the manse as the sun set.

The hall was so packed with clansmen and clan alliances that there was barely any room for Meg to breathe, let alone sit. She squeezed her way past some MacLeod warriors and took her seat next to Ewan.

She still felt awkward, claiming such a position next to her Laird, but this Laird was now her husband, and that thought continued to jolt her when she brought it to mind. It almost seemed a game or a joke that she, wee Meggie Lachlan, should wed the Laird of her clan. She reached for Ewan's hand and held it gently.

She was also saddened that her family would not be at the gathering that evening. While any clansmen were welcome to attend, she knew from her mother's visit that morning that her father would not be there. It was her mother's clan, not her father's, and for some reason, her father never seemed to abide well in that circumstance.

Her mother was a MacLeod, and for all that her father loved her mother, it did not seem to help matters much. Meg sighed deeply and moved her thoughts back onto the gathering itself. She had never seen one and looked forward to the feast.

Food was served; everything, it seemed, from trenchers of dripping beef to platters of roast venison, warm loaves of bread, berries and small apples, and pitcher after pitcher of ale was brought to the tables.

Ewan turned to her, holding a steaming half loaf of bread. Instead of taking it from him, she leaned slightly and bit off a small piece. The warm bread melted in her mouth, and when she looked up at Ewan, his eyes smoldered. He placed his other hand on her thigh, possessively, and then bit a small piece of bread himself. They were so entranced with each other that they forgot they sat at the head table of a crowded hall.

Meg was pleased she could bring some measure of happiness to Ewan amid all the chaos of the last few days. Only when Gavin forcefully nudged Ewan with his elbow did Ewan finally tear his gaze from Meg's.

After that, the meal passed quickly, punctuated by several toasts and calls of "Here, here!" Mugs clashed together, men talked loudly, and laughter erupted frequently. All too soon it was over, and men dragged tables to the sides of the hall, creating a large space in the center. Ewan moved his chair a bit, positioning it at the front of the room. Meg stood to leave his side, but Ewan grabbed her by the hand and dragged her and her chair next to him. He then held her hand tightly in his as he raised his other hand for silence in the hall.

"My faithful clansmen!" Ewan's voice bellowed throughout the hall. "I would present to ye my beloved wife, Margaret MacLeod!"

At the sound of her name, raucous cheers went up in the hall, causing Meg to blush violently. Ewan then stood before his people and pulled his claymore from the scabbard on his back.

"My fellow clansmen," Ewan bellowed again. "I come to ye as Laird of the Clan MacLeod. My dear father passed from this life into the next not two days ago, and I have followed in his footsteps. God grant me his strength and wisdom to lead the MacLeods as he did."

With that, Ewan held the sword tip to the ground. MacLeod men came to him, swearing oaths of body and blood to the clan. Lairds of bordering lands came to him and swore alliances that they had sworn to his father.

Once the oath-taking ended, Ewan called for grievances and challenges to be settled. Since this was also the swearing of Ewan as Laird, the men declined to respond, many choosing to reserve addressing their issues until the following day. At the oath-taking, however, there was ale to drink and a wedding to celebrate. The festival was about to resume when a screeching voice filled the hall. Meg cringed at the sound of it.

"I have a grievance for ye, MacLeod!" Elayne cried.

Meg heard Jenny next to her mumble under her breath, "Sweet Mary, who let loose the harpy?"

Ewan turned to MacNally.

"MacNally, if ye canna control your daughter, I shall have to do it for ye."

"Elayne!" shouted MacNally, "get ye wicked self back to your room. We leave on the morrow!"

Elayne ignored her father and marched up to Ewan. The rest of the hall watched in silent fascination.

"Wicked? I am no' the witch! I have proof for ye, Ewan! That woman ye wed is a witch!"

Elayne pulled something from the folds of her skirt and threw it at Ewan. It was the satchel of herbs that Elspeth had left for Meg. Ewan caught it with one hand, and shifted his eyes briefly to his wife, then back to Elayne.

"A wee bag means my wife is a witch? What say ye, Elayne? Ye make no sense. Get ye gone," he told her.

"A wee bag wi' a potion to make ye blind to all but her!" Elayne stuck a finger at Meg. "Her mother is the witchy midwife who practices black rites! Can ye no' see it, Ewan? Look at how she controls ye! She has put a spell on ye, I can tell!"

Elayne's father came up behind her and took her arm. Elayne jerked from him. "Dinna touch me!" she screamed.

"Stop!" Ewan roared. "Ye will no' speak of my wife this way!" Elayne suddenly grew quiet.

"So, that is to be the way of it?" Elayne reached out to her side and dragged the priest from the crowd in front of Ewan. The priest looked embarrassed, and Ewan's whole visage darkened.

"What is the manner of this, Elayne?"

Elayne drew herself up in front of Ewan, staring him straight in the eye.

"I have seen her chambers, Ewan. She has strange, witchy potions hanging about. Potions she used on ye. Her mother helps her and brings her more to keep ye at her will. We will have the priest use church methods to show ye that she be the witch I say."

Meg paled. She knew what Elayne meant by her threat of the church. To bind her hand and foot and throw her in an icy burn, and if she proved human and sank, while she would not be a witch, she would be drowned. Otherwise, she would be burned at the stake. Heaven forbid anyone else harbored similar feelings, or Meg would soon feel the hard grip of death. Witch hunt or not, Meg was frightened beyond belief.

Ewan, however, had just married his wife and was not about to lose her yet. He would kill Elayne before he let her strange ideas take root and threaten his wife. Fortunately, the priest saved him from having to stop the witch hunt himself.

"Elayne," the priest spoke. "I ken for a fact that the woman is no' a witch. I married her yesterday in a holy kirk, gave her the body and blood of Christ myself. I would have noticed if the body was rotten, or the chalice burned as if by fire. As such, I deem Margaret MacLeod no' a witch in the eyes of the church."

Both Meg and Ewan breathed a sigh of relief. Elayne, however, screeched once more and pushed the priest aside. Suddenly, a dirk was in her hand, and she was aiming for Meg.

"Ye shall no' suffer a witch to live!" she screamed and lunged at Meg. Ewan threw himself in front of her, and the blow glanced off his arm. Ewan knocked her to the ground as MacNally ran to his daughter. Crouching by the stunned Elayne, he looked up at Ewan.

"My apologies," he said quietly. "I did no' intend my family or clan to make a mockery of your celebration. We shall depart on the hour."

Ewan did not argue yet restrained his father's old friend while MacNally's clansmen helped Elayne to her feet and led her away. He grasped MacNally with his good arm.

"Is she unwell? What has caused her to act as such?"

"I dinna ken," MacNally responded. "She has become shrewish with womanhood and lost many suitors. Methinks her lack of a mother is now showing." MacNally smiled weakly. "I dinna ken what would make her think she was to wed ye. Again, my apologies to ye and your lovely wife."

With that, MacNally followed his men out of the front hall. Meg took Ewan's hand in hers, tugging gently. Ewan looked down at his wife and gave her a flashing smile.

"'Twould seem, my love, that we were meant to share blood more than once for our marriage," he joked.

"I wouldna ken to be sliced so many times in one day. Come, milord. We must staunch the wound."

Ewan allowed his wife to lead him above stairs, with Jenny following. He felt pity for the poor man in having such a mad daughter.

Jenny left after binding the wound, noting it was not very deep, the Lord be praised, but still could lead to fever. She wrapped it in fresh linen and bade Meg to change the bandages daily. Gavin stood in the doorway as Jenny left. Meg noted how Gavin's doe-like eyes followed the young maid before redirecting on Ewan.

"And how are ye, man?" Gavin asked. Ewan flexed his arm, testing the bandage.

"As well as could be expected. 'Tis little more than a scratch, but Meggie insisted it be bound as though my arm hung from naught but a thread." Ewan threw a wicked smile towards Meg who tossed her hair at him in response.

"Shall ye rejoin the festivities? The men would like to try to drink ye under the table again."

Ewan gazed at his wife as she poured water from the pitcher into the wash basin. He sighed heavily.

"Aye. I will join ye below for a short time. However, I must cut the evening short, as I have deeds to tend to this night."

Meg blushed as Gavin chortled from the doorway.

"I'm sure ye do, Ewan. I'm sure ye do." Gavin then left a blushing Meg and a contrite Ewan and headed for the stairs.

Ewan barely began his second cup of ale when Hamish led old Keith into the main hall. The man was shaking as he held onto the young man, and Hamish's eyes were wide and alert. Leaving old Keith with fellow clansmen, Hamish approached his brother with the news.

"We have a problem on our land, brother," Hamish began, his dark head close to Ewan's. "Unknown enemies have taken advantage of our oath-taking to wreak havoc on crops and crofter. Methinks none are dead, but three families are wi'out shelter," he gestured to old Keith, "and several crops burned. We dinna ken how the stock fares."

Ewan's demeanor lit with fury at Hamish's news. To reive off a man's land was an accepted practice, but to burn homes and crops needed to live was unacceptable, and to do so on a night such as this was unheard of.

"English?" asked Ewan, tersely.

"I dinna ken. Duncan shall be bringing th' families here for shelter, but they dinna ken who attacked. 'Tis been a while since they have encroached on our land, but ye well ken that doesna mean they are gone. Could very well be English, and the manner of attack speaks of their vile ways."

Ewan was silent for a moment, rubbing at his forehead. Most of the festivities had halted, with well-wishers waiting to learn the cause of the intrusion. He called Gavin to his side.

"I think I ken why 'twould be English. Gather our forces and ride through the glen near th' small burn. Look ye for signs of camps, and if ye see any English, bring them here. There is a conspiracy afoot, and we must rid our land of these English bastards."

Ewan turned to Meg, grabbed her around the waist and, pulling her to him, kissed her fiercely.

"I shall join ye tonight," he promised again and stormed off with his warriors.

The night stretched long without her husband. Many of the clansmen prepared to leave with the morning light and camped outside in the warm spring night. With the MacNallys out of the house and camped at the far end of the gate, Meg felt more secure in her own home. Meg found herself dozing slightly when the door to Ewan's chamber, *our chamber*, she corrected herself, was thrown open. She rose to assist Ewan with undressing for bed.

Meg remained silent, waiting for Ewan to tell her, in his own way, what occurred. He skin was warm, a thin layer of perspiration covering his entire body. He retired his claymore, placed it near the hearth, and turned to Meg in the near darkness. The last bit of candlelight gave her enough light to attend to Ewan. She removed his dark leather boots, slid his plaid from his shoulder, and pulled off his tunic.

Ewan remained silent and still, allowing her to minister to him. He had not expected her to be awake, much less aid him in undressing, and he found this aspect of marriage with his new wife to be completely enticing.

That she was caring for him, placing his simple need of being undressed above her more important need for sleep, caressed his heart, and her fingertips on his skin caused his loins to throb. His breathing became a rasp as she finished removing his kilt.

Meg left him suddenly, and he watched as her silhouette moved to the table with the wash basin. When she returned, he felt the coolness of the wet linen on his chest as she washed the wear of the day from his body. Moving silently, her hand and the linen wiped him softly from chest to back and down. The sensation of her touch was too much for him to bear.

Unable to endure her quiet, thorough attendance, he crushed her to his nakedness, kissing her with all the passion he had pent up throughout the day. His damp body wetted her thin shift and he could feel the outline of her body against his, as if she wore nothing.

She clung back to him and every fear he had of losing her, every want he had of bedding her, and every need he had to be near her went into his kiss. His tongue caressed her lips and tongue before moving to her jaw line and creamy neck. He carried her to the bed and restrained himself from ravaging her, reminding himself that she was untried as of the night before.

Wordlessly, he stroked her face and neck, working her nightclothes down her body to caress her breasts. When his lips found the first one, she arched her back, breathlessly calling out to him. Unable to control himself, he ripped the remainder of the shift from her. He put his lips to her breast again, sucking and kissing one, then the other, until he heard her moans and could feel her quiver beneath him. His lips moved back to hers. He trailed his fingers down her stomach and lower. She was damp and more than ready for him.

Ewan settled between her legs and thrust himself into her. Once there, tight, and hot, he continued to thrust, not gently as he felt he should have but urgently, forcefully, trying to lose himself in the glory that was her.

Meg anticipated pain for her second night with her husband. He was being especially rough, taking her frantically, but she found no pain. She was more than ready for him when he entered her, clinging to him, breathless and moaning from the pure pleasure that now was this intimacy.

As he thrust harder and faster, she rode the waves of pleasure he gave her. Only at the bursting sensation, when she thought she would die from it, did she cry out his name, loudly and passionately. Feeling her climax, Ewan ballocks tightening before he exploded, pouring himself into her, calling out to her. Then he collapsed, covering her tiny body with his own.

When his breathing slowed to normal, he moved to the side of her, pulling her close. There were no other words spoken that night.

Meg woke early the next morn to help see the clansmen off with a meal to warm their bellies on the way home. Certain Jenny and the kitchen maid Fiona would like the assistance, she dressed quickly, this time in her now more common green gown, and rustled down the stairs.

To her surprise, Elayne sat in the main hall on a low bench near the hearth, fingering the fine trim on the sleeve of her chemise. She donned a regal blue costume, her hair bound back, covered by a shimmering blue veil held in place with a dainty silver circlet. Elayne shifted towards her when Meg reached the bottom of the stairs but did not bother to rise. She gestured to Meg in a condescending manner and, not knowing any better, Meg walked over to her, stunned and confused.

What was Elayne doing inside the keep when her family and clan were supposed to be camped outside? Why was she dressed like the lady of the manor? Meg's stomach sank to the floor as Elayne shook her head in disapproval.

"Well, little crofter lass," Elayne spoke in a harsh whisper. "I should have known that ye would not ken any better."

"Any better about what?" Meg demanded. She already harbored ill will with this woman; she did not want her resolve about her marriage or Ewan to be shaken any more after all this woman had tried to do.

"He laid wi' ye last night, am I right?" Elayne's mouth twisted into an unpleasant smile, and Meg did not respond.

What occurred in her marriage bed was between her and Ewan. She would not bring this crazed woman into her life. Since Elayne was set to leave in a few hours, Meg thought she would not have to encounter Elayne again.

"I should have ye know he sought me out first, but my father had moved us far from the keep. Ye see, little girl, I am wi' child." Elayne paused to let the words have their effect. Her smile was now full and didn't reach her eyes. "Ewan's child. I only told my father last eve, as I thought to tell Ewan first. Now ye ken, and soon Ewan will ken as well. Then he will have your marriage annulled and we will wed."

Elayne looked directly into Meg's eyes, her beady, angry look kept Meg rooted into place. She could not help but listen to this evil woman's lies. She knew in her heart they were lies, but as often happens, her head did not want to listen to the heart. It wanted to listen to Elayne's vile falsehood.

"Ye can save us all some trouble and leave now, before anyone wakes." Elayne rose and grabbed Meg's arm. Suddenly Meg was drawn back to her senses.

"Aye, leave. Dinna bother to pack your belongings. Just go back to your croft and dinna return to be humiliated," Elayne hissed at Meg.

"If that is so true, Elayne, then where is your father to support your claim?" Meg asked softly, her anger tempered with her knowledge that something was greatly amiss with Elayne's story. "Your father should be here, screaming at Ewan at the top o' his voice, but he is no'."

Meg pulled her arm away from Elayne. She did not know that Ewan had risen and was on the stairs, listening to the entire exchange, or that Fiona and Jenny had been listening in the kitchen. Jenny opened the door to keep watch out for the new mistress of the MacLeods, while Fiona ran like the wind to retrieve MacNally himself.

"I ken my father would have tracked Ewan down last night, Elayne," Meg's voice was barely above a whisper. "But where is your father now? Nay, I dinna think ye speak the truth. Methinks ye are a sad, jealous woman. Methinks ye should go home."

"Nay! I am no' jealous! I speak the truth and ye will get yourself gone from this manse this very morn if I have t'drag ye from it!" Elayne screamed at Meg, then grabbed her sleeve again and began to pull Meg towards the door by her arm.

"Here! What is this?" Meg yelled at Elayne, trying to peel off the gripping hand that held her.

Elayne barely made it across the room when Ewan stepped from his hiding spot on the stairs to take control. However, before he could come into view, two doors opened into the room. At the front door of the hall, MacNally appeared, shocked and enraged at being drawn from his slumber to the sight in the hall.

This was immediately followed by the kitchen door, thrown open by Jenny, who raced over to Elayne, grasped her arm, and pried her loose from Meg. For good measure, Jenny thrust Elayne toward her father. Elayne stumbled and fell. Her veil had worked loose, and anger alighted her entire face.

Jenny then realized what she had done – she had attacked the daughter of a neighboring, powerful Laird. She put her hand to her mouth in shocked awareness, when Gavin burst in, sword raised, and moved in front of Jenny. What started off as a quiet morning had turned into a fiasco.

It was then Ewan stepped around the wall of the stair, surveying the exploits before him. He rolled his eyes in exasperation, and to his pleasant surprise, Meg rolled her eyes in response. Ewan bit back a smile and approached Gavin. It was Jenny who spoke first.

"My apologies, my Laird." Her delicate voice was barely a whisper. "I only thought for the safety of Meg. I didna mean --" but Ewan cut her off with a wave of his hand.

"There is naught amiss, Jenny. Ye were protecting my wife; 'tis all I ken." Ewan focused on MacNally, but the look on the man's face caused Ewan's sharp words to die in his throat.

"I, too, apologize, Ewan MacLeod. Never has my family been embarrassed as such."

MacNally strode over to Elayne and roughly dragged her to her feet. She was blubbering to her father, but he would have none of it. One look from MacNally quieted Elayne. "If there is ever anything we can do to make up for the spectacle she has caused, ye only need ask."

Ewan nodded and with that, MacNally hauled Elayne from the hall by her arm. They could hear him gather his men and then scuffling as they readied their horses.

Both Meg and Ewan noted how Gavin escorted the fair-haired Jenny back to the kitchen, talking in low tones to each other. Ewan took Meg's hand in his and kissed it.

"Are ye hurt, my Meggie?"

"'Tis only my pride, methinks." She then turned her fierce smile on Ewan. "What manner of people have ye brought me into, my Laird?" she asked in mock astonishment. "If I am no' being attacked, then I am accused of witchery, all within the past two days!"

Ewan could not help but laugh out loud at his wife's comments, agreeing with her that the past few days had been especially trying.

"Well, ye can no' ever say ye are wanting for entertainment, now can ye, Meggie?"

CHAPTER NINE

Little Boy Lost

EWAN LATER TOLD MEG that they had found some campfires the night before, but no English. Deciding that the worst was over for the moment, the MacLeod men returned to their homes and families and began rebuilding the destroyed crofts that day. Most of the stock was not hurt, and some new crops were planted. It took almost a week to rebuild all three crofts. Those without homes either stayed with families or returned with Ewan to stay at Broch Lochnora. No one saw hide or hair of any English, and most thought that they left for good. Only Ewan, his brothers, and Gavin knew any different.

Ewan acknowledged that he must have a leak among his people. Someone had to inform the English that most of the men and many of their families would be at the oath-taking, leaving homes vulnerable. He tried to think of a clansman who would betray his people but could not. The most difficult part was trying to see how Meg tied into the English. She seemed to be an object of their attacks until she came to the manse. Now the attacks focused on the land itself. Ewan knew no one would ever drive him or his clan off MacLeod land. The coastal route must be of the utmost importance to try to force a whole clan of people to bend to the wishes of the English, and Ewan thought that a note penned to Robert the Bruce, informing him of the current events, would not be uncalled for, even if only to apprise the Bruce that the English had not truly gone away.

Now that the English seemed to have departed for the moment, life began to move smoothly after Ewan's tumultuous start. His wedding on the heels of his father's death, and the oath-taking the next day, followed by the rebuilding, left little time to take in his new situation. However, as spring quickly became warmer and turned to summer, Ewan fell into the everyday dealings as Laird. He collected rents, settled disputes, and assisted wherever he was needed.

At night he came to bed with his beautiful wife waiting for him, loving him as he had never been loved. Ewan began to see how powerful love could be which gave him new insight into his father's nightmare of losing a wife. Meg had done more than make a mark on his heart, he felt cleaved to her, as though they were truly one person. She gave him solace when he had none, and he yearned for her from the moment he woke until he took to bed at night. They enjoyed discovering each other, and Ewan adored the look in Meg's eye when she explored his body, to her something new and unseen, and he hoped she would never lose that look.

As for Ewan, he could explore Meg every day and never get enough of her. Occasionally, he had managed to sneak away with her during the day, and once they made love in the stable, not far from the young ears of William the stable lad. Ewan smiled as he recalled kissing her as she found her pleasure, ere she cry out and bring the household upon them.

He was beginning to realize how much she cared for him as well. Meg left flowers on his pillow and scented his basin water with a fresh pine oil to invigorate him. She worked in the garden daily, digging up roots and clipping herbs to keep the household and the rest of the clan in good health. If she were not in the gardens, she was in the kitchen baking and cooking, or sewing by an open window.

Ewan often found himself searching her out. He could not tear his eyes from her. If she entered a room, Ewan lost whatever conversation he was having and followed her with his eyes. It became a joke with Gavin and his brothers, and Gavin would usually exclaim, "Smitten!" to recapture the Laird's attention.

Meg, too, became accustomed to life as the Laird's wife. No longer did comments about her status arise, as they had when she had inadvertently eavesdropped before her wedding. People made her feel important by coming to her for advice or recommendations, and even Ewan asked for her input on nearly a daily basis. Ewan did everything in his power to help make the keep her home, and she found herself loving him for it. In fact, it had begun to feel too perfect, and when she found Ewan one afternoon in early summer, she was shocked at what she saw.

She came downstairs to help begin the evening meal when she caught Ewan standing near the doorway. Thinking he was alone, she approached him, only to see a small boy standing outside the door. She paused behind Ewan, patient for him to finish his discussion with the lad.

The boy was exceptionally frail and looked no more than five years in age. A grimy thing, layers of dirt that would take several baths to scrub away coated every inch of skin. She was certain she saw lice crawling in his hair, even from so far back. The lad also had a sad, uncared-for look that was too plain for anyone to miss, so she was shocked when she heard her husband turn the child away.

"Git gone wi' ye, lad. We aren't needing ye here for a time. Christ, ye can barely walk, let alone hold a weapon. Come back when ye've grown a bit."

Ewan walked away from Meg, leaving the lad stranded by the door of the keep. She watched the boy's lower lip quiver, and then large tears streaked the dirt on his face. He dragged his feet as he trudged away from the door.

Meg was astonished to hear her husband talk as such. He seemed the gentlest of men, when he was not trying to be a warrior and wage a battle with the English. Especially when they were alone, he spoke soft words to her. For him to now turn away this child who so obviously needed help, to speak so coarsely to him, was outrageous. Meg raced to catch her husband and grasped him by the arm.

"Was that truly necessary, milord?" she demanded of him.

"Was what necessary?"

"The way ye treated that lad!" she fumed. "Could ye no' see the lad was in need of help, and ye, as his Laird, turned him away? How do ye think the poor lad feels? Where will the lad go? Obviously, no one cares for him as 'tis, and now he thinks his Laird does no' care for him either!" Her voiced raised to a fever pitch. Ewan gave an exasperated sigh.

"Do ye ken what th' child wanted?" he asked her. "He wanted t' train as a warrior. To be a soldier in my army, he spoke. The child could no' carry a pail, let alone a sword, and ye want me to train him?"

Meg stared at him unbelievingly.

"How can ye be so blind, milord?" she asked, her hand over her chest, trying to register her shock. "Do ye even ken whose child that was? Or if he had someone to care for him? Could ye no' find a place for him here, in the keep, lest he grows strong enough to train wi' ye?"

"I admit, wi' all the bairns that have been born as of late, and the issues I have faced, I do no' recall the lad." Ewan paused, sighing as if in deep thought.

"Could ye find a place for him here, then, 'til he is ready to train?" she asked.

His eyes riveted on his wife, and they were hard and unyielding. She had not seen him ever look at her with such hardness.

"Milord, I do no' mean to displease ye," Meg whispered, bowing her head.

She realized too late that she tried to go against the wishes of her husband, and while she was used to being loved by him, she did not know how to make her wishes known when they went against what he decided.

"'Tis no' displeasing me that I worry over, Meggie. I am no' used to having to explain myself to anyone, least of all a wife. I am no' used to my decisions being second guessed, which has been happening too often as of late. Least of all, I am no' used to having to admit when I may, *may,* have made a mistake."

She grinned to herself at his small admission. With his finger, he took her face and tilted it back up towards his. Once again, he was shocked at how she affected him, and how she was willing to say what she felt was right, regardless of the consequences. He kissed her, then took her hand in his.

"Come. Let us find the bairn and see if he would like to assist the stable lad for the next few years."

Meg smiled grandly at his words and nearly yanked him off his feet as she took off after the child.

⟫⟫⟫⟶ ⟵⟪⟪⟪

They found him in an empty crofter's hut to the east, just outside the glen. There was no food in the hut, and child had been making his bed on a pallet of filthy straw, using more straw as a blanket. Meg's heart lurched at the sight of the poor boy and silently vowed he would never live like this again. Ewan wanted to know how he came to live this way to begin with.

"I dinna ken ye, lad. Are ye no' a MacLeod?" The boy stood there, his dirty head bent low. He traced a pattern in the dirt with a grimy toe and shook his head slowly.

"Did ye leave your clan then?" The boy nodded, keeping his head down. Ewan sighed heavily. This could take all day.

"How did ye come to be here?" he demanded, receiving a warning look from his wife over his tone.

"My name is Davey," the boy's voice was barely above a whisper, and both Meg and Ewan strained forward to hear him. "Davey MacDonald. My mother died and my father's a drunk. When he drinks, he hurts me, hitting me about the head, pushing me into the walls. I was afeared, so I ran. I found this place. Ate some berries. But I am hungry and scared, milord. I heard ye were a good man, and ye wed a good wife. If I could work for ye, earn my keep . . ."

Davey's voice trailed off as the tears began to flow freely, and Ewan regretted more than ever the harshness of his words. He had truly thought that the lad was a local crofter's child, trying to get out of work at home. He never imagined such a story as what the lad was telling him.

Meg needed to hear no more. She went to the lad and swept him into her arms, patting his back and making gentle shushing noises. She had seen her father angry, but never enough to strike her mother, though she knew such things did happen in other households, sometimes quite often. Meg cut her eyes to her husband, imploring him.

Seeing her hold the lad, knowing that one day she would do the same for their child, wrenched Ewan's heart, and he sighed deeply again.

"Will your father be coming to look for ye, lad, seeing as ye are a runaway?" Ewan asked the child.

"Nay, I dinna think so. Most times I dinna think he kens he has a lad, 'cept when he is wanting to hit something."

"Come now, lad. Ye'll no' stay here any longer. Ye shall earn your keep wi' us until ye are old enough and I shall train ye myself. But if your da or clan comes for ye, I can no' keep ye. Ye ken?"

The boy nodded and used his sleeve to wipe his face. Meg shifted Davey to carry him back to the keep, but Ewan stepped forward.

"I'll carry him. Ye lead the way."

They settled the boy at the manse. After a bath of hot water and strong soap, to which the boy protested loudly, some clothes were found that fit somewhat, and then Jenny led him to the kitchen for his first real meal in days. Meg began to follow Jenny and Davey, but Ewan put his hand on her arm to halt her.

"I must thank ye, for seeing t' the lad," he said quietly. "If no' for ye, Davey would still be alone and hungry. Thank ye for having the courage to face me, even when I was angry for such a small reason, to help that child."

Meg brushed her fingers against her husband's. "Nay, milord. I think had ye no' been so busy as of late, ye would have seen it for yourself. I thank ye for giving him a place when many others would have no'."

He gathered her close to him, wishing that it were night already so he could take her to bed. He had never met a woman such as Meg. She never denied him, never shied away from him, not even on the first night.

She even stood up to him when she felt that he was wrong. Ewan knew he looked dark and menacing. He heard of men that cowered at the sight of him, and boys who hid, even though his reputation for kindness preceded him. Ewan believed that was one of the main reasons he wanted Meg so much when he first met her – she was willing to go against him, tell him he was wrong, if the case warranted. It intrigued him, that she, little golden Meggie, should be the one who feared him the least. He rubbed his fingers across her palm.

"Well, my Meggie. Do ye have plans this aft noon? I think we need to see to some concerns in our bed chamber."

She giggled at his audacity, his brazen lust. It did not seem to her that other men were so obsessed with their wives, and she was overly flattered at the amount of attention her husband bestowed upon her. She tugged at his hand, guiding him towards the stairs as she glanced about the hall to make sure no one saw them take their leave. While she felt as lusty as he, she did not want all of the clan to know it.

They had started up the stairs when Gavin burst into the hall, screaming for Ewan at the top of his lungs. The fire of lust in his eyes turned to anger when he heard Gavin's words - an anger that frightened even Meg.

"The English are attacking! A man has been hurt by the glen, and men are riding now to track them!"

Ewan pulled Meg aside, crushing her to him. "Stay within these walls, wife," he spoke against her lips, then released her abruptly. He spun to Gavin and rushed out the doors, his hand clasped around the hilt of his sword.

It had been nearly a fortnight since any movement from the English had been detected, and while other clans in the area had not been taunted, the English seemed to continue to wreak havoc on the MacLeod Clan. This worried Meg, not necessarily for herself anymore, but for other maidens of the demesne. If she could have been attacked, so could any lass -- her mother or her sisters.

She still couldn't understand what the English hoped to accomplish; the MacLeods would never leave the land, but the English seemed bent on antagonizing them.

Meg pressed her fingers to her lips. They still tingled from Ewan's touch, and she marveled at her body's response to him. He came to her every night, sometimes the slow and gentle lover, sometimes rough and quickly, aching with need for her. Even his kisses sent her mind reeling. She had noted that he never left the manse without kissing her. Not only kissing her, but forcefully and possessively claiming her.

Her mind on Ewan, she set out for the garden to tend to the plants in the warm weather. It was beginning to be hot out, especially aft noon, and she did not want to dally too long in the heat. Midsummer would be upon them soon enough.

Meg looked forward to the celebration, clutching her abdomen as she walked. She knew of several fertility rites for midsummer, but many she had been using already, including keeping several stems tied with ribbon under her pillow. She hoped that by midsummer she would have wondrous news for Ewan. God knows, they didn't want for trying.

CHAPTER TEN

A Fox in the Hen House

IT WAS NOT AN attack as Gavin and Ewan were led to believe. One man and his cottage were attacked, that was the extent of the damage. The English brigands had ridden off immediately, and this time, the clansmen tracked the English south, close to the MacNally land not far from the sea, then lost the tracks amidst the rocks, and there were no further signs of the instigators. They cursed themselves for not finding a single one.

The man they had beaten would be fine, and they were taking him to Elspeth's for care. As the men began to ride for home, Ewan kept his horse reined by the border of his land, and the stallion pranced about with disdain. He did not like being reined in while the others trotted off. Gavin rode up next to Ewan, surveying the land with him.

Ewan remained silent. Tracking the English to MacNally land gave him cause for concern. After the problems with MacNally's daughter, he did not want to believe that his father's longtime friend could be harboring the enemy.

He knew that the problems with the English began before his wedding to Meg and Elayne's fit over it, but seeing the English tracks lead to MacNally gave Ewan cause for doubt.

Was it possible that his father's close friend was an English sympathizer? Did MacNally have a claim if the land went to Argyll, giving the English a foothold in the Highlands? Could that be a reason MacNally and Elayne had hoped for a match with the son of MacLeod?

Ewan shuddered; he could not picture anything much worse.

Gavin finally spoke. "Have ye noticed, Ewan, these English seem to have attacked us when we were most weak? When most men where otherwise preoccupied or indisposed?"

He paused to let the thought make its mark, wondering if Ewan had considered that or not. Gavin decided not to press the matter. Ewan would make the connection to a possible traitor in the clan, even if he did not want to admit to it.

Gavin continued, "Ewan, what shall ye do?"

The question was a weighted one, and Ewan did not know how to answer. Especially now, with a wife he cared for deeply, he wanted to do naught that could jeopardize his future, but he could not forsake his land or his clan for that. He was Laird, after all, and with the title came responsibility.

Another thought came on the tails of the first, *A wife, and perchance a babe as well.* He could not ignore that a child would be the eventual result of his attentions to his wife, and that bairn would come sooner as opposed to later. At least he hoped it would. Ewan thought of his family and sighed heavily.

"On the morrow, we will ride to MacNally and confront him. If he has naught to hide, he will help us locate the English. We can no longer wait for them to raid us and try to retaliate. That has been for naught. The next raid may cost a life or more, and I would no sooner risk the life of a clansman as I would my wife's. We must drive the English from our lands." He paused. "Other than Meg, we will tell no one."

With that, Ewan reined his mount around and galloped for home, with Gavin at his heels.

They arrived at the hall in time for the eventide meal. Gavin left to wash, and Ewan found his wife at the table eating and talking to Davey. Ewan surveilled the scene for a moment, realizing that was how his wife would look when she had children that age. He observed her mannerisms, how she patted his head and gave him another helping of bread.

Soon, my wife, he thought. *Soon I will see ye be a mother to our bairns, and I canna wait for that day.* He walked over to her and greeted her with a kiss. He tousled Davey's hair. Davey had finished eating, and Meg sent him off to help in the kitchens before bed.

Ewan dropped into the vacated seat next to her. The hall was packed with people eating and talking, but the sound was subdued and no laughter rang in the hall. He didn't want his words to be heard by all, so he leaned close to Meg,

"We followed the tracks to the MacNally land. We will ride there on the morrow and discover what MacNally knows."

"Ye should speak t' the man who was beaten. William was taken to my mother's house, and he may be able to tell ye who he saw wi' the English, if MacNally men were there."

Ewan smiled at his wife. "Ahh, my Meggie, how did I get a wise wife such as ye? Ye are wise beyond your years." He kissed her forehead, then tore into his evening meal. It felt as though he had not eaten in days.

Meg finished her wine and rose for bed. Ewan promised to join her after a time, and she headed for the kitchens in search of Davey. She found him helping set slops for the pigs. When he was finished, she sent him off to wash and then to bed down in the hall. She gazed upon the wee lad as he ran off, and Jenny found her there, resting against the doorway.

"He is a wee, soft lad," Jenny said to her. "I will keep my eye on him to see he stays out of trouble."

"Aye," Meg replied. "He has seen enough of trouble, methinks. I am just grateful that we found the lad afore he starved to death, from either lack of food or attention."

"Ahh, lack of attention. That is one thing ye can no' claim of Ewan, eh?" Jenny asked suggestively, and Meg blushed to the roots of her hair. Jenny laughed and came up to Meg, hugging her fiercely.

"Ooch, Meg, the blushing bride. I am glad that ye have control of the house, but ye have to learn to laugh at the jokes, lass!" Jenny's laughter was contagious, and Meg giggled through her blush. "So, does he have ye wi' a bairn yet?"

Meg's blush deepened. She had a difficult time realizing that all the clan would watch her to see if and when she conceived. She shook her head.

Jenny gave her a playful pat. "Well, if no' yet, then soon enough. I hear ye canna even go to the stable . . ." she trailed off, laughing uproariously at Meg's shocked expression. "I ken it is difficult to be private wi' so many watching what ye do day to day. It will wear off soon. Ye should feel blessed to have one like Ewan, who attends to ye so much . . ."

Jenny's voice trailed off again, but this time not into laughter. Her eyes were turned away, and Meg followed the gaze to see Gavin as the focus of Jenny's attention. Meg gave her a soft smile.

"Dinna ye fret, Jenny. I ken all too soon, we will be comparing babes." Then Meg changed the subject. "Ewan and I shall attend William at my mother's house tomorrow.

I will see to Davey afore I leave. Will ye see that he does what he is told?" Jenny nodded in agreement, and Meg pressed forward.

"Ewan says that he is to go to MacNally's soon. And I fear, I mean . . . Do ye think? I mean, will Ewan . . ?" and Meg found she could not voice her fear. Jenny understood anyway.

"I think that, even if Elayne threw herself at Ewan with nary a piece of clothing betwixt them, Ewan still would no' see her for your vision would dance afore his eyes."

Tears burned in Meg's eyes as she thanked Jenny for understanding and trying to put Meg's fears to rest. Had it been anyone but MacNally's daughter, Meg would not have worried, but with Elayne, she could not be sure. Fortunately, she trusted Ewan, and that assuaged her fears even more. She bid Jenny good eve and went to her chamber for bed.

When she entered their bedchamber, she found he had made it there before she did. He was already undressed and sat on a small stool near the hearth.

The evenings were nearly as warm as the day now, but sometimes fog or a cool breeze could come in from the sea, and a fire banked at the hearth was not amiss in the early morning. The window tapestry was pulled back to reveal a clear, starry night.

"It looks like ye will have fine weather for your ride tomorrow," she said quietly to Ewan. He did not speak but nodded his head. She fastened the chamber door behind her and moved to him.

"Are ye worried?" Meg ventured quietly. Ewan did not respond immediately. After a moment he turned to her and spoke.

"I guess I dinna ken what is truly going on," Ewan sounded bewildered.

While he put on a strong façade for the rest of the clan, he often took off the "great Laird" mask when he and Meg were alone. This he did now.

"The Englishman we caught told us that Argyll wanted the land to aid English movements, but why our land? Is it because we are small? But so is our land. For movements like that, they would want more exposure to the sea, more land, more cooperative men. Why does Argyll no' offer to pay for the access? Many clans would take gold or silver for access to the sea. I dinna ken what is going on here. These unprovoked attacks make us angrier, and less willing to tolerate any English at all."

He turned back to the fire and sighed.

"Would ye?" Meg asked. "Take gold for the use of the land?"

Ewan looked at her sharply. "Nay! Of course no'!"

Meg nodded in return. "Then how can ye be sure any other clans would? We've only just thrown off the yoke of the English, and still battle them heartily in the south. Accepting gold would only put that yoke back on, no?"

"Aye. Your thought is clear on that, my little Meg. And a larger clan, wi' more influence, would undoubtedly complain about such attacks as we have seen."

He paused and regarded Meg with his pensive blue gaze, then stood to embrace her. She laid her head against his bare chest, enjoying his warmth and his musky scent. She touched his chest, marveling at the strength beneath his furred skin.

"Aye, Meg. Ye do well to help me see clearly. Our clan lands are near perfect to overtake for coastal access. But, how do they expect us to leave wi' such small attacks? Surely, they ken a few burned crofts will no' make us want to leave?"

Ewan stroked her head, letting his fingers run through the coppery softness of her hair. His forefinger caught on a lock entwined with a ribbon and curled it around his fingers.

"Unless it is to keep us off guard, milord," Meg responded. "Is there a greater target they could strike to hurt the whole of the clan? Like the kirk?"

"Nay, Meg. The MacLeod clan is the people, and they havena killed or really threatened anyone. They've barely wounded those they have attacked!" Ewan sighed again, resting his chin atop Meg's head. "I dinna ken what is going on."

Meg pulled back and took Ewan's hands in hers. "Well, then, come to bed and sleep on it. My mother always tells me 'tis best to think wi' a clear head."

She then guided him to bed, closing the window tapestry as she went.

※

Davey found Meg in the kitchens early that morning. She was bending low to stir some oats in a large pot over the fire. He waited behind her until Meg rose and turned around. He looked up at her with eyes that belonged to a lost pup.

"Och, Davey! What brings ye here this early in the morn?"

Meg smiled at the little boy. Davey brought one of his hands from around his back, and in one hand he had several stems of white heather and pale rosemary. He shyly held them out to her. Meg went to her knees in front of him.

"Oh, little laddie," she gushed. "Did ye pick these for me?"

Davey nodded and gave Meg an awkward hug. Fiona, one of the kitchen matrons, entered, and Davey turned at the sound of her entrance. He released Meg and went to

Fiona. In his other hand, he held another bouquet of heather and rosemary, which he presented to Fiona. The buxom woman suppressed a condescending smile and gave Meg a sly wink. She then reached down and took the blooms from Davey's up thrust hand.

"Davey, lad," she crooned, "these are the most beautiful flowers. Shall we place them in the window?"

Fiona led the boy to the far end of the kitchen, and Davey placed his hand in hers. Meg had wondered what Fiona's reaction would be, after losing her own youngest to illness and fever over a year ago.

Meg had feared the sight of that lost little boy would remind Fiona too much of her lad, but Fiona seemed to warm quickly to Davey, and like Meg and Jenny, had been helping him adjust to the keep. In fact, it was Fiona who prepared his meal of bread, milk, and meat. After his bath, Davey ate hugely of the meal as Fiona kept watch. Meg thought that maybe Fiona had needed Davey as much as Davey needed her.

After breaking her fast, Meg accompanied her husband and several of his men to her mother's house. The man would live, praise Hosts, but was wounded nonetheless, and would have to remain abed for several days. After Elspeth hemmed and hawed over William, the injured man, she and Meg left Ewan to talk to him. Meg followed her mother outside to collect some healing herbs near the woods.

Meg observed that her mother seemed pensive and less talkative than usual and broached her.

"Mother, what ails ye?"

Elspeth remained silent for a moment, her hands working mutely among the greens she collected. Then she spoke, her voice soft and shaking.

"Methinks your father is in more trouble than I ken, my wee Meggie."

"Trouble? What trouble?"

Fear grew quickly in Meg, for if her father had problems, those problems affected her whole family, and Meg would be distraught should anything happen to her beloved family.

"Methinks 'tis wagering. He has been gone oft of late, as I have told ye. But yester eve, he was late returning from tending the sheep. I left Mairi with the bairns and searched for him. He was no' far past the stable, speaking wi' another man. Your father claimed, 'I have none,' and the man spoke, 'have some soon, or your house will be next.'"

"Oh, Mother!" Meg exclaimed.

This seemed odd to Meg, and she wondered if her mother thought so as well. She had never seen her father gamble, or heard her mother speak of it. Had they been hiding it? It did not make sense to Meg, for her father doted on his family, giving to them before he took for himself.

Why would he forsake a family he held so dear for a recent bout of wagering? Perchance she could ask Ewan to lend her the money to cover her father's debts, to save her family.

"Do ye ken the man?"

"Nay. I dinna see him at all. He spoke oddly though. Not Scottish, this man. English, methinks."

English! Is father gaming with the very men who tried to assail me? Meg feared it was the truth. Meg knew Lachlan's family was the most important part of his life; why would her father wager with those who threatened her? What was going on?

She didn't voice her fears to her mother. She knew it could only make matters worse. Instead she would try to pay off her father's debts and stop his affiliations with the English as soon as possible.

Ewan and his men were leaving the cottage when Meg and her mother returned. He spoke briefly to Gavin, who turned back toward the other men. Elspeth took the fresh herbs to steep in hot water for William's injuries. Ewan approached Meg.

"The man doesna ken if he was attacked by English or Scottish. He doesna recall much. He did say that he can no' recall seeing MacNally plaid, so that is a good start."

"'Twas an English attack, then?" Meg questioned. Ewan gazed off into the trees, considering.

"'Twould appear so. Still, Gavin and I ride to MacNally this aft noon to learn what dealings he has had with these English, if any."

Ewan bowed to Elspeth, bidding her good day, and giving his thanks for the care of the injured man, then took Meg's arm and led her to her little horse. While she was a more accomplished rider than when she had first rode with Ewan, she still feared larger beasts, and was content to waddle along on a stout pony. It was a source of great amusement to Ewan, but now he made no comment about her mount.

"Come. We will ride back to the hall. I should return tonight, but if 'tis late, ye will no' see us til the morn. I would like to say goodbye to ye properly."

Meg's heart surged at the suggestion his words implied, but she still harbored a small worry that Elayne would try to work her wiles on Ewan. This thought depressed her even more, and she was quiet for the short ride back to the keep.

He escorted her up to their chamber, collected his dirk and coin for his sporran, then turned to face Meg.

He took her hand and pressed her fingers to his lips. The warmth of his lips sent a surge of fire through her, and she marveled that, even in worry, she could react to him so. He slid his lips up her arm, over her shoulder to the mounds of her breasts that pushed against the fabric of her gown. She wore a simple yellow kirtle, as most of her clothing was selected for ease of wear in the gardens, but he thought she looked as elegant as a queen and told her so. He tugged lightly at the fabric, exposing more of her breast, and found the nipple with his lips.

She gasped at his touch but still could not wrest the image of her husband with Elayne from her mind. She found herself pulling at him, grasping at him, silently begging him to prove that it was she he wanted, herself and no other. Ewan felt her eagerness and pulled away, chuckling.

"If this is how ye say goodbye, Meggie, I shall have to leave ye more..." his voice trailed off as he saw the tears that glistened in her eyes. He touched a fingertip to her face as one began to fall. "Meggie, what is this?"

Meg had no voice for her thoughts. She undoubtedly would sound foolish, and he would be angered that she could not trust him. She bowed her head low, running her hands over her husband's backside, feeling him shiver under her fingertips. He was as vulnerable as she when it came to such an intimate touch.

"Meg?" Ewan lifted her face to his, leaving the question in the air.

"Love me," she whispered to her husband. "Love me well and promise me to remember this loving whilst ye are away."

"Remember --?" he began, then realization settled into his face. "Oh, Meggie," he almost laughed. "Ye canna mean ye are worrit about Elayne?" He did laugh when she nodded. "Oh, my wife," he hugged her close, kissing her forehead, her lips, her neck.

"If I searched all the rest of my days, I would never find another like ye, love," he explained to her. "And of all the women I could possibly search through, how could ye think Elayne would even come close?"

"Weel," Meg began, "'tis no' ye, necessarily. I mean, ye were quite the rake afore we wed. Ye canna deny that," she gave him a sidelong glance that made him laugh more. "But 'tis

002

no ye I worry about, 'tis *her,* my love. If she came to ye in the night, with naught but the skin she was born wi', would ye reject her?"

She regretted her words when she saw the shocked and hurt look of Ewan's face.

"Reject her? Oh, my wife, I would run for the hills and back to ye afore a blink of the eye should that woman, or any woman, come wantin' to bed me! Can ye no' see? Have I no' made it clear to ye this season past? I want ye, only ye, all the time, wi' every breath of life in my body! How can ye fear a harpy when 'tis your sweet words of love I hear in my head all the day?"

He leaned to her, claiming her mouth with a burning intensity that surprised her. He seemed so earnest, yet when he kissed her it was urgent and demanding, forcing her to accept the truth of his words.

He slid his lips back down to her exposed breast, kissing and licking softly. "Ye are like the sunrise, soft and fresh, and all other skin is likened to dust when compared to yours."

Meg found herself melting into him, his kisses and his words making her want him more, believe in him more, making her love him more.

He undid the laces on her gown and slid it and her chemise to the floor. He pressed her back toward the bed, never taking his lips or hands off her body. Kissing her stomach and navel, he removed his kilt and stopped touching her only long enough to yank his tunic over his head. Then he was on her again, his lips between her thighs as she moaned her pleasure.

"Ye taste of the sweetest fruit, my love. A blessed fruit, the perfect fruit, given only to me. All other food is bland as oats to your lush sweetness."

With that, he moved his tongue between her private folds, and the sound of her pleasure nearly undid him. He reared up, covering her with his body and taking her lips with his.

"When I dream, I dream only of ye. When I yearn, 'tis only for ye, Meg. None other can make me rise as ye do or make me feel the man that ye make me feel."

Then he pressed into her, slowly, and she pulled him more closely to her as if she wanted to feel all of him, take all of him. Then he was completely sheathed, and he stilled, taking in the feel of her, the warmth of her.

She moved her hips slightly, calling out to him in her soft voice, and then he was undone. He thrust hard and fast, trying to touch every part of her at once, loving her as fiercely as she had wanted until she cried out his name over and over, clinging to him. He then found his release, calling out to both her and God in one breath, panting and shaking as though it were his first time.

He slowly gathered himself, still inside her, and held her face with his hands. Her brow was damp with perspiration and her skin glowed. Her green eyes glistened at him, not with tears this time, but with pleasure and contentment.

"'Tis your image that occupies my mind, your name that is always on my lips. But 'tis my heart, wee Meggie, that had claimed ye for mine own. For me, all else is for naught wi' out ye. The goddess of the wood could dance as free as the day is long, but none would sway me. In fact, 'twould most likely anger me to be so detained when I could be home with my love in my arms and in my bed."

Meg wanted to cry, for never had she heard such words of love spoken, and never did she think such words would be spoken to her. She reached up and traced his lips with her fingers, marveling that he spoke such heartfelt and endearing words.

"Oh, Ewan, ye truly want to make me weep. Just as I am in your heart, ye—" she stopped short as a fierce knocking came at the chamber door.

"Ewan!" Gavin cried. "Do we ride to MacNally, or do we tell him ye are detained and as such canna ride at all?"

"Insolent joker," Ewan mumbled to Meg as he rolled off the bed and donned his plaid.

"Else have ye already ridden?" Gavin continued to yell through the door. "And are now too tired to—" He did not finish the thought as Ewan rushed through the door to silence him, leaving Meg to laugh behind the bed curtains by herself.

⤞⤞⤞ ⤝⤝⤝

Ewan returned with Gavin that night, long after the evening meal. Jenny and Meg waited in the hall for the entourage to arrive, with Meg in the doorway, looking out past the gate to the road that Ewan would ride back to her.

The night air grew clammy with mist and the air smelled of damp earth and heather. The bright green grass bloomed for summer; she could see it near the steps in the torch that blazed outside the door. White and purple heather, thistle, and lavender scented the night air and rustled in the breeze.

How different this view was from her parent's croft, where her evening vantage from the doorway was peppered with trees. From there, north of the village and off the main road, she would hear sheep baying the night, and some nights, if the breeze was just right, she could catch the smell of the sea she had never seen. How different this life was than the one she had grown up in. She still worked hard, cooked, cleaned, and sewed, but something else persisted. Here she was in the center of the MacLeod's, where everything bustled in a way nonexistent at the remote croft of her parents.

Then also the way people treated her. As the Laird's wife, others granted her a sense of respect she'd not felt before. She still was not used to it and did not think she would ever be. To call a crofter's daughter *milady* or *Lady MacLeod?* It seemed like a joke to her, and Meg shook her head at those thoughts, still trying to believe she had truly married Ewan MacLeod, that it was not all a lovely dream from which she would soon wake.

She smiled to herself at the thought of Ewan's return, knowing he would not want to be parted from her for too long. She heard the jokes among the men and even some of the house help. They called Ewan smitten, and Jenny had made a "bewitched" joke to her once or twice.

Meg, however, was the smitten one. She looked forward to every moment she could spend with her husband, almost moping while he was away. She did not know if it was like this with all married women, but she knew that Ewan lit up her life in a way she never thought possible. Do other women feel this about their men?

Meg glanced over at Jenny. She marveled at the spry girl who befriended her when Meg most needed a friend. Jenny pined for Gavin, Meg knew, and she continually pondered on how to bring the two of them together. Gavin seemed focused on his duties as Man-at-Arms, Ewan's second in command since his brothers were too young, though she was certain she had seen Gavin turn his gaze on Jenny more than once.

Meg also discovered that Jenny requested to work at the manor to be close to Gavin. Meg thought Jenny, and the entire household for that matter, fortunate that Gavin did not keep a woman at the hall, for it would most likely destroy Jenny. Since both Gavin and Jenny were not wed or betrothed, and they were attractive and determined to serve the Laird of Clan MacLeod, Meg thought they would be perfect together.

She smiled at the idea of playing matchmaker, another position new to her. Meg came up with the plan to have Jenny take a more assertive role in getting Gavin's attention. When the men arrived, Meg motioned to Jenny to assist Gavin with his weapon and plaid, making sure Jenny attended Gavin more than anyone else could. If that didn't get his attention, Meg was going to have to come up with something even more overt.

As Jenny attended Gavin, Meg rushed to Ewan, happy to have him back, and especially happy that he did not have to stay the evening near MacNally's daughter. The men were weary from riding all day, and Jenny retrieved some oatcakes and cheese from the kitchen. All the men ate heartily, then slowly dispersed for their homes.

Meg tugged at Ewan, entreating him to follow her upstairs. Not only did she want to know what was going on, she wanted to give Jenny a chance to speak privately with Gavin. Meg gave Jenny a scheming grin as they left, thinking to herself, *'tis a poor chaperone I am. 'Tis good that Gavin is the gentleman.*

Ewan followed Meg into their chambers and let her serve him. She stripped him down to his plaid, motioned for him to sit in a chair near the hearth where only a few tapers were lit, then began to wash away the sweat and grime of the ride with a cloth and warm water. Slowly the weariness eased, and he began to talk.

"'Tis no' the MacNally's," he began. "They welcomed us with open arms. 'Twas obvious they had nothing to hide. I spoke to MacNally, and he was enraged to find the English had been camping on his lands. He was more than willing to help after all the dramatics his daughter had caused. He vowed to put out more guards, and I did the same." Ewan sighed deeply. "Ahh, Meggie, how is it ye ken how to comfort me when I need it most?" He sighed again as she ran the warm cloth over his face and around the back of his neck.

"Well, milord, if it had been me on the back of a horse all day, riding for all I was worth, I think nothing would feel better than a bit of cleanliness."

"And that scent of the cloth?" Ewan noted the scent when she first brought the cloth over his face.

"Lavender in the water, to calm and relax ye. I thought 'twould be useful this evening."

"Ahh, my wife, 'tis most welcomed this evening, and also serves as a wonderful excuse for us to retire, leaving poor Gavin in the grips of a wanton female?" Ewan's statement and soft chuckle took Meg by surprise, and she bit her lips to stop from laughing out loud.

"'Twas that obvious, my husband?" Meg asked.

"'Twas obvious to me, love. Gavin, on the other hand, seems most oblivious to everything but serving the clan. Jenny has quite a job of wooing him before he will woo her."

"Do ye ken why he is so focused, milord? 'Twould seem that he misses out on some of the simpler pleasures as a result."

"I dinna ken his motives. I do ken that he has been my right-hand man since childhood, and he probably believes that is the only position he holds with me. Not that he has been my closest friend almost since the day I could walk. Perchance the Jenny lass will turn his head. Then perchance he could enjoy the simpler things." Ewan paused, cocking a weary eye at his wife. "Do ye have some flowers and twigs ye could put on his doorstep to entice him to Jenny?"

Pretending indignation, Meg threw the cloth into the shallow bowl, splashing water on her husband. She then led him to bed, pulling him down on her. He pulled her chemise over her head as she fumbled with his kilt. Finally, he reached beneath and removed his kilt, throwing it to the floor. He moved his head over her body, kissing her lips, neck, breasts, and stomach. Suddenly he stopped and grasping her by the hips, rolled over so she sat atop him. Meg let out a small squeal at the movement.

"Ewan," she exclaimed in a hushed voice. "What are ye doing?"

"I want to see ye, *a leannan*," he whispered.

Her skin caught in the dancing firelight, and her entire being seemed to shine in a coppery glow. He moved into her soft, slippery warmth and moaned at the tight pull of her nether lips. Meg's hair hung down, flowing over her shoulders, partly covering her breasts before brushing his chest like fine fingertips. He began to move inside her. Meg relaxed and began to move with him, pressing her hips into his, taking him deeper.

She tipped her head back, and her hair tickled his thighs. He moved his hands from her hips to her forward thrust breasts. Both the touch of her and the sight of her in one moment was nearly too much to bear, and he began to thrust harder as she ground her hips. He forced himself to hold back for her, but she began to cry out his name.

"Oh, Ewan. Ewan!"

Then he could hold back no more and grasping her hips, he surged up, deep into her, crying out her name in his own release. She shifted forward to lie on top of him, panting, her body hot with her own pleasure. Meg reached her hand down to grasp his, their fingers entwining. They fell asleep in that position, barely moving until morning.

Elspeth was worried when her husband was late again coming to bed and decided to follow him to the place she found him last time -- past the stables, speaking with the English. It was a warm night; midsummer would be upon them soon. Elspeth had already noted that her daughter had yet to quicken with the Laird's child, so her mind was occupied on the best remedy for that. She was almost to the stables when she caught Lachlan making his way back to her. His face was heavy until he looked up and saw her. His face changed to a mask of fury, so much so it frightened her in a way she had never before known.

"Christ's Blood, wife! What are ye doing out here?" he raged at her.

"Looking for ye! What have ye been doing this eve? Where ye wi' those men again?" Elspeth decided to rage back at him. Lachlan was harboring a secret, and she was determined to know what was taking its toll on her husband.

"'Tis none of your affair, Beth! Ye stay away from this! And ye had better no' tell anyone what ye are mixing in that head o' yours! Do ye ken?"

"None of my affair? Why Lachlan - 'tis my house and my family - and ye! My husband! How can ye say—" Suddenly Lachlan lunged at her, his hand upraised. Elspeth gasped and pulled back.

"Ye would strike me, husband? This affair, 'tis so grave ye would beat me?" She whispered.

He had never struck her before, though there were times she was sure she had given him cause. Lachlan was a gentle hand, and that was one of the things she loved best. Now, he stood with his hand upraised, ready to strike her over words spoken by an Englishman, and she was sorely frightened.

Lachlan turned and struck an already tilting fencepost, He roared in anger, then grasped his wife fiercely.

"No' a word, Elspeth. If ye care for the wellbeing of this family, ye will let me handle this and speak no' a word."

He then thrust her aside and strode to the croft. Elspeth sat on the dewy grass, her eyes filled with tears. For once she did not know what to do and did not have a concoction to remedy it.

⋙⋙⋙ ⋘⋘⋘

The very next day Elspeth confessed her predicament to Meg. As her mother, Elspeth would normally never tell Meg about Lachlan's dealings with the English; however, as the wife of the Laird of the clan, Meg should know in case Ewan needed the information that Meg had. Elspeth would not, she had decided, ask for help. She was a proud woman and did not beg, neither for money nor assistance, least of all from her eldest daughter who should be enjoying the wonderful life she now lived.

Elspeth left early for the manor, before the heat of summer could grip the day, a covered bowl in her hand containing a tincture made of berry leaves and heather to help ripen Meg's womb to accept a child of the Laird. Elspeth knew well enough about the jokes of the attention Ewan showered on his little wife, and if Meg hadn't ripened in these past months, it was time for more drastic measures.

Meg met her mother at the door to the hall, happy to see Elspeth so early in the morn. Since she came to live at the manor, she only saw her family every few days, and this was a harsh thing for Meg to accept. Her mother at the door made Meg's heart soar.

"Mother!" Meg cried, throwing herself at Elspeth like she was a young child. Elspeth caught her in one arm, trying to balance the bowl with the other.

"Meggie!" her mother reprimanded. "Ye are no longer a child! Ye should no' cry out like that." Meg squinted at her mother, then dismissed the reprimand. She was more curious to learn what was in the bowl, peeking under the cloth. Her mother leaned in close to her.

"'Tis a drink to make ye quicken wi' child," she whispered. "I think ye may need a bit of help. No' that Ewan isna doing his part." Elspeth winked at her blushing daughter.

Meg led her mother to a table, and Elspeth mixed the herbs into a drink for Meg. She listened to her mother's words of child-making wisdom as she drank it down.

"And dinna forget to put your bed facing north, for that will help as well. Can ye remember all this?"

Meg nodded, noticing that her mother looked tired and worried - more than she should about child-making. Her face was drawn beneath her head covering, and blue-gray smudges stained under her eyes, a sure sign that she was sleeping little.

"Mother, is something wrong?" Meg asked quietly. People had begun to fill the hall to break their fast, and Meg watched as Jenny took her time to serve Gavin his morning porridge. Meg smiled inwardly, then turned her attention back to her mother.

Elspeth was introspective for a moment, her eyes cast downward, then spoke.

"'Tis worse wi' your father. Methinks he is in much debt to these English, for they keep harassing him. Yester eve, he threatened me should I speak of it to anyone." Meg was shocked, for her father was not a violent man.

"Yet ye speak of it to me?"

Elspeth nodded her head. "Please, lovey. Dinna say a word to anyone. I dinna like to think of what could happen to your father."

"But Mother," Meg protested, "shouldn't I ask Ewan for help? Perchance he would pay off the English, to speak wi' them—" Meg trailed off as her mother shook her head.

"I swore to your father, lovey. Please. No' a word to anyone. But if Ewan needs to know to keep the clan safe -"

Elspeth hugged her daughter close before leaving. "Your father is a strong man, Meg. A proud man. 'Tis best if this matter is left to him. Nothing good ever came of meddling."

Meg nodded in agreement, still apprehensive. Elayne wiped her eyes and walked toward the door, wishing Meg good luck. Meg blinked back tears as her mother left.

At least Meg was not at home to see the shame that had become her beloved father and family, but her heart pained that she was not there to help, and even worse, that her mother did not want her help. She sighed and went to the kitchen to help with the morning meal.

Davey sat near a pile of apples, eating them one at a time. The sight of Davey, especially with Fiona, managed to brighten Meg's day after the disappointing news about her father. *'Twas a match made in heaven,* Meg thought.

Fiona had been diligent in nursing Davey back to health, and now the young lad was all but Fiona's adopted son. Meg had not seen Fiona this happy since she came to the keep. She had learned Fiona's son had fallen ill and died, and Fiona had not regained her happiness since that time. The sight of Fiona and Davey together, happy and well, made Meg's heart swell.

Meg caught Davey by surprise as he was about to take a large bite out of a shiny red apple nearly the size of his head. She snatched it out of his hand and bit it herself. Davey's eyes widened in shock, then crinkled with laughter as Meg tossed the apple back to him.

"Methinks ye could eat a whole orchard, Davey," she told him. "Are apples all ye eat?"

"Just about!" remarked Fiona, pounding her fist into the dough, making flour fly everywhere. She had a smile on her face lately, and for one orphaned little boy, a bushel of apples to appease his appetite. Davey, in return, always had a smile and a grateful look ready for Fiona.

Meg took some of the bread dough from Fiona and began to knead it herself. The texture of the soft dough between her fingers was calming, and the smell of the yeast made the large house more like a home.

"I like apples," protested Davey. "And I dinna eat too much to make me sick!"

Meg and Fiona laughed in response to the little boy.

"And what are ye doing today after ye eat all these apples?" Meg inquired.

"Hamish said he would teach me t'use a sword!" Davey's eyes widened even more at this prospect.

Now that he was no longer malnourished and sickly, thanks to the attentions of everyone in the house, Ewan and Gavin had granted their permission to learn how to use a weapon, but only if he kept up with his work in the stables. He adored being a stable lad, almost as much as he adored Fiona.

In the evenings, Davey would often find an unsuspecting elder, Meggie, Ewan, Jenny, even poor Gavin, who seemed to have little tolerance for small children, and retell every event that happened in the stables that day. In his excitement, he talked so quickly that they often only heard half of what he said, but the shine in his eyes more than made up for his excited rantings. There were small wagers placed nearly every night over whom Davey's poor audience would be.

So far, Hamish had been the most fortunate; he often took his evening meal with his intended and her family or ate at the keep then immediately left to visit them. Meg would wager that the day Hamish stayed for the evening meal would be the day he got an earful of Davey. Meg was waiting for that wager.

The lad in question took another bite of his apple, drank some milk, and was off and running to find Hamish, his red hair shining in the sunlight. Meg sighed to herself, content that Davey would grow as big and strong as any other little boy in the clan. She grasped a loaf of bread and pulled off a piece to eat.

She walked to the gardens, noting the sun already warm in the late summer day. She sat on a small rock near the lavender, and the heady scent made her suddenly dizzy and sick at the same time. Dropping the rest of her bread, she spun and vomited on the lavender bush next to her.

Still feeling uncomfortable, she rose and went back inside to her chambers. The early morning heat taking its toll on her, Meg was sick one more time before she lay on the bed to rest. *So much for gathering blooms today,* she thought before she sunk back into sleep.

She awoke later that morning to a gentle tapping at the door.

"Meg?" Jenny whispered through the door. "Meg, are ye well?"

Meg pushed herself up in the bed. "Yes, Jenny. Please come in." Jenny pushed the door open slowly, carrying a tray of mead and honey.

"Ye weren't seen all morning," Jenny remarked, "and now I find ye abed in the middle of the day. Is there something ye may be hiding from us all?" A small smile played at Jenny's lips.

"Nay, Jenny. 'Tis only my worries of Ewan and the McNally's, all. Shall ye stay for some mead?"

Jenny declined, shaking her head, smile disappearing. "I must get downstairs. Rest ye well."

Meg moved from the bed to the table where Jenny placed the tray. Ewan's sack from the night before was on the table in a rumpled lump, and as she moved it to the floor, she noticed something lacy inside. Forgetting her drink, she reached in and extracted a frilly handkerchief, embroidered with a bold capital E. Meg's queasiness rose once again.

"So, ye didna see her, eh?"

Throwing the handkerchief, she barely made it in time to be sick in the chamber pot.

Ewan walked in on Meg cradling the chamber pot. Jenny had reported the state of Meg's health to him after leaving the bedchamber. Ewan raced to her side to help her up, wiping her face with his plaid. She rinsed her mouth and spat into the pot, then looked up at him.

"Meggie! What's amiss?"

Worry etched Ewan's face, and as sore as her stomach was, her heart felt better. She knew there had to be another reason for the lacy piece of fabric. The look on Ewan's face reassured her heart what her head already knew.

"'Tis a bit o' queasiness, husband. Naught that is serious."

"Why are ye sick, then?" He helped her to the bed and she sat heavily.

"I dinna ken. Perchance 'tis only the heat. I first felt sick outside."

She did not tell Ewan of her concerns about his travels to the MacNally's. With everything else on his mind, the last thing he needed was to hear the rantings of an overly jealous wife.

Ewan turned to pour some water from the pitcher and saw the handkerchief on the floor.

"Ye dropped your cloth, Meggie," he said as he stooped to pick it up.

"'Tisn't mine, husband," she told him softly.

Ewan cast her a confused look, then held the fabric between his fingers and thumb. Seeing the E, he cursed under his breath, "That bitch!"

He looked imploringly at Meg, who sat passive and pale on the bed. Ewan assumed she would be outraged and wondered why she didn't rail at him.

"She came up to us as we left the stables. She leaned close to pat Fire Foot. I did no' think on it. She must have put it in my bag. I'm sorry, *mo annsachd*. Please believe me that I did naught wi' her."

"Ye do no' have to explain to me, husband--" Meg began.

"Ye can ask Gavin, if ye doubt me, my love. He will vouch for my honor."

Ewan crushed the handkerchief in a fist and knelt before Meg.

"Nay, Ewan, I—"

"Shall I retrieve him for ye?" He sounded almost panicked.

Meg caught Ewan's jaw in her hand and turned his face toward hers to gaze in his eyes.

"Ewan," she smiled at him. "I ken what ye say is true, for I had to bathe ye yestereve, ye stank so of horse. Elayne is quite perfumed, and I would have smelled her on ye and known the truth then, had aught happened."

She leaned forward until her forehead touched his and traced her thumb over his lips.

"I dinna need Gavin to tell me. I ken the man ye are wi' me."

He kissed her, deep and hard, throwing the handkerchief to the floor with no more thought. Wrapping his fingers in her hair, he groaned as her fingers moved under his shift, light and feathery as a bird's wing, then more urgently as she yanked at his tunic to pull it over his head. He paused for a moment, considering.

"Ye were just sick in here, Meggie. Are ye well enough for this?"

Her stomach was still a bit heavy but had improved with Ewan's presence.

"I am feeling much better, milord," she told him.

He raised up his arms to assist her in removing her shift. He took her nipple in his mouth and she gasped. Then he lay her back on the bed, unwound his plaid from his hips, and joined her. He trailed his mouth down her stomach, licking at her warm skin and he tugged off her skirt. With his own sudden sense of urgency, he rose up over her, and as he put his mouth against her, he entered her soft warmth. She lifted her legs around his hips to accept him more readily, and he groaned hoarsely.

"I love ye, Meg," he chanted as he moved inside her. "I love ye."

CHAPTER ELEVEN

A Banshee

It should not have been a shock to Ewan to discover Elayne had arrived only days after they left MacNally's, but it was. Elayne rode into the village around noontide with a small entourage, and the news of her approach spread to the Laird's house more quickly than Elayne did. Ewan's loud groan of disdain did not surprise Gavin and Hamish when they informed him of the arrival of her Ladyship.

Would she stop at nothing?

Elayne entered the village of Lochnora with her head held high, as if she owned the town herself. She wore a shimmering blue cape, even though it was midsummer and quite warm, and her hair was piled high on her head and held in place with a fine gold mesh that sparkled in her rich dark hair.

Even her horse was similarly decorated, with heavy ribbons in its mane. Many MacLeods peeked out their doors to watch Elayne ride by. The women commented to each other that it was obvious Elayne was out to impress someone, and they all knew who. The men remarked on the poor horse beribboned in the heat.

Elayne rode in with two men by her side. Several recognized one of them as MacNally's man, James MacNally, Elayne's cousin, a short weasel-like man whom MacNally himself trusted very little. The other rider nearly everyone recognized, if not the man, then his occupation. The second rider was a priest.

Ewan knew all of this before Elayne presented herself at the gate. Ewan, Gavin, and Hamish went out to meet her and Ewan felt better having both his closest friend and his brother by his side. *Reinforcements,* he thought to himself.

He dreaded this meeting and all but dragged his feet like a petulant little boy. Dust kicked up as he did so, and Gavin gave him an elbow in the ribs, a signal to shape up. Ewan would rather have met an armed cavalry with naught but a dirk than meet this loud, troublemaking woman. *I ken why she brought her cousin, but why the priest?* he wondered.

Elayne rode up to Ewan and his men, looking regal upon her horse. She waited there momentarily, and when nothing happened, she signaled to James, who quickly dismounted. He ran to Elayne's side, put his hands about her waist, and helped her slide down.

Ewan was certain she hoped for a more significant entrance, and her awkward dismount caused Gavin and Hamish to cover their laughter with a quick succession of coughs. Elayne dusted off her gown, which Ewan noticed matched her cape perfectly, and he wondered how much MacNally paid for that.

She cast her gaze up at him, and a brief look of annoyance crossed her features before she managed a smile for Ewan. He knew he was being rude, but he did not greet the woman, and her annoyance returned.

"Is this how ye greet a neighbor-woman, MacLeod?" she screeched, and Ewan, Gavin, and Hamish cringed at her shrill voice. In retrospect, Gavin was now even more relieved that Ewan had not married Elayne. Having to listen to her shrill voice every day would drive any man insane.

"Greetings, Elayne. What brings ye and your kinsmen here?" Ewan responded grudgingly, nodding toward the coterie.

While the appearance of Elayne was enough to raise Ewan's hackles, bringing her worthless cousin and a priest with her was even more puzzling. What did the woman want?

Elayne pulled herself up to her full height and flipped her hair over her shoulder in, what looked to Ewan, a practiced move. She gestured to her cousin.

"Surely, Ewan, ye remember my cousin? James, ye recall Ewan, do ye no'?" James nodded in Ewan's general direction but remained where he was. Obviously, Ewan was not the only one lacking manners. When Elayne began to introduce the priest, Ewan leaned over to Hamish and whispered in his ear. Hamish ran off toward the keep.

"This man, Ewan, is the reason that I am here. He is Father MacNally, my father's second cousin." The priest also nodded at Ewan but remained rooted to his spot, making the sign of the cross. This move made Ewan suddenly more wary than annoyed. Why did they not approach him?

"State your business, Elayne." Ewan's words were short and clipped.

He was wary, annoyed, and angry. After all the problems Elayne had instigated, first the day after his wedding, then with the kerchief trick, the last person Ewan wanted near himself or his wife was this she-bitch. What trouble would she cause now?

Elayne took a step forward, her smile increasing, and both Ewan and Gavin noticed that smile did not reach her eyes. She held her hand out to Ewan, as though he should take it as an escort.

"Why, Ewan. 'Tis no manner to be speaking to a lady." Ewan bit back a sharp insult and allowed her to continue. "Should we no' retire inside? Methinks this conversation should be more *private* in nature."

Her dark grey eyes glittered, and Ewan felt the best way to get rid of the beastly woman was to let her have her say, then have her escorted out, in the most expedient manner possible. The easiest way to do that was to have the woman come inside; she would not open her mouth out here by the gate.

Ewan nodded once, turned his back on her to climb the steps and went inside, leaving Elayne with her gaping jaw to find her own way into the house. Ewan's manners left much to be desired, but he was not happy about Elayne's visit and wanted her to know it.

James and the priest followed Elayne as she scuttled after Ewan. Once inside, she settled herself on a bench near the hearth and motioned Ewan to sit next to her. He remained where he was, shaking his head in disbelief at Elayne's gall to be so informal with him.

Ewan took a quick peek around the hall, then gave a silent thanks to God that Meg was not present. Hopefully, she was in the gardens, away from the gossips of the house help, or better yet, at her mother's, far from the nearest waggling tongue. Ewan did not presume himself to be that fortunate, but God knew the last thing he needed was for his wife to see him in conversation with MacNally's daughter. It would do naught but add flame to the fire.

When Ewan did not sit on the bench, Elayne sighed as if aggrieved, then waved her hand toward the priest. This time he did step forward, closer to Elayne, and she began to speak.

"It seems I am no' the only one who thinks ye have a witch amongst your people, Laird MacLeod. Since ye dinna believe me, and I dinna trust your own priest, I have brought my own priest to test your wife. If she proves no' to be a witch, then may ye both live long and well. If the truth comes out that she is a witch, she will be dealt wi' accordingly by Father MacNally, and your marriage shall be annulled."

Gavin and Ewan were stunned into momentary silence by Elayne's words. So were most of the kitchen help eavesdropping from the doorway, and Jenny, who was on the stairs. She leaned in closer to better hear what Ewan and this woman said to each other but wanted to remain as hidden as possible. Jenny had come to truly love Meg, like a sister she never had, and she would do almost anything to keep Meg safe. If Elayne came bringing strife, Jenny would do all she could to see it set to rights.

"Your own priest?" Ewan barked a short laugh. "Why is my priest biased, yet yours not? What of your priest's own bias to ye?"

"That is the reason for my cousin. He is here in my father's stead to see that all is done fairly, and that no harm comes to me from your witch."

At that, Ewan lurched and had to stop himself from throttling her. If Elayne had been a man, Ewan would have killed her for those words. While he was not a Laird of a great and powerful clan, he was still Laird, a position that demanded respect, and Meg was his wife, thus she commanded as much, if not more, respect than he.

Before Ewan could respond, Hamish rushed in with Father MacBain. The priest's visage was dark with anger, both for having to defend Meg again, and for having his very integrity as a man of God put into question.

The moment Hamish told him who was at the gate, Father MacBain knew what trouble Elayne was bringing. To make a point, he grabbed his more elegant stole for High Mass and the gold embossed Bible as he and Hamish left the rectory. Father MacBain had never been in the position to accuse anyone of witchery, let alone *defend* someone against it, so the priest wanted to make a marked impression on those in the hall.

When he entered, Father MacBain went straight to Ewan, holding out his ring. The Laird immediately dropped on one knee and kissed it. As he did this, Father MacBain bent low, as though saying a prayer over Ewan, but instead whispered in his ear, "Does Meggie yet know?"

Ewan shook his head as he rose, and the priest turned his full furor on Elayne and her cousin. "What brings ye here to hurl such accusations at this good man and his wife?"

The MacNally priest stepped forward to answer. "The good lady, Elayne, daughter of the great Laird MacNally and of good word and reputation, has discussed wi' me what she has seen and heard. She tells me of a woman here who dances with demons in the moonlight, who places nearly everyone she meets under a witchy spell to make them bow to her will. Elayne tells me that this is how this witch, a lowly crofter's maid, managed to ensnare the Laird of her clan and marry him. She tells me that the witch is the daughter of the nearby midwife, who is rumored to be a witch as well. As the higher-ranking priest, I shall conduct a series of tests to determine if she is a bride of Satan. If she is, I will oversee her burning at the stake."

Those final words left Father MacBain in stunned silence. *Higher-ranking priest? Burning at the stake? Meggie? He canna be serious?*

Ewan, however, had no problem reacting to the priest's statement. He lunged at the priest, aiming to crush his poisoned head with a harsh blow, but Gavin managed to grab his friend before he could assault Father MacNally. Gavin had to use his entire weight to throw the giant man back, so Ewan managed to only grasp the front of the priest's robe.

Ewan shrugged his shoulder to release Gavin's iron grip on him, pulling the priest close to his face. When he spoke, his voice was rough, and Gavin saw that Ewan was using every last bit of restraint to not kill Father MacNally.

"Let me grant ye some information of the 'good lady' Elayne, as ye called her. Do ye ken why she falsely accused my wife of such actions? She is no' good lady; she is a jealous one. At our clan gathering, she walked into *my home* and commanded *my people* as if she were already lady here at Lochnora. When she heard of my wedding, she demanded I have it annulled. So much for her 'good words.' As for her reputation, she tried to make it look as though I had lain wi' her on my last visit wi' her father by putting her kerchief in my saddlebag. She tried to make it look as though I committed adultery—if anyone is a sinner or witch, it is she, as she covets and bears false witness."

At that, Ewan all but threw the priest across the room, then turned on Elayne, who was cowering near her cousin.

"How much did she pay ye, James?"

"Why, I—" he stuttered, but Ewan cut him off.

"MacNally doesna trust ye more than he trusts a fly."

Ewan flicked his eyes to Elayne and back to James. "Get ye, all of ye, out of my lands. I will see all three of ye dead, woman and priest included, before I let harm come to my wife."

Ewan stepped back to gesture towards the door when there was a noise on the stairs. Ewan felt his stomach sink. *Oh no, Meggie. Dinna come down yet.*

But she was there, with Jenny right behind her. She wore a white *airisaidh* that some of the clanswomen had given her as a belated wedding gift. Her hair was loose with no adornments, not even her beloved ribbons, and she was pale from her sickness. As such, she resembled an angel straight from Heaven, and when Elayne saw her, she raced toward Meg. Ewan made to go after her, then paused as he watched Jenny moved to stand in front of Meg.

Elayne stopped short of the two women.

"I ken what ye truly are, ye *crofter's maid,* witch!"

Then, to everyone's surprise, Meg stepped next to Jenny, right in front of Elayne, and looked up at the tall, angry woman. She put a bored look on her face, and Ewan had to bite back a smile when he saw it.

"Ye forget yourself, Elayne. I'm Mistress MacLeod. Now, if ye would kindly take yourself and your company to the door, I think ye are no longer welcome here. We dinna want your unpleasantness to put a pall upon our day."

Then Meg stood in that position, full of dignity, and waited for Elayne to take her leave. Elayne spun around in a huff and stormed off out the door. James and the priest, knowing they had been duped, looked abashedly at one another, and followed Elayne out the door. At the last moment, Father MacNally turned back toward Meg and bowed slightly.

"My apologies," he told her, and walked out to the overcast daylight.

Everyone was silent for a moment, letting out a collective sigh of relief, when Ewan tipped his head toward Gavin.

"Have a rider send a message to MacNally. He must be fast; I want it there before Elayne returns wi' her cousin. He must tell MacNally what his daughter did today, and let him know that if she ever returns, he will have one day to collect her before she is hanged."

"Aye, Ewan," Gavin responded, grabbing Hamish as he ran for the yard.

Chapter Twelve

And Two Become Three

WHEN MEG'S ILLNESS DID not abate two days later, Ewan sent for her mother. It was nigh on summer and Elspeth arrived at the house, sweaty, out of breath, and full of fear at the health of her eldest daughter. Not sure what to expect, she had Ewan rush her to Meg's chamber. She saw little Davey hovering near the door, wanting to be near Meg but at the same time, not wanting to disturb her. Elspeth gave Davey a little pat on the head as she reached the door and gestured to Ewan.

"Son," she said in a low voice so Davey could not hear, "take little Davey out to the yard and keep him busy, wrestle with him, anything to take his mind off Meggie." She looked at Ewan's strained face and continued, "Might do ye some good as well t' get out into the fresh sunshine."

Elspeth winked at Ewan, then walked into the room and, giving the boys a shove down the hall, closed the door to the chamber.

Meg perched on a stool near a small table, drinking some of her mother's tincture. A slice of buttered bread sat before her, yet to be eaten. Elspeth stood very still, taking in her daughter's appearance. Meg's face was strained, and the room smelled vaguely of vomit. Were her breasts larger as well? With all seriousness, Elspeth asked Meg, "My daughter, have ye yet had your monthly?"

Meg's brow furrowed deeply. "What would that have to do wi' my being sick--" Meg then paused and slight shock registered on her face. Elspeth's face broke into a huge smile and she started cheering.

"Huzzah, Meggie! Ye are wi' child!"

Elspeth danced over to Meg, helped her out of the chair, then hugged Meg and cheered and chanted all at once. The tincture Meg had drunk sloshed around in her wane and she felt slightly ill. She pulled back from her mother, and grasping her by the upper arms, looked Elspeth straight in the eye.

"For sure? Ye ken for certain?" Meg's lower lip quivered, and she wasn't sure if she would laugh or cry at the news.

"Aye! As certain as I can be at this point! So, daughter, what do ye think?"

Meg let go of her mother and sat heavily on the stool.

"In truth, 'tis no' so wonderful if vomiting is all I do. I ken it's no' true, but on the now I feel that it canna get much worse than this."

Elspeth laughed at her daughter's candor and patted her head.

"Ach! 'Tis no' only bad on the now, but gets worse!"

And again, Elspeth cackled with glee. She was going to be a grandmother --a wise-mother-- possibly to the future Laird no less! She was in grandmotherly heaven and was not about to let Meg's complaining of a bit o' sickness get the best of her. Elspeth felt as though her lips, no matter how much she willed it, would never stop smiling. She then had Meg lie on the bed and checked her to see if anything was amiss. Elspeth was pleased to discover the pregnancy seemed absolutely normal.

"Is there anything I canna do? Anything I should stop doing?"

Meg's face was a bit pinched with nervousness, and she settled back into her tea. Her stomach felt calmer, but she was unprepared for the news of her condition and reeling from it.

"Nay. Ye are a strong lass. Ye take after your mother, ye ken?" Elspeth winked at Meg, and Meg managed a small laugh. "Ye shall be fine, I will tell ye what must needs be done as your time draws nigh."

Elspeth paused with expectancy.

"When will ye tell Ewan? He best know by the by, ye ken."

Meg looked up warily from her cup. Elspeth could still see the shock on her face, complete with an undertone of burgeoning happiness over the impending little stranger. She rose and took her mother's hand.

"Well, Mother, if Ewan has no' taken Davey too far off, I dinna see no reason why we can't be telling him now."

Ewan was in the yard outside the hall and led her mother out of the room in that direction. As she walked, her excitement began to build, knowing that once she told Ewan, it would be real between them, this child, the family they had created. Her feelings were probably not unusual to a newly pregnant woman, especially with the first child. However, she still felt special, honored, to be with child, almost as though no woman had ever been pregnant before now.

Ewan crouched on the grassy part of the yard, a bit away from the path, teaching wee Davey to fight. Meg lips downturned. *Wasn't Davey lad too young to learn how to fight?* She had felt her mothering instinct set in with Davey, but now it seemed to come on even stronger.

Several clansmen, mostly younger men, formed a ragged circle around the Laird and the boy, shouting out tips and advice when deemed necessary. Even Gavin watched the festivities from outside the loose circle of men. While he didn't have a smile on his face, at least he wasn't frowning. When Meg stepped up with her mother, it seemed that, overall, Davey was not fairing too well.

"Dinna run, wee lad!" she heard Ewan shout. "Ye must face me to fight me!"

Meg watched as Davey tried to swing at Ewan, his little face strained and earnest, and Ewan jumped out of the way in a swish of tartan while giving Davey a push back.

"Now, ye try again," Ewan commanded.

Meg decided it was time to step in. Leaving Elspeth at the edge of the circle, Meg approached Ewan lightly, with a sly smile on her face. Ewan, turning only his head to her, beamed at her presence.

"My husband, I have news for ye."

"Aye? What news is that, Meggie?"

Meg leaned in close to him as his body was still mostly facing away, preparing for little Davey. His look of interest died abruptly as Davey, only following the orders of his Laird, continued his efforts with a swift kick that landed between Ewan's legs.

Ewan squeaked in a shocked, pained response, cupped himself between the legs, and fell to his knees with a groan, his clansmen grabbing themselves and cringing loudly in sympathetic response. Unable to support his weight, Ewan then slumped to his side, and lay on the ground, curled up around his wounded manhood. Davey came up to him with a look of accomplishment on his face.

"I got ye, I did! Aye, milord?" Davey asserted proudly.

"Aye, lad," Ewan squeaked. "Ye did. Run along now."

Davey, chest puffing out and ready to gloat, ran off in the direction of the kitchen, hoping to receive more apples as a reward.

Meg stepped over to Ewan's head, and sat on the ground, running her fingers through his hair to try and soothe him. The misting rain of the gray morning had gathered in his hair, giving it a slippery texture, and Meg wondered if the child would have Ewan's rich, dark hair. Ewan let out another squeaky groan.

"Christ, the child has the legs of a bull on him," Ewan managed to croak. "I can only hope the damage is no' permanent, or I may never give ye bairns." Meg put her face close to his to whisper into his ear.

"'Tis no' worry if it is damaged, my love. It has already done its job."

Ewan tried to turn his head to look at her.

"What do ye—" he stopped and a shocked surprise registered on his face. His eyes were as wide as the moon. "For certain? Ye are with child for certain?"

Meg nodded. "Mother says that ye shall be a father before spring."

Ewan maneuvered himself as best he could with his aching ballocks and gathered his little wife in his arms. He then kissed her hard, and the audience of clansmen responded with raucous approval. But when Ewan stood (albeit shakily, Christ, the child had good aim) and announced that the new Laird would be born next year, the approval turned into outright cheering.

And Elspeth, still beaming with happiness only a soon-to-be grandmother can feel, helped Meg escort the aching Ewan to his chambers to rest his wounded pride.

Beginning the very next day, Meg noticed Ewan treating her as though she were made of glass. He actually tried to forbid her to leave the bed but to use the chamber pot. Meg, after using that very bowl to be sick, felt well enough to laugh in Ewan's face. His injured look of shock then caused her to bite the laughter back a bit.

"Ewan, love. I dinna have to stay abed all day," Meg told him gently.

"But what of the child?"

"I asked my mother, of course, about the very same thing. She told me 'tis better for a woman ripening to be busy. She says it can be a lot o' work when my time comes, and the more work I do now, the better prepared I shall be."

"Aye, Meggie, your mother would know best, but for me, would ye rest now and again when ye feel tired?"

His face was so full of worry, and she was blessed that he should care so much. She patted his knee with a gentle hand.

"Aye, my husband. I will."

Ewan kissed her, then left the room quickly in a swirl of plaid. He and the other men of the clan had been busy rebuilding crofts and barns and trying to patrol the land at the same time, and Ewan was beginning to show signs of weariness and concern. He now had the responsibility of a new babe and the health of his wife to add to that weight.

Meg wanted nothing more than for Ewan to not put his efforts into worry over her and the babe, and she was determined to make sure that happened. She had a smile on her face and a kind word for him every time he saw her. And it was not just for show. Not even her mother's concern about her father's possible gambling debts could bring her down from her cloud of happiness. She was the Laird's wife, and now she would bear him a child. The life she was living exceeded anything she could have dreamt.

However, after the evening meal, when most everyone had left or retired for the evening, her mother's words returned. She and Ewan sat in front of a low summer fire, using its light for quiet work. Ewan had a small table near him. He was comparing figures and making notes on parchment. Meg listened as the quill made its *scritch scritch* sounds. The only other noise was the fire crackling and popping at the hearth and the cat purring at her feet.

Meg was busy sewing swaddling clothes for her babe. This was a fairly simple job for Meg, something that came almost second nature as she had helped her mother sew similar clothes for all her brothers and sisters. As a result, Meg found her mind wandering, and she could not get her mother's concerns from her thoughts. Meg frowned, biting her inner lip in consternation. She wanted to tell Ewan about her father's gambling debts, but she feared what his reaction would be. With the worries the clan had with the English, and Ewan spending his days either patrolling or repairing burned crofts, she was not sure how he would take the news of her father's entanglements with the English. What if his temper got the best of him?

Also, Meg hated the idea of her family being indebted to the Laird, her own husband, if Ewan did repay the debts himself. After deep consideration, Meg decided that, for the moment, discretion was the better part of valor. She would not say anything.

"Meg, are ye well?" Ewan's voice interrupted her thoughts, and she near jumped out of her seat.

"Oh, aye," she replied quickly and looked down at her sewing. "I am only concentrating on these swaddling clothes. The stitches have to be so little, ye ken."

Guilt at her white lie spread through her, but she could not bring herself to tell her husband the truth. At least not yet.

Ewan smiled at his wife. "Well, do not let it tire ye too much. I trust I would rather have the child bareback in the sun than his mother fall sick over sewing his clothes."

Ewan rose and banked the fire and held his hand out to Meg. The kitten that had curled up at her feet for warmth and attention rose, too, and arched her back in a leisurely stretch. It trotted off to the kitchen in search of leftover milk.

Fiona, originally upset at having a cat take over her kitchen, had come to love the "little beastie," as she called him, for this small kitten had made quick work of all the mice that tried to come near the food stuffs. Pleased that the cat worked for its room and board, Fiona often left a bit of milk for it after the evening meal was done. Meg watched until the kitten was out of view, then turned to Ewan.

"Come wife. Let us retire to bed. I can find better things to occupy your fingers," he said with that same wicked grin, and Meg could not help but smile.

"Aye, milord," she replied, taking his hand and following him up the stairs.

⟫⟫⟫⟩ ⟨⟪⟪⟪

Gavin sat in front of that same hearth the next morning, talking in a quiet voice to Hamish. Jenny hid in the shadows of the kitchen until Hamish left. She felt almost embarrassed; she was not the type to hide from anything. All too often, people told her she was rather outspoken.

Her interactions with Gavin MacLeod, or rather, his rebuffs of her interactions, made her feel self-conscious -- something she had never really encountered before. Her affections for Gavin belied her normal esteem, and she found herself relying on Meg to intervene more and more. Jenny wanted to kick herself, because that was not like her, and thus she found herself hiding in shadows, admiring from afar.

Once Hamish was out of earshot, she meandered toward Gavin, hoping he would notice her before she had to speak and afraid that he would look up and see her approach. He continued to stare into the fire, so she spoke.

"Gavin," Jenny called softly. "Have ye a moment?"

Gavin shifted slightly to glance at her, then returned his gaze to the fire. His hair and beard caught highlights of the fire, making his light brown hair blaze with red highlights. Jenny took a deep breath and strengthened her resolve.

"Gavin, I have tried for a time to show ye what I cannot seem to say, yet ye dinna seem to hear it. So I must say it to ye plain. I find ye a strong, handsome man who does not have a wife. Ye dinna seem to have an interest, and I thought to let ye know I would be willing, if ye would consider me."

Her voice trailed off and she hated herself for it, begging for affection. Gavin did not seem to acknowledge her words. Feeling rebuked, she moved to leave.

"I ken how ye feel, Jenny."

His voice was light, softer than she had ever thought possible. She couldn't bear to look at him, hoping he would say the words she longed to hear, but knowing in her heart she would be disappointed.

"I have known from the first time ye tried to make it clear. Ye have me in a bind, and I dinna ken what to do."

Gavin rose and faced her. She averted her gaze, glancing at him from the corner of her eye. Her embarrassment and emotional fear, combined with the heat of the fire, formed perspiration that left a trail of sweat trickling down her back.

"I dinna have a wife and have not been searching for one. I tried to pretend that ye were just nice, that ye did no' have any affection for me, but I can no' hide from the truth."

He grasped her hand and turned her face to his. She held her breath in hopeful anticipation, completely unprepared for what came next.

"Look around ye, Jenny!" Gavin exclaimed at her. "Look at these men who are worrit for their loved ones! These men have wives and children they love more than their own lives, and they live in constant fear of these attackers who have plagued us these past months! Yea, this in our land, MacLeod land, and they fight and search every day to protect this land, but it is more than the soil and the trees! It is the people who live on the land! These men search and fight every day to protect the women and children they hold so dear. And I canna do that - I canna be as brave as these men are, as brave as Ewan is. I canna live every moment with a fear that all I love and care for, my own wife, could fall to the same torture and death as Ewan's mother! The old Laird was never the same after her death, and he is the bravest man I could ever imagine."

Gavin paused in his speech, and Jenny took the moment to peer around the hall at the men who remained, most of whom had families.

"I fear that if I ever failed ye, I could no' live with myself," he added in a quieter voice.

Gavin squeezed her hand and gazed into Jenny's hopeful face.

"I do care for ye, Jenny. More than I care to admit. But until these scourges are done with, I canna do right by ye."

Gavin pulled his eyes from the hurt look on her face and made to leave, but Jenny held tight to his fist.

"Ye speak in fear, Gavin. And I pity ye for that. Ye have the chance to do something great, to have something wonderful, and ye will throw it all away out of fear? Ewan lived with what his father went through, yet still took the risk to hold what he loves most. I canna believe a man would rather live without something great, than feel blessed for the greatness he is permitted to hold, no matter how brief."

Jenny released his hand and took a step back.

"I hadna thought ye such a coward, Gavin."

Now it was Jenny who turned and walked away, leaving Gavin in the hall. He was at a loss for words, having never been called a coward before. He watched Jenny's back, shocked that one little woman would have the gall to call him a coward. Try as he might, he was unable to stop a small smile from lifting the side of his mouth.

Gavin departed for his croft before anyone could see him grinning like an idiot.

CHAPTER THIRTEEN

The Sins of the Father

THE NEXT DAY WAS market day, and everyone in the keep bustled about. Ewan collected the necessary parchments to bring to the village to make accountings, while Meg gathered herbs and flowers she had collected from the garden and dried in her rooms. She knew her mother would come to the village as well, and her mother did not grow some of the treasures Meg had discovered in the Lochnora garden.

Fiona had spent the entire day before baking enough bread to feed an army and enlisted Davey to help her wrap it in linen and bring to town. Jenny helped Meg gather the rest of her things and joined them as the women walked the short distance to the village center. Ewan, Gavin, Hamish, and Duncan had all ridden ahead to set up tables in the market square for tenant payment and other accountables.

The market fairly buzzed with activity when Meg arrived. First, she visited Ewan, leaving him with one of Fiona's loaves since he would not have the opportunity to eat otherwise. Her mother was not far from Ewan, sitting next to the village healer, Cuspin, offering advice to the variety of women who came to her for help. While Elspeth despised Cuspin, who thought all women's maladies were superficial and a result of "women's nerves," she nevertheless worked right next to him on market day.

Sometimes, menfolk did not want their women to see Elspeth, commenting that she was nothing more than a witch. But Elspeth noticed that if Cuspin were present, the men felt more comfortable letting their wives visit her. Plus, if she were near Cuspin, she could address any women before they reached the healer and provide them with some herbs or advice they could actually use.

And, of course, women talked more readily to a woman than they did a man. These women would sooner bite their tongues off than admit to a man, especially one like Cuspin, that their monthly time bled heavy, or of the pain in their lower belly, or that intimate relations with their husbands were painful. Cuspin would most likely recommend ale and to lie back and think of Scotland.

Elspeth shook her head in wonder at how some men could be so ignorant, especially one who called himself a healer.

This thought about men brought her back to her own husband, and how Elspeth never before encountered difficulty talking with him, including issues that were a bit embarrassing. She recalled before Innes was born of their sadness in having lost two babies in a row before Elspeth even reached her sixth month of pregnancy.

Instead of brushing off her concerns as "womanly nerves," Connor had held her close and murmured that, in God's plan, those babies were yet meant to be with God. Then came Innes, pink and perfect. Connor had smiled at his son and told Elspeth that God's plan was good to make them wait for so perfect a child and thusly appreciate him all the more.

Elspeth blinked back the tears that came with thoughts of how Connor used to be. She wiped them away with the edge of her skirt as she saw Meg walk toward her, Fiona, Davey, and Jenny in tow.

Meg gave her mother the herbals Elspeth desired, and they discussed their uses. Elspeth had once hoped that Meg would follow in her footsteps as town midwife, but the wife of the Laird could never be such. Thus, Elspeth contented herself with teaching Meg all she knew about herbs in hopes that she could heal members of the clan if the need ever arose.

Fiona and Jenny, with Davey right behind them, moved farther down the marketplace to look over some kippers brought in by a clansman and his cousin who fished with the clan Lee. Ewan had provided Jenny with some coin to purchase fish and salt, and she consulted Fiona on how much to buy.

As they were in deep discussion, neither of them noticed the filthy, smelly man who walked up behind them. Without looking at anyone else, he grabbed Davey, who had moved to

one side to see the fish himself, by the ear and dragged him out of the market square. When Davey let out a loud yelp, several people turned in response, searching out their own children. Fiona and Jenny turned together and watched in shock as a strange, bedraggled man pulled their wee Davey off.

Meg also turned at the strange sound. To her surprise, right in front of her, the most degenerate man, with a stench that brought tears to her eyes, was dragging Davey past her. Davey wrapped his hands around the man's wrist, trying to relieve some of the pressure on his ear and wriggled desperately to free himself. Oddly, since the initial yelp, he had not made a sound.

Without thinking, Meg stepped forward and put her hand on the grimy man's arm. He halted and glared at her.

"What do ye think ye be doin'?" he croaked out in his raspy voice, and Meg almost swooned at his breath.

It smelled as though the man had been living in a vat of ale, and cheap ale at that. With a sudden sinking sensation in her belly, Meg realized who this stinky man was. Ewan's words came back to her ears.

"If your father comes for ye," Ewan had told Davey, and that probably accounted for the look of absolute fear on Davey's face. That and the pain this man inflicted after not seeing his own son for many weeks. While most parents would have greeted a lost son with a hug and tears, this man greeted Davey with a twisted ear and stinking breath. Meg was horrified by the man, and regardless of his relationship with Davey, she could not let this stranger steal little Davey away. Fiona's mental stability alone necessitated it.

"I would ask ye the same," Meg spat back at him. "Take your hand off the lad. He is no longer your concern."

"No longer?" the drunk's bloodshot eyes opened wide, and before Meg registered movement, the man's filthy fist struck her face.

She felt the pain shatter in her eye and fell back to the crowd that had collected around them. Jenny and Elspeth were there to catch her, and the moment Meg released the man's arm, she heard a bellowing sound that chilled her to the bone.

Ewan was approaching Meg and the man to see the cause of the ruckus when the drunk hit his wife. *Hit his wife. Hit his beautiful, pregnant wife.* Rage boiled up inside him like he had never before felt, and he launched himself at the drunk who still held tight to poor Davey's ear. The unsuspecting man turned at the sound and Ewan struck him in the head with such force that he released Davey and crumpled to the ground. Davey, shocked and afraid, ran toward the safety of Fiona's skirts, where she hid him and comforted him with little pats and cooing words.

Ewan had his hand on the man's throat, wanting to choke the life from him while also wanting to torture him for his actions at the same time. Panting hard in anger and effort, Ewan loosened his hand a bit to allow the man to breathe while he thought out the situation in his head. How best to turn this into a good situation? Ewan knew his wife, and Jenny and Fiona for that matter, would be sorely upset if Ewan let Davey go back with this cruel drunkard, but Davey was not Ewan's son, or truly Fiona's son, or even a son of this clan.

He peeked at his wife, who was holding a damp cloth over her eye but looked otherwise well. Ewan, of all things, winked at his wife. *Winked at her!* Meg's brow furrowed in confusion as a slow smile pressed at Ewan's cheeks. He looked back at the drunk he held down.

"Do ye ken who ye struck?" Ewan asked in a low voice.

"I dinna care! 'Tis my son--" the drunkard tried to say, but Ewan closed his hand tighter around the man's throat. He leaned close and asked again, louder this time:

"Do ye ken who ye struck?"

This time, the drunk's lip quivered as he tried to speak. "Nay," he choked out, breathing his foul breath on Ewan. The Laird wrinkled his nose in displeasure and sank back on his heels. He then gestured to Meg with his free hand.

"That lady," Ewan stressed, "is the wife of the Laird of the clan." He paused to let his words sink in, and the man's pink face paled.

"Do ye ken who I am?" Ewan then questioned the drunk. The man nodded slowly.

"The Laird," he whispered. Ewan's smile was large and frightening at the same time.

"Aye. The Laird," he repeated. "And what do ye think I shall do to ye?"

This time the drunk swallowed hard. Ewan could feel it under his hand.

"Ye willna kill me?" the drunk whispered again. Surprisingly, Ewan shook his head.

"Nay. Ye are a stupid, stupid man, and I can no' bring myself to kill a man too ignorant to know better. But ye shall have to apologize and offer me recompense."

With that, Ewan hauled the man to his feet and dragged him to the group of women near Meg. Davey, still trying to hide in Fiona's skirts, shrunk down even farther away from the disgusting creature he called father. Ewan thrust the man in front of Meg and demanded an apology. The drunk suddenly found great interest in his feet.

"I am verra sorry, milady," the drunk said with a touch of humility and irritation.

"Think on it no more," Meg responded.

Elspeth pulled Meg away from the stinky man and settled her on a stool to look at the wound once more. There would be bruising for certain, but the eye looked good and intact, so she repacked the willowbark to the cloth and reapplied it to the eye. Hopefully the willowbark would take away some of the sting, and the cool water would keep the swelling down.

Elspeth spied Ewan watching her, and she gave him a small smile and nodded, letting him know Meg was fine. Ewan turned back to the man he still held in place.

"Well, now, that was no' too bad, was it?" The drunk shook his head. "Now there is the matter of recompense. Assaulting the wife of the Laird is a grave offense, ye ken? Others would be put to death for such an offense."

The drunk nodded in agreement this time, willing to give almost anything to be able to leave the village of Lochnora and never lay eyes on it again. The ale was watered down anyway, in his opinion.

"Thus, we must consider an appropriate recompense. What do ye have that would come close to the value of the Laird's wife?"

Ewan looked at the drunk expectantly, as if he truly expected the man to have a significant amount of coin on his person. The drunk's eyes narrowed, for he knew the Laird noticed his poor condition. Coin was out of the question and Ewan was playing him as a cat toyed with a mouse.

"I dinna ken," the drunk replied. "I have naught."

Ewan shook his head at this, clucking his tongue. "Now, that isna entirely true, is it?" Ewan gave the man a sly grin. "Ye do have something, ye ken."

This time the drunk glared at Ewan, anger building at what the man was forcing him to do, and in the presence of an entire clan!

"Aye, ye have a fine, hale son, whom I ken would serve nicely as payment, seeing as how my wife and my house have already taken him into our fold."

Ewan put his finger on his cheek as if he were thinking of the idea and its merit. The effect was almost comical, and many people in the crowd chuckled under their breath. Both Fiona and Jenny had to cover their mouths with their hands, and Meg could not stop the smile pulling at her face.

"My son?" the drunk asked.

"Yea, I think that your son will fare well in the house of MacLeod. That exchange will work well. What say ye, man?"

Ewan stuck out his hand and the drunk looked at it stupidly. He could not believe it as he put out his own hand. Ewan grasped the man's forearm and it was sealed. The drunk was almost stricken; he had just sold off his son to save his own hide. He was angry and embarrassed, and his eyes drove daggers into these people he now considered enemies.

Ewan maintained the lighthearted persona, as though they agreed on the price of a cow, as they walked to the edge of the village near the road. Once there, Ewan took the drunk's hand again, but instead of shaking it this time, Ewan pulled the drunk close, his eyes dark with anger, his hand squeezing to the point of crushing the bones in the drunk's arm.

"If ye ever return to this land, I will kill ye with my own hands," Ewan growled at the drunk man, then shoved him with such force that the drunk stumbled into the dusty road.

"Get ye gone from my land," Ewan called over his shoulder as he walked back to the crowd and his wife.

⇶⇶⇶ ⇇⇇⇇

The bulk of the crowd dispersed after that, allowing Ewan to see for his own eyes how hurt Meg truly was. Having been on the receiving end during several scuffles as a younger man, Ewan could easily evaluate a blow to the face. As it turned out, Elspeth had been right in her own estimation; the blow to Meg's face, applied by a slovenly drunk, had been a glancing one at best. While there was some purple bruising, the swelling had already diminished. Her eye, still bloodshot, looked up at Ewan.

"Thank ye," was all she said as she grasped his hand and put it to her face.

Ewan tried to shrug in an offhanded manner, but the slight blush that stained his own cheeks said he was not overly comfortable being caught in a good deed.

"Will ye be well?" he asked. Meg nodded, and Ewan gestured to Fiona and Jenny. As they approached, Jenny stepped ahead and addressed Ewan.

"Yes, Laird MacLeod?" she asked. Ewan turned back to Meg.

"Methinks we have had enough excitement for one market day. Will ye have these fine ladies escort ye home, Meggie? I shall join ye afore the sun sets."

Again, Meg only nodded. Jenny took her hand and helped her off the stool. Elspeth reapplied the willowbark to the linen and handed it to Meg with the order to continue to reapply throughout the day.

"I heard what happened wi' Elayne MacNally," Elspeth said before Meg departed. "Wi' all that has occurred these past few days, methinks ye should rest a wee bit. 'Tis no' good for the babe's mother to be overly excited, ye ken?"

Meg squeezed her mother's hand in response. She was grateful her mother spoke to her thus; Meg had been unaware that too much excitement could be harmful to an unborn babe. She turned to Ewan, who gave her a small kiss on the lips but hugged her hugely. Then Jenny took her arm and, with Fiona and a very confused but happy Davey, they started back to the keep.

Davey was more talkative on the way home, and he kept asking Fiona if his father would ever come back. When Fiona would respond nay, Davey would skip and dance ahead, content to be staying with his new mother and her gentle ways.

Conversely, Meg was unusually quiet. When prodded by Jenny, Meg stopped walking and looked at the two women.

"I think I am a wee bit shocked," the most she had spoken since the incident. "I've been smacked afore, by my mother and father, and had my hair pulled and such, but I have never been struck in the face."

Her wide eyes and tone of voice, soft and surprised, conveyed her shock. It was when Fiona chuckled that brought Meg back to reality.

"Ooch, dearie," she said. "My brothers and sisters and I, we used'ta fight something fierce, with punches and scratches and the like. Then, my parents would lash us for fighting, so we'd get it all again!" She laughed out loud at the memory. "O'course, we were only mad for the day. When we woke then next morn, 'twould be naught but a memory, and we would start fightin' again."

Then Davey spoke up. "Aye, and when ye wake up in the morn, ye won't even think on it!" he exclaimed, his voice full of smiles. However, the sadness of his statement made Fiona pull up short. She picked Davey up and settled him on her hip as if he had always belonged there.

"Now, my sweetie, dinna think any more like that. Ye come wi' Fiona and we will spoil ye rotten wi' honeyed apples. Would ye like some?" Davey nodded, and Fiona blinked back tears as she walked ahead, the small boy clinging to her shoulder.

Later that evening, after Broch Lochnora had settled for the night, a disheveled, smelly drunk fell into a pub at Glendare, a small village south of Lochnora nearer to the coast. He was a short man with dark, matted hair. His clothes were so filthy, most men would have thrown them out long ago, but this man still wore them despite the stench which rivaled the popular herring meals served in the pub.

The drunk stumbled up to the counter where the serving man was engaged in a heated conversation with another patron. The drunk rapped on the counter for attention, but the serving man behind the counter did not even glance his way. Tired and already angered at the course of his day, the drunk rapped again, louder this time, and voiced his wants.

"Barkeep! Ale, if ye may."

Again, the man behind the counter did not look to him, so the drunk leaned over to the serving man and grabbed his tunic.

"Barkeep!" the drunk yelled this time. "Ale, if ye may!"

The serving man pulled away from the drunk and looked him sharply in his reddened, bloodshot eyes.

"Sir," the serving man tried to keep his voice level and not wrinkle his nose at the drunk's odor. "Ye are a stranger to this place and seem to need more care than ale can give ye. I would ask that ye leave this establishment. We dinna want any trouble."

"What is it wi' ye people? I've come from north o' here, and the treatment there was no better! Then I come here, wi' my coin, and ye willna serve me ale? What manner of people are ye?" The drunk was near screaming now, and the serving man came about the counter to forcibly remove the man from the pub. Then a large blond appeared and intervened.

"I apologize for my friend's demeanor."

The blonde man pulled out a leather purse and handed a silver coin to the barman.

"I will take him to my table and calm him down, if you would be so kind as to deliver some ale to our party?"

The blond man had a smile on his face that was more of a smirk. The serving man considered the silver piece laying in that large hand. Against his better wishes, the serving man snatched up the coin and waved the blond man back to his table.

"Bertha will bring ye out a pitcher."

The barman turned his back on the drunk and his blonde friend, washing his hands of the two of them. As long as they did not make trouble in his pub, he didn't care what they did together.

The blond man led the drunk to the back of the pub, where two other men sat at the small, worn table. The blond man gestured to a stool and the drunk sat heavily. He was apprehensive, looking wildly at all three men and wondering what they wanted with him. No one bought a drunk ale unless they wanted something from him. The drunk perched at the edge of the stool, waiting to see what they wanted and for the drink to calm his nerves.

The blond man waited until the ale arrived, gave the serving wench an obligatory pinch on the bum, then addressed the drunk.

"My good man!" the blond man exclaimed as if the drunk were an old friend he had not seen in years. "Where have you come from that treated you so poorly?" The drunk eyed the blond man and his associates with suspicion.

"Who are ye and why do ye want to ken?" the drunk asked.

"My apologies, good man. I am known as Montgomery." He gestured towards the men sitting with them. "This is Ward and Nichols, old friends of mine. We've had dealings a bit north of here, with poor reception. If you were also treated badly, we would like to know, so we could, well, commiserate – if you will."

"Commiserate?" the drunk asked.

"Aye." The blond man pushed a cup of ale towards the drunk. "Commiserate."

The drunk took the offered cup and downed the ale, spilling some on his filthy tunic. When he finished, he wiped his mouth with the back of his hand and started to speak.

"Weel, I came to this village, and 'tis market day, ye ken? And there is my missing boy! Relieved to see the lad, I rushed to him, anxious to hug the boy, when this lassie grabs my arm. After I push her away, her husband, the *Laird*, Christ curse my luck, says I offended his wife. I had to give up my son 'acause she liked the lad and wanted to keep him."

The drunk's words came out in a rush, and they could not have stopped his speech if they wanted to, which they didn't.

"He 'ad me by the throat, he did! Raving that I offended his wife, a wench who couldna mind her own affairs anyhow! Christ I canna abide by a man who cottons to a wench like -- he doesna have his own ballocks, that man! She's got'im good! Stinking wench! If I ever..."

Montgomery and his compatriots were no longer listening. His eyebrows rose with the drunk's angst-ridden ramblings, and his comments about MacLeod's young wife were the fuel for the fire that Montgomery had been searching for. Never having been smitten himself, Montgomery did not think to look to the wife as means to their end. They may not even have to kill her.

Montgomery regarded Ward and Nichols, then jerked his head toward the door. They all rose, leaving the sotted drunk to his ale and his own conversation, and exited the pub. They had much to accomplish before their job in this harsh Scottish Highland was finished.

Montgomery's mood was improved, however, for he finally saw an end to this job, coin in sight, and he could soon leave and join civilized society back in England. Montgomery rubbed his hands together as he approached his horse, and for the first time in many months, he genuinely smiled.

CHAPTER FOURTEEN

The Evil Ye Ken

ELSPETH AWOKE LATE AT night, a dull light on the far side of the room attracting her attention. It was Connor, stoking the fire at the hearth. He held his head in his other hand, a look of desperation etched deeply on his face. She started to move toward him, then paused. She didn't want to anger him and awake the children. Instead, she faced the wall of the croft in bed, placed her face in her hands, and cried herself back to sleep.

Connor, unconscious of his wife's eyes on him, was a man in dire straits. Montgomery began to make more personal threats against Lachlan's family, even to Meg again, though she was the wife of the Laird. He had no information to give the man, save for a strike on Meg would be a blow to the clan. But no matter how afraid he was for his whole family, he would not sacrifice his daughter like that. He would give his own life in a moment to protect his first born, his golden daughter. However, how could he turn to the Laird when he would be hung as a traitor and injure Meggie and his family's hearts? Connor feared for his family. Oh, how he feared.

His nights were restless as he tried to think of a way out of this impossible situation. What had begun as a bargain for his family's safety, especially Meg's welfare, had turned into a nightmare. Connor was certain that the threats could not last much longer. Montgomery would soon turn to violence, and Lachlan was powerless to stop him.

Suddenly Connor Lachlan felt older, older than time itself, and not for the first time, considered the possibility of the ultimate sin to rectify all. Suicide was oft on Connor's mind, but then he thought of his wife and his bairns, and while he was nearly powerless now, he could do nothing for his family if he took his own life. Lachlan closed his eyes. Utter defeat infiltrated his entire being, and tonight was another sleepless night thinking of how he could extract his family from this terrible, terrible mess.

The next morning, Elspeth, now desperate herself as she watched her husband fall apart, walked to Broch Lochnora. The sky seemed to mimic her feelings; the gray clouds blocked almost all the sunlight. A slight rain, little more than a mist really, wetted her clothes as she walked and turned the dirt of the road to mud which clung to her hide boots and flung onto her legs. The weight of the world hung on her shoulders, trudging through life as she did the mud. *Was this all?* She wondered. Was she in this life to live a gray, troublesome existence, only to die with nothing to show for it?

She found Meg in her chambers, sipping ale and fingering a pale green ribbon that lay on the small table near the window. A few fat, waxy candles sat in the window itself, casting a glow over Meggie that bathed her in shimmery light. Like much of Elspeth's life, it seemed that Meg was the sun in an otherwise bleak existence. How terrible that the happiness of such a successful wedding match should be shrouded in troubles with her father.

"Mother, what ails ye?"

It only took a moment, and Elspeth poured everything out to Meg. She hated herself for it, placing all these worries on her daughter's shoulders when she should celebrate her new family and coming bairn, but Elspeth did not know where else to turn. Her husband was becoming a stranger, one enslaved to foreign Englishmen who haunted her family. There were still five children at home, the youngest naught but a bairn, and Elspeth could no longer shoulder the trials she faced. For the safety of her family, her children, maybe even Meggie and her own bairn, she had to tell all.

Meg was quiet as her mother sobbed her story. Her mind, however, worked the whole time, trying to discern the information as her mother unfolded it. How did her father get into debt, if that's what it truly was, so deep? Why did he turn away from his family and toward these English in such a way?

When Elspeth's crying ceased, Meg wiped her mother's eyes with a damp linen and offered her some of the spiced mead she had been drinking. Elspeth took the proffered cup, sipping once, then inhaled to gather herself. She offered her daughter a small smile and a simple thanks. Meg escorted her mother down the stairs.

"I will figure out what to do, Mother. Methinks 'tis best to tell Ewan what is amiss."

Elspeth sighed heavily at Meg's words but knew talking to Ewan to be for the best. She felt as though she was betraying Connor, but what else was left? What other action could she take? In her mind, Connor had already betrayed his own family; she was doing no worse. What would he have done with his English ties if events had ended differently for Meg? Elspeth nodded and stepped out the door into the mist. It would be a long walk home.

Ewan came upon Meg and her mother as Elspeth was leaving. After a quick embrace, Elspeth walked the wet lane, head down, despondent. He watched Meg wipe at her eyes and knew it to be something more than a woman's pregnancy tears. He placed a hand on his wife's shoulder and put his arms around her as she turned to him.

"What is it, my Meggie?"

She was silent for a while, trying to find ease in Ewan's arms. Finally, she could keep it from Ewan no longer. Her shoulders and her mother's weighed heavily under the worries about her father. She did not want to risk her father's health or life to those vagabonds he gambled with, and perchance Ewan could help her father, or at least take some of the weight from her.

"Oh Ewan, I dinna ken. Mother is worrit about father. She thinks he owes gaming debts to the English - or some trouble as such."

Ewan was immediately on alert. The English? For the love of Christ, could his wife's own father be involved with the attacks that had been happening as of late? And she thought it was gambling? He didn't want to let his thoughts go to the idea of treason, but Ewan's mind worked quickly as he studied his wife, then spoke as cautiously as he was able.

"Trouble wi' the English? More than what the clan has seen to now?"

"Aye, Ewan. I didna say anything' to ye before, as I thought my mother was being overly worrisome, and she asked me to no' say a word. But now, ye ken, she feels it is worse. She has seen him speaking to them. And," she added in a desperate voice, "he has spoken violently to her for even mentioning it. My father is no' a violent man." Her voice slipped into a sigh.

She put her hand to her forehead and leaned against the door. Lachlan, with his croft at the end of the MacLeod lands, Elspeth's concerns, the attack on Meg . . . and a light dawned on Ewan. And Meg's stay and eventual marriage to Ewan, the Laird himself. Ewan's head was spinning. Could a father do that? Risk the sacrifice of his own daughter for his own gain? Spy on his own people - treason- for mere pennies? Use his daughter in such a way? There had to be more to this, Ewan knew.

He gathered Meg in his arms, praying he was wrong. He kissed the top of her head and sent her to their chamber to rest, but she had seen the look on his face and fear overwhelmed her. It was a look of frightening power, only this time she understood it would not be checked. Would her father suffer for these English? Would it come to that?

She tried to have faith that her husband would not harm her father, but she was not truly convinced. There was, after all, the safety and security of the clan at stake, and Ewan did not take those concerns lightly. Meg wanted to beg and plead her father's case, only she had no excuse to give and found she had lost her tongue. Unable to speak, she disappeared up the stairs, before Ewan ran for the stables, bellowing for Gavin.

He found Gavin engaged in a mock battle with Duncan, with several of the younger lads looking on. Hamish sat inside with barn, fixing some used reins and watching the combatants.

As Ewan approached, he heard Hamish yelling from inside the barn, "Dinna take it easy on the lad, Gavin! A five-year -old English lass could beat the lad as he is now!" The humor in his voice was not missed, and the other lads laughed while Duncan grimaced at the joke made at his expense. Ewan's hand jerked Gavin back, and Duncan's thrust went completely awry.

However, no one laughed at Duncan's attempt; the look on Ewan's face preempted all light heartedness.

"I must talk wi' ye now, man." Ewan's face left no room for argument, and Gavin tossed his weapon to Duncan.

"Take care o' it, lad. I'll return shortly."

Ewan dragged Gavin from the cluster of boys, hoping beyond hope he was over-reacting, and that Gavin could give him some perspective. He laid it all bare: the suspicious actions of Lachlan, his treatment of Elspeth, trading his daughter for something from the English, using his own daughter as an unwitting spy, and feeding any knowledge he had to the English - resulting in the attacks and fires. He spoke in a rush, as though the thoughts would slip from his mind as sand slipped from fingers. Only when he mentioned Meg as the "unwitting" spy did Gavin raise a hand to stop him.

"Dinna anger at this, Ewan, but are ye sure, truly sure she was unwitting? Look deeply, good man."

At the mere mention of that notion, Ewan felt a sudden urge to bludgeon his oldest and dearest friend, but then he stopped and looked Gavin straight in the eye.

"If she was a willing participant, why would she mention her father, of all people, to me at all? She would say nothing, or direct suspicions on another to protect her and her father's interests, ye ken?"

He managed to keep his voice in check, but Gavin could read the fury in Ewan's face. While he was sorry the anger was there, he did not regret his words. He would never hide the truth from Ewan.

Gavin eyed Ewan for a moment, then nodded. "On that ye are right. She would not lead ye right to the source, her own father, if she was witting. My apologies."

Ewan bowed his head once. "Forgiven. I recall your worries when we were first marrit. I thank ye for being forthright." He paused, looking around at the house and stables, and the young men who were watching the discussion with obvious interest.

"What do ye think? Am I correct in my assumptions? And if I am, we must stop Lachlan."

"What do ye propose?" Gavin asked.

Ewan mulled over the situation for a moment as Gavin looked on.

"We must catch him in company wi' the English. We must catch him wi' his hand in the fire." Ewan stared into the afternoon light, then faced Gavin. "Perchance Elspeth might ken her husband's routine. Mayhap she can be the lamb t'lead us to the wolf."

Gavin moved to leave, and Ewan turned to follow when a disturbing thought came to his head. He recalled the night he told Meg, *MacLeod is the people.* Ewan blanched in horror as he realized that was no longer completely true. MacLeod is the people, but there *was* a greater target that the English could hit, one that Ewan realized the would-be traitor knew about. Ewan dared to cast a glance up at the window to their bedchamber.

Connor Lachlan was Meg's father. Meg was the Laird's beloved wife; that alone was a greater target. And Meg was carrying the MacLeod Laird's child. Oh, God save him, there *was* a greater target.

The need to catch the traitor came to a head only a few hours later. Meg was worrying everyone in the house about Davey. She had not seen the lad since breakfast, and neither had anyone else. Typically, at least the widow Mary MacLeod, the kitchen help, saw Davey stealing apples throughout the day, but he had yet to make a single visit. Fiona had been asking about him since he missed his midday meal and was worried beyond compare. She knew he liked to go exploring, especially to pick flowers for his two favorite ladies, but to miss a meal was not like Davey at all.

After giving the house a thorough search, panic began to set in. Had his father returned and risked death for his son? While Meg could not believe the drunken sot capable of anything of the sort, it was not beyond the realm of possibility. After her frantic search, she raced for the door to look outside and collided with Ewan as he entered.

"Ewan! have ye seen the lad? Davey?"

"Nay, I have no' been near--"

Ewan was cut off as Keith burst through the front door with Davey in his arms. Davey appeared unconscious, his head and arms hanging limp from his body. His clothes and skin were dirty, bloody, torn. Meg screeched when she saw him, which brought Jenny from the kitchen, Fiona on her heels, just as Keith asked for her.

"Jenny! We need ye, lass! He's hurt, hurt badly! What can ye do for him?"

Jenny directed Keith to place the boy on a cloth near the hearth. Fiona's reaction mirrored Meg's, screaming when she saw Davey laid low. She rushed towards him, tears streaming down her cheeks. Her heart was breaking again, as it had with her boy whom she lost years back. *No' again. No' again,* Fiona chanted to herself as she bent over the lad.

His face was bloody, and his arm bent at an odd angle, but his deep and steady breathing mildly reassured Fiona. When her son passed on, his breathing was so shallow; she couldn't tell when he took his last breath. Meg moved behind her, gently rubbing her arms and murmuring encouragement into her ear. Fiona took a deep breath and regained her composure. Someone handed Meg a pot of hot water while Fiona pressed cloths into Jenny's hands. Davey lay limply on the floor, unmoving.

Jenny surveyed the damage. He seemed to have a broken arm and numerous cuts and bruises, but the reason for his deep sleep was a large, bloody knot on the side of his head. She decided to treat that first. The room was silent as she barked out orders immediately followed by even the Laird himself. Davey continued to sleep as Jenny set his arm, but woke, disoriented, while she bathed several cuts about his face and neck. He moaned, blinking a few times to clear his eyes.

Jenny looked to Ewan. "I canna do much more for him here. Best Elspeth sees to him."

"My Laird?" Davey croaked. Meg knelt on the floor beside the lad as Ewan moved close to him. He crouched low to hear what Davey had to say.

"Who was it, laddie? Who did this to ye?"

"They were no' Scots. 'Twere English. Nearer to the coast," Davey paused to moan as his head throbbed from speaking, then he continued. "The leader was tall, blond, mean. Wi' a scar."

Meg paled at Davey's description, recognizing it as the man who harassed her at the well. Ewan sat back on his haunches, his fists tight in anger.

"English? Ye ken they were English?"

"Aye. They said if they could no' burn or raid ye off the land, they might as well kill ye off it." Davey moaned again, and Jenny signaled to Ewan to stop the questions.

Ewan nodded and rose, walking toward the men gathered near the door. He felt more than guilty over what happened to Davey. After telling Davey's own father that Ewan and the clan would care for him better than a drunk old man, his words seemed to come back and haunt him. If he could not keep his promise for a little boy in his own house, what was he to do for his wife or unborn child? A sliver of fear pricked him.

"See that Davey is sent to the midwife to heal. We need men along the coast to watch for boats, horses, men. That's why we couldna find them. They are as slippery as silkies. Hamish and Duncan will stay to guard the house. Ye dinna let anyone in or out til we find these English." Ewan strode off in a storm with Gavin at his heels. "We beat them once. We willna let them take even one grain of Scottish soil!"

⟿⟫⟩ ⟨⟨⟨⟵

He returned with his claymore strapped to his back. Meg had a sack of food ready for them and met Ewan at the door. He pulled her to his chest and spoke hoarsely into her ear.

"Dinna leave this place - no' for naught." He let his fingers trail through her hair, fingering a strand twined with ribbons. "I love ye, Meggie."

She rose up on her toes and kissed him soundly. "Take care, my husband. I will be here when ye return. I love ye."

Then Ewan released her and signaled that it was time to depart. A small party lifted Davey to transport him to Elspeth, while a larger group of men gathered outdoors as news of the English's location spread. Gavin, Hamish, and Duncan held back. Gavin bent toward Jenny who stood near the kitchen and flung an arm towards Davey in desperation.

"Do ye understand now, Jenny? Do ye see why I canna lay my heart open? What if that were your son, Jenny?" His eyes bored into her, and Jenny felt herself shrinking under his stare. He suddenly reached out and touched her cheek. "I am sorry, Jenny," he said softly, then followed Ewan out the door.

Ewan and most of the other MacLeods approached the coastline at sunset. He assigned men to different places among the rocks and trees. Ewan had settled in to watch when he saw a lone man paddle up to the shore, then pull his boat under a rocky overhang and hide it with rocks and brush. *Boats?*

Cursing himself for not thinking of such a possibility, Ewan watched as the man climbed up a rock face not more than twenty-five yards from Ewan's very spot.

However, there had to be more to it. From where did the horses come, and where were they kept? It could not all be done with boats, could it? How did they move inland on horseback so quickly and quietly? Surely someone would have seen boats afore this day. Ewan wanted to attack the man as he climbed. Kill him ruthlessly and end this minor reign of terror, but he had to know if his suspicions were right. He had to know if one of his own men, his wife's very father, would betray him and his people.

Ewan groaned inwardly as the man headed north toward Lachlan's croft.

He signaled to Gavin and to two men close by, brothers James and Simon. They followed Ewan as he tracked the path of the Englishman. Keeping a good distance, creeping slowly, staying near the trees and low brush, he tried to convince himself that there had to be another reason, another excuse for the man to head north, for Lachlan to be in trouble.

The closer they came to Lachlan's relatively isolated croft, the more apprehensive Ewan began to feel. He didn't want to believe it, and he tried to hold onto the idea that something or someone else was to blame. The man halted and stood silently in the shadows, as if trying to hide from what was left of the sunlight.

Ewan signaled the men to hold back as he crept a few steps closer. Sweat dripped down his neck and back as Ewan watched motionless, crouched in the brush. It was near the end of summer, and the scent of warm sun, heather, sweat, and salt from the sea hung in the air.

A loud rustle broke Ewan from his thoughts, and he looked toward the right to see the origin of the noise. It was Lachlan.

Ewan hung his head in defeat. He could hear the strange man speaking, and he was definitely English. Straining to hear their words, he took a small step closer to listen better. Some branches crunched with his step, and the Englishman's head snapped up. The man broke for the forest, heading back toward the shore.

Ewan saw Lachlan run towards home and, against his better judgment, Ewan chased after Lachlan. He yelled and motioned for Gavin and his brothers to give chase to the stranger, but he knew they were too far back to catch him; the Englishman moved like the wind and had a good lead.

Lachlan's strained breath allowed Ewan to track him easily. Near the glen where he first encountered Meg, Ewan leapt, hitting Lachlan, knocking him to the ground. They rolled in the grass as Lachlan struggled. Ewan moved on top of Lachlan, forcing his face into the ground and hiking his arm behind his back.

"Cease! Cease, man!" Ewan's breath was ragged. "Ye are caught!"

Ewan stood, pulling Lachlan to his feet with him. Lachlan stood with his head held low, motionless before his Laird, knowing well the penalties for treason. Ewan glared at the humbled form before him, resisting the overwhelming temptation to smash his fist into the older man's face.

"Have ye naught t' say for yourself?" Ewan's voice was wild with anger. "Have ye any reason for betraying your people? Your family?" Lachlan opened his mouth to speak, then snapped his jaw closed. Any reason, no matter how grand, would only seem like lowly excuses now. He remained silent. Suddenly, Ewan grabbed his arm and pressed his face against Lachlan's.

"And Meg?" He had to know if his own wife, the mother of his child, was part of the treachery. "Is she a party to your schemes?"

Lachlan gave Ewan a look of absolute horror, which relieved Ewan considerably. "My wee Meggie?" Lachlan's voice choked. "Ye think my Meggie a traitor? How can ye?"

"I don't," Ewan responded. "I wanted to hear it from ye or see if ye were low enough to accuse your own daughter." He released his grip on Lachlan's arm, but held tight to his plaid. "Come on," he ordered. Lachlan followed without argument.

Ewan and his men brought Lachlan back to the manse. Thankfully, Meg and much of the keep had retired for the night, so Ewan and Gavin dragged Lachlan to the cells below the keep with little fanfare. However, he knew secrets did not keep well in a tightly knit community, nor a tightly knit house such as his. While Meg may be in her chamber for the night, he had no guarantees she was asleep. He had to make sure it was he who told her of Lachlan, not some of the house help. He grabbed Gavin by his jerkin before they left the lower level.

"I need some time. Dinna let anyone tell Meg where her father is. Do ye understand me?" Ewan's voice was still harsh with anger and exertion.

"Aye. I will keep Jenny and th' others from her. Ye will be back soon?"

"Aye. I must speak wi' the midwife."

Gavin regarded him with doubt. Ewan glared back, then turned in a swirl of kilts and left the manse.

He rode for Lachlan's croft, pondering his words the entire time. He was sure neither Meg nor her mother had any idea of Lachlan's actions. By Meg's own words and her mother's fears, they thought he was heavily in debt. *In debt, for certain,* Ewan thought, *in debt to his clan, bartering wi' his soul.* By the time he arrived, the moon was full high, bright, and lighted his way.

As he approached, he could see Lachlan's oldest boy lingering by the door. His wife's younger brother. Could he resign himself to seeing a boy raised without a father? And what of the midwife? For all Lachlan's faults, surely, she still loved the man. Would he take Lachlan away from her and her family? Kill his own wife's father? These thoughts weighed heavily on his heart.

Her son left the door and Elspeth appeared, lines of worry etched on her face. He dismounted and strode to her, taking both her hands in his.

"What is it, MacLeod? Is it Meg? Is it the babe?"

Ewan looked around her, verifying that the children were in the house and away from the conversation.

"Nay. Meg is well. How is Davey?"

"As well as can be expected. Only time will tell. Why are ye here, MacLeod?"

"It concerns your husband, Elspeth. Do ye ken where he is?"

"Connor?" Surprise, followed by despair, showed in her eyes. "He was to be wi' the beasts. He was to be on his way home. Do ye ken -?" Ewan nodded slightly.

"Forgive me, Elspeth. Lachlan is jailed for now. 'Twas no' debts he was involved in, but the English troubles we've had. I'm afraid he was caught conspiring wi' the English. I have him in the dungeon at the manse."

"English?" Elspeth breathed. "Surely no, no' the same who troubled Meggie?"

"Aye. The same. 'Twould seem the English wanted her at the house to serve as an unwitting spy." Ewan paused, shaking his head. His own reputation may have found him his wife, but it left him exposed to the conspiracies of the English. "Do ye ken if he was paid? Did ye notice if he had more coin? Furs? Anything?"

"Nothing of the sort, my Laird, I swear on Christ's Body. If he did, he hid it well, for I saw naught at all."

"No pay? Are ye certain?"

Elspeth only nodded. She bit her lower lip to hold back the tears but failed. She used her sleeve to wipe the wetness from her cheeks. Ewan told her she would hear from him soon, then left. He did not think the woman would want anyone to see her tears or shame.

Ewan was more than puzzled about Lachlan's behavior. If he was not paid in monies, then why would he deceive his family, betray his clan? He mounted Fire Foot. It was now time to go home and tell his wife.

When they returned to the manse, those still awake were all eyes as Gavin led the horses to the stable and Ewan checked on Lachlan in the cells below. Meg's father cowed in the corner of the cell, a sad vestige of a man sitting on the dirt floor. Ewan didn't want to imagine what Meg's reaction to the news that her father was a traitor to the clan and used her in the plans to boot. It was a dubious situation at best.

While Meg rested in her chambers awaiting Ewan's return, he cringed inwardly. What kind of son jails his father? *The sins of the father are reaped upon the son,* he thought grimly, sliding the cell door in place. He wanted to race upstairs as quickly as possible, before anyone else let Meggie know the awful news. Even she knew that traitors were put to death.

"Ye will stay here, Lachlan, 'til I decide what to do wi' ye."

There was no response from the other side of the door. Ewan sighed, then started for his chamber.

Low whispers echoed as he walked through the hall toward the stairs leading to his chamber. He could not bear to look anyone in the eye as he passed, for fear of losing his temper on some hapless kitchen maid. Jenny caught the corner of his eye, and that gave him a bit of relief. If she were here, she was not upstairs spilling the miserable news to Meg.

At his chamber, Ewan paused at the door, feeling his stomach clench. He knew 'twould be impossible to placate his wife in any way, provided no one had yet to tell her. God help him if someone had already shared the miserable news.

He pushed the door open slowly. The room was dim, and she was hidden in the shadows thrown by the tapers. The scent of late summer blooms was heavy in the air. He closed the door behind him, then adjusted his plaid. He stopped fidgeting, suddenly abhorring his job as a Laird, a man, a husband. He wanted to be a little boy again, safe with his mother, knowing his father would make all the right decisions. He did not feel wise enough or strong enough to be a leader - to be a man.

He sat on the stool nearest the fire and grabbed a mug of warm ale off the table next to him. In the shadows of the window his wife rested against the sill.

"Meg," he called softly. She turned from the window and regarded him cautiously.

"What is it that no one will tell me, my husband?" Meg's voice wavered. "Ye have someone in the dungeon, yet no one will tell me. I am frightened at what ye will tell me." She took a step forward, coming into the candlelight, and he could see her eyes watered.

"Who do ye have below?" she whispered.

Ewan sighed heavily, averting his wife's gaze.

"'Tis Connor, Meg. 'Tis your father."

Her eyes shot open wide as the shock registered within her. *My father?* She thought wildly. *Da's naught but a poor man o' the land! My father?*

"Why?" she cried. "Why would ye arrest my father? His debts? Why?" Tears streamed down her face, and those tears pulled achingly at his heart.

"'Twasn't his debts, Meggie. 'Twas the English. He was working wi' the English to run us off our land."

"NO!" she screamed at him. "Ye lie! My father would no' side wi' the English. 'Tis a mistake! A horrible mistake!"

"'Tis no' a mistake, Meggie," his voice rising slightly. "He was seen wi' them, wi' their leader. They elude us and abuse us, Meggie, and your father was lying abed wi' them. He has made his bed; now he lies in it. He is in the dungeon where he belongs!"

"But ye can't!" she protested. "He is my father! What of my mother, my sisters?"

"He is where he deserves to be!"

Ewan charged, rising towards her as he grasped the table, flinging it and its contents aside. Once again, that fiery power consumed him. Ewan seemed larger, making Meg seem smaller in comparison.

She shrank in fear from the angry heat that flared from his eyes and look of anger that contorted his features. That fearsome power, both as a man and Laird of the clan would be held under control no longer. His entire being had been threatened by her father, a poor crofter, and Ewan would not likely forget it.

"'Twere he anyone else, he would be dead already!"

His fists were clenched as he approached her, and Meg shrank away from him, clinging to the wall for safety. She had never seen him with such fury and hatred in his face, and she was desperately afraid. Fearing the very man she loved and cleaved to passionately, she did not think it possible he was the same man.

"Would ye beat me now, my husband?" she asked quietly, looking away and raising her hands to her stomach. "Would ye beat this woman who loves ye and carries your child?"

Ewan planted a fist against the wall near her head and ran his other hand through his hair, clenching it at the crown of his head. His breath came hard and fast, his anger pouring out in puffs of air that beat against her face. Firelight flickered behind him, hiding his features, making him look even darker than the anger and pain that ravaged his face. He leaned in near her, pressing his lips close to her head as though he would kiss her.

"He was aiding the English," he growled in her ear. "He associated with murderers. He aided those monsters who hurt Davey. He aided the English, the same who accosted ye, the English who ravaged my mother and killed her. He—"

"He's my father," she whispered, bringing her eyes to meet his and blue met green. The tears flowed freely now. "He is still my father. I can no' help but feel he had a reason for what ye say he did." Meg paused and tentatively reached for Ewan's face, as though the darkness that was there would attack her. She traced her finger along the rough stubble of his jaw. "Can ye no' ask him?"

The anger went out of Ewan's shoulders, and he slumped, resting most of his weight against the wall. He traced Meg's jaw with his own hand, his heart breaking at the sight of her tears. The darkness, his fearsome power that held him, fled at her plea.

"Ahh, Meggie. Ye make my heart ache, I love ye so," his voice was hoarse. He wiped one of her tears away with his thumb. "I canna promise ye anything, *mo annsachd*, but I will talk wi' the man."

Meg rested against him, pressing her forehead to his chest. "I thank ye, my husband."

Ewan looked up towards the starry sky on the other side of the window.

Dinna thank me just yet, Meggie, he thought to himself.

Ewan helped Meg to bed, placing a gentle hand on her belly as he kissed her goodnight. She was overly distraught for anything but sleep, and he was too restless to lay beside her. He also did not think himself ready to confront Lachlan. Brushing at her hair with his hand, he rose and left the room.

The gardens beckoned him. Ewan stepped out into the warm evening air, his thoughts troubled. His wife, his wee Meggie, had all but begged for her father's life, pleading with him for mercy, yet he still felt nothing but murder in his heart for a man that would betray clan and kin, who would risk the safety of a beloved daughter. What reason drove a man to damage to those who loved him most? At that moment, Ewan felt lost. How did his father do it? How did he make difficult decisions? Keep his head when everything around him seemed to be on a downward slope to hell?

He raised his eyes to the sky and asked God and his own father for the wisdom and fortitude to do what his position as Laird commanded of him.

Ewan stopped his pacing and paused near the heather that had yet to collect evening dew. He inhaled the heady scent, one that called to his mind images of Meg who so often carried the scent of wildflowers on her person. Second only to his gift of ribbons, herbs and flowers were favorites of Meg's. Sighing in despair, he thought of Meg and the babe. Could he ever tell his son that he killed his grandfather for betrayal? Would Meg forgive the man who killed her father?

At that moment he knew he would not kill Lachlan, no matter how much his honor and position as Laird called for it. He could not live with his wife, after seeing the look on her face, knowing he caused her that pain. The murder of his future son's grandfather, regardless of how worthless the man may seem, would not try his conscience. He sighed again and started for the cells below the keep.

Lachlan slumped against the wall of the cell, his chained hands draped between his legs, his head bowed in defeat. He had tried to do the right thing to save his family. He had done all he could to protect his daughter and her virtue, and while it saved her and got her married to the Laird of the clan of all things, it also got Lachlan what he deserved - a night in a cold empty cell with death hanging over his head like the moon. At least when his time came, he would die knowing he kept his daughter safe.

He raised his head at the sound of the key turning in the lock. Ewan MacLeod himself walked in, kilt and sword swinging, his face hard and dark. Lachlan knew it was time.

Ewan said nothing as he walked to the man he presently detested. He came to the wall where Lachlan was chained, holding his hands behind him to prevent himself from throttling the man. Ewan's voice sounded harsh against the silence of the cell's nighttime darkness.

"Why, old man?"

Lachlan let the question settle in the night air. An opportunity to explain himself? It was the last thing he expected, and he felt his hopes raise a bit. He may not meet his maker this night.

"Close your eyes, Laird," he told his son-in-law. Ewan eyed him suspiciously for a moment, then complied.

"Close your eyes and listen to the tale of a man with three daughters. A man with three sons by the hearth, and a lovely and devout wife rocking them gently." Lachlan's voice with rough with emotion as he tried to tell the leader of his clan why he would betray it.

"Close your eyes and listen to my tale of a man with no options but to go against those he is sworn to in an effort to protect those he loves most." Lachlan paused, contemplative, and continued.

"I live on the very edge of the forest, where there is naught to see for distances in every direction. It is myself, my wife, my daughters, and sons. 'Tis a poor life, a quiet life. I have a few sheep and goats, some nice crops, and mayhap a prospect for my eldest daughter. Then, one day, men ride to my land, our land. English, ye ken? They come upon me whilst I am wi' the sheep, Meg off in the distance looking for her flowers before she tends the garden, and what was I t' do? An old man, alone? I brace myself for the worst.

"This heavy, blond man looks at Meg, my wee Meggie. He speaks t' me, but doesna look at me. He looks at my Meg whilst he speaks, as he proposes an offer t'me. He offers me my family, just as they are, unharmed, if I will remain silent t' all but him. To him, I am to provide information about our land, do we have weaknesses? When and where will the men be occupied? He stops speaking and watches Meggie walk away. 'She is beautiful,' he says t'me. 'Twould be a shame for harm to come to her.' So I agree. What could I do? They could kill my whole family, burn my home before I could return from even telling ye about them. Again, what was I t'do?

"So I agree, and he comes by with his men one day, then two or three days later. Always, it is near the sheep, my family in view. Always it is the same questions, when will the men be away? What is no' being watched? What could cause th' most damage to us as a clan? Then he notices the Laird's son takes an interest in my daughter, and this man thinks, why no' press the advantage, so he and his men begin to bother my daughter, threaten her purity, threaten her life, to get to the Laird, for if my daughter is in the Laird's house, then she can tell me more about what the Laird does than I can divine alone. And their plan works! My daughter is wed to the Laird, and this Englishman has a stronger hold on me - where are the crops kept? Is there any gold in the house? Who is watching the animals this eve? Then more fire and destruction, more people hurt, and again I ask ye, what could I do?

"Naught, for I am an old man, whose gravest sin was t' love his daughter and family more than his clan. And God forgive me, as a result, I have hurt them all."

With that ending, Lachlan began to cry like a child. Unsure what to do with the weeping man, Ewan watched him for a moment, then turned on his heel and left, leaving the cell door wide open in his wake.

Gavin and Hamish waited outside the cell as Ewan walked through the door. He looked up at his younger brother and his oldest friend and felt an argument brewing. Avoiding their gaze, he studied his hand that rested on the wooden door. The hate in their eyes burned into him.

"I shall let him go," he said and braced himself for their fury.

"Nay!" Hamish exploded. "Are ye mad? He betrayed us! He betrayed his clan to the English, and ye would let him go?"

Gavin was quiet as Hamish raved and tried to collect his own thoughts. His suspicions and anger toward Meg quietly flourished and came to a head with the actions of her father. He gave little credence to crazed Elayne's words, but now her screams of "she bewitched ye!" ran in his head. Truly, it seemed to be the only reason. Ewan's actions were not those of the man he knew. Gavin said he accepted Meg, and when it was announced that she carried the heir, he put aside his reservations altogether.

Now, with her father's behavior, those reservations came back thousand-fold. Was his closest friend bewitched? He waited until Hamish stormed off down the hall then spoke.

"Ewan, has she witched ye? Ye canna truly think to release a man who has wounded us so deeply. Think of Davey, man. Think of Ian. Think of your fa-"

"*Dinna say such things to me!*" Ewan's angry shout surprised them both, causing them to flinch back. Ewan resembled a wild animal, his black hair standing on end, his chest heaving with anger, hate, and the weight of his responsibilities. He fought to control his emotions; the last thing he wanted to do was cause strife in his clan, among those he loved most.

"I said release him."

CHAPTER FIFTEEN

Atonement

EWAN DID NOT IMMEDIATELY go back to Meg. He knew in his heart that he had done the right thing, but had he made the proper choice? He could not say for certain that he had, and that hung over his head as he left Broch Lochnora.

It was a starry night. The crops of oats and vegetables fared well, all encounters with the English considered, and Ewan paused in the evening air to breathe deeply. He needed more counsel than could be had by Gavin, his brothers, or his own mind, so he did something he could not consciously recall ever doing before. He headed for the church to seek out the priest. Perhaps a man of God would provide answers, or at least support, for Ewan's actions.

God knew, Ewan did not feel he had either at the moment. Was he betraying his people, those who had lived and worked on this very land for generations, his good mother and father included, by letting Lachlan go? Was he thinking with his heart, or God save him, his cock? Was he doing the right thing for his people as a whole, not just himself or Meggie? Or was he forsaking his countrymen, *his clan*, to please his wife?

Father MacBain was still awake. He sat near a nubby candle, trying to read a rather thick book. Ewan knocked on the door of the chamber, and the priest's squinting eyes popped open wide at the noise. He rose and turned toward Ewan, his arms inviting the Laird into the solitary room. Ewan hesitantly stepped in, feeling a bit like an intruder. This was the priest's personal space. Perhaps he should have waited 'til morn?

"Come in, Laird MacLeod. Come in," the priest invited, then paused, reading Ewan's face. "Perhaps ye would feel more comfortable under confession?" Relief flooded Ewan.

"Aye. Can ye take confession this late in the evening?"

"I can take confession anytime. Come. Let me gather my stole, and we will go into the kirk."

The small church had the typical altar in the front, and Ewan knelt before it. He reflected on the last time he knelt at the altar-- it was at his wedding to Meg. He looked up at the Crucifix hanging above and crossed himself and asked for guidance. When he turned toward the bench for confessions, he noted that Father MacBain was already seated and appreciated the man's ability to be unobtrusive on another's private moment. Ewan went to the bench and knelt before the priest.

"Forgive me, Father—" Ewan began, but Father MacBain waved him off.

"What is it that troubles ye, young Ewan. Both God and I know how long it has been since your last confession, but we won't dwell on that," the priest added with a wink. "What troubles ye, lad?"

Ewan took a deep breath, bowing his head.

"Father, ye ken the problems we've had wi' these English. Ye may have heard that Lachlan, my Meggie's da, was aiding them. Yet, when he was caught and confessed, I stood there and did nothing! Nay, worse than nothing! I let him go! I set a traitor to my own people free! And now there is this conflict wi' in me, should I have killed him like I would have killed most any other in the same bind? Have I done rightly by the clan, or only by my wife? I am torn, father. I fear I am letting my heart and my loins lead when I should listen to my head."

Now it was the priest's turn to take a deep breath. As Laird, Ewan should always put his clan first, but he found himself in the terrible predicament of having to essentially choose between a much-loved wife and the loyalty of his clan, at least so it seemed. But was it truly as to-the-point as that? Father MacBain did not think so and told Ewan as much.

"Methinks the good Lord would have agreed wi' your decision, my son."

Ewan looked up at the priest in shock, and Father MacBain patted Ewan's shoulder. "The good Lord gives us life and a few commandments to show us how he holds all life dear. The fourth commandment is, 'thou shall honor thy mother and father.' Wi' the marriage to Meg, is Lachlan no' your father too, if only by marriage and no' by blood? Also, 'thou shalt not kill.' Ye were truly only following the commandments of the Lord when ye made your decision. Ye can tell that to anyone who would question what ye have commanded -- ye commanded no less than the very Lord our God, have ye no?" Father MacBain patted Ewan's shoulder again, then rose to leave.

"Ye have made your confession, Ewan. Now say one 'Our Father' and go wi' God."

The priest turned and walked back to his chamber, leaving Ewan kneeling in the kirk, alone.

⟫⟫⟩ ⟨⟨⟨⟨

Ewan returned to the chamber he shared with Meg. She lay on the bed, facing the wall. She seemed to be dozing, though Jenny had told him that she had been crying most of the night. Jenny also told him that Meg had yet to leave the chamber, even to eat. While the risk to the babe was minimal at best - he knew that she had been sick enough to miss meals before, the thought of her skipping a meal in her condition upset him all the more.

Still torn over his decision to release Lachlan, he knew in his heart that he made the right choice, that his father would have agreed, and none in the clan would question his decision, at least not publicly; however, the idea that a traitor lived among them ate at his soul.

The fire burned low, telling him that she had not moved for some time. The heavy tapestry that covered the window was pulled back, and an untouched meal of cheese and wine sat on a low table nearby. Obviously, someone was caring for her, though she did not seem to notice the effort. He stepped toward the bed, ready for either anger or tears. She remained motionless at the sound of his entrance.

Unprepared for silence, Ewan neared the bed and stood over her momentarily, looking down on her light form. He noted that no ribbons adorned her beautiful hair and that hurt his soul as well. She was curled in a fetal position, covering the babe she held and looking so much like a bairn herself. The words seemed to find themselves behind his lips.

"He's no' dead." Still, she did not move. Meg steeled herself for bad news. "I let him go."

At that, she spoke, her voice low. "Ye didna keep him locked below?"

"Nay. He told me a story. A verra sad story, and I could no' keep him locked up any more than I could kill him."

Meg rolled to face him. "A story? What story?"

Ewan was again quiet for a moment. Red, wet eyes, streaks of tears on her cheeks, the worry marks on her forehead cast a pall on her pale face. Yet another knife cut in his gut and he wondered how one man carried the weight of so much. He had a much deeper, abiding understanding and sympathy for his father, who had lost so much, but carried on with great composure. *Christ's Blood, father! How did ye do it?*

"He did no' approach the English. They approached him and made him a terrible offer," he paused again, choosing his words carefully. "They gave him a choice, ye ken. Given the rather remote location of his croft, he could communicate with them easily. He was to tell them of clan weaknesses and of opportunities of thievery and pillaging. They want us off the land, Meggie. The Duke of Argyle is no' an honest man and is using English deserters to gain land, money, and prosperities by claiming non-clan land. If we are no' on the MacLeod land, it makes for an easy case that it is no' MacLeod land. Damn Hebrides."

"Ye said there was a choice. What did he have to choose from?"

"It was either agree to aid them, or they would ravish and destroy his whole family, and let him watch. Ye ken 'twas a terrible choice? Either a traitor to the clan or destroy his family. Tell me, Meg, which do ye think he chose?"

Meg's hand went to her throat, her eyes wide. "The Englishmen. The ones from the glen? The ones from the well?"

"The well?" Ewan stood up straighter. "What happened at the well?"

"Naught of import, to tell the truth. But I was set upon by these English; the leader spoke, commenting on my hair, and that I was alone. I was fair frightened, for he was a large man, much like ye, my husband, with heavy blonde hair--"

That was all the description Ewan needed to set his teeth on edge. Not only had the men been harassing the clan and his future wife, the leader himself had threatened little Meg.

His mind flashed back to how she looked when he first saw her in the glen. How fortunate she was that Ewan and his brothers decided to take the long way back home, or how Duncan had to piss, and couldn't wait til they returned. How small yet fierce she looked next to those dirty men.

To now discover that the head of these brigands had approached her, used her as an unwitting spy, would have violated and killed her had Ewan not taken her into his home, made him want to vomit. The anger he felt towards Lachlan for being a traitor was nothing compared to the hatred he felt towards the Englishman who would wreak havoc without a care. How typically English.

"Ewan?" Meg's voice broke him from his thoughts.

"Meggie, I released your father with the hopes that these English will try to contact him again and we will be ready and waiting. If we can destroy these interlopers who would kill us all for a wee bit of land, we can hopefully live in peace. If we dinna stop them now, these men will go to greater lengths to rid this land of us, and we canna let that happen." He paused, searching her face.

"I will no' apologize for imprisoning your father. 'Twas the very least he deserved for what he did. I will only ask that ye realize my position and try to understand that I did what I felt I must. Can ye do that, Meggie?"

Meg sat back and regarded her husband. As much as she hated to admit it, Ewan was right. Imprisonment was the least that her father deserved; he was fortunate to escape death. Though she had thought of nothing but her mother, herself, and her family, she did see the position Ewan had been in. Inasmuch as he had duties to her as a husband, he had greater duties to the clan as a whole. He'd released her father nonetheless, and she felt sudden pity for his lot in life.

"Did ye send him home to mother?"

"Aye."

"Then come to bed, love. The nights are cold without ye."

She flipped back the covers, and Ewan quickly lost his tunic, kilt, and shoes. He climbed in next to her, pulling her lithe form close to him. She tossed the covers back over his body, enveloping him. The warmth was soothing to her after the worry and concern she had been through this evening. She could only imagine how torn Ewan must have felt, and she was more than grateful that he decided her father was not dangerous enough to leave imprisoned, or even kill.

Pulling him closer, she kissed his cheek, touching her leg to his. His body, which seemed to always radiate heat, felt even warmer. He turned his head to kiss her full on the mouth, moving his tongue against hers as he stroked his hand over her breast to her belly. It was not the first time they had lain together since she told him of the babe, but worry still wore on his face.

"Could I hurt the babe?" he asked softly, not wanting to break the moment. He felt rather than saw her shake her head in the incandescent light of the moon that poured into the chamber.

"Nay. Mother says we are well for a long time yet."

Ewan nodded in ascent and moved his hand back to her breast, rubbing his thumb over the enlarged, dusky nipple. He kissed the soft curve of her neck, then lower and caught her other breast in his mouth. When she moaned into his hair, he smiled to himself. Her lingering inhibitions humored him. Meg tried to refrain from crying out or moving too much. She had started to touch him more, be a bit more daring, but he knew it would still take some time before she felt truly comfortable touching him intimately.

He trailed his kisses down her belly to the rise of her woman's mound. He parted her gently and placed small kisses and licks between her velvety lips. As she whimpered her delight, Ewan felt himself pulling and tightening and could control it no longer. He rose above her and thrust deeply into her, reveling in her smooth tightness, gritting his teeth to retain some semblance of control. He moved in her, slow, but when she began to gasp and move her hips under him, he buried his face in her hair, taking in her smell and touch.

He wanted to ride her long and hard, to take his anger toward her father out on her body, but in the end, he succumbed to her. Ewan heard Meg cry out his name and, panting and sweating, he felt his own explosion and poured himself into her. He strained for a moment, then collapsed, covering her as if to protect Meg and the bairn from the evils of the world. He whispered, almost to himself, "Meg. Oh, my Meg," then rested his head next to hers. She entwined her fingers in his hair and nestled him close.

They lay together, unspeaking for a long while, listening to the still air of the night.

Gavin caught up with Ewan the next morning.

"Well, now we ken they are using the sea to their advantage. That is something at least."

"Aye, we wasted much time looking toward the MacNallys. Set up a light patrol along the coast. Keep most men near home, should the English step up the attacks here."

"And what shall ye do today, MacLeod?"

"Well, I must calm the clan's fears, and I must see to Davey. Meggie desires to ken how he is. We will meet back here midday to assess the situation. Tell everyone to keep their eyes and ears alert."

Ewan and Meg rode to her mother's soon after Meg felt well enough. Lachlan met them at the door and hugged his daughter, but did not meet Ewan's eyes. Elspeth soon appeared, and after coddling Meg and asking after her health, led her to Davey. Ewan followed.

Davey lay on a cot at the edge of the room. His sunken eyes cast shadows on his pale face, but Elspeth assured them that he was doing well and would regain full health with the proper care. As Meg crooned to Davey, Ewan pulled Elspeth to the side and asked about Connor.

"How is he?"

Elspeth looked around nervously. He noticed that she had aged since she had asked him to look after Meg, and that saddened him.

"Lachlan is no' the same man he was, but that is to be expected."

"Do ye think the English have contacted him as of late?"

"Nay. he has no' been away from the house but to feed the sheep. I dinna ken if that is good or no."

"If he does, ye send your young James to me rightly. Aye?"

"Aye," she responded quietly.

Ewan retrieved Meg. She gave her family parting kisses, and they left the croft. Ewan was helping Meg mount when Duncan rode up like a bat out of hell.

"Ewan! Ewan! ye must come now! The farms, the stables, the horses, homes, and families! It is all alight! They struck hard and fast!"

Ewan acted quickly. He grabbed Meg and dumped her on the back of Bedbug, then mounted Fire Foot.

"Ride wi' Meggie home. Then find Gavin and have him meet me near the coast. He'll ken where."

Ewan nudged his horse forward. His hand grasped Meg by the back of her head and he pulled her to him, kissing her roughly. He let his finger trail through her hair, tracing a ribbon -- pale pinks and lavender today.

"Get ye home, Meggie," he said in a harsh command. "I would have ye and the babe safe." Then he smacked the haunches of Duncan's horse and off it went, trotting at a quick clip.

Though he still felt like a small lad inside, Duncan tried to sound like a full-grown man, "I'll see ye safe to the house, and Ewan will be home rightly. Dinna fash, Lady Meg, all is well."

Meg wanted earnestly to believe Duncan, that this would be the last affront, that Ewan and his men would rid these foreigners from their homeland, but in her heart, she knew different. If they were able to seduce her father to treason, who else was aiding them? What if they did find a way to strike deep enough to run the MacLeods off the land? What if these attacks only got worse, and more people were harmed? The thought of any of her loved ones at the hands of the English sent a shiver down her spine.

"Are ye well. Meg?" Duncan asked at her quiet introspection.

"Aye, Duncan. Just anxious to be home."

They were nearly halfway there. Out of deference to Meg's still lacking the finer horsemanship skills, Duncan moved the mare at a slow pace.

They were past the glen, approaching the bend in the road where they would head south towards the keep, when three men broke out of the bushes and grabbed at Duncan and his steed. He turned frantically to Meg.

"Do ye recall what Ewan taught ye?" he yelled in a rush.

"Aye, but—" Meg began, but Duncan stopped her mid-sentence with a swift slap to her mare's haunch.

"Then ride, Meg!" he screamed as her horse took off in a sharp gallop. Meg grasped the reins to regain her balance and hunched over Bedbug's mane, as Ewan had shown her, racing back to the keep. Midnight barn fires or isolated assaults were one thing, but to attack a small group in the middle of the day did not bode well. She turned her head over her shoulder to see how Duncan fared when he called to her.

"Ride Meg—" Duncan's words were quickly cut off with the sound of a rock hitting a tree. Duncan fell awkwardly off his horse, his head bashed in with a good-sized tree limb.

"Duncan!" Meg screamed. She began to slow the horse to assist Duncan then thought better of it and faced forward to ride harder. A shockingly familiar figure emerged from the trees in front of Meg.

Montgomery was atop a dark stallion of his own, and Meg tried to rein Bedbug around him but didn't make it. Poor little Bedbug slammed into the stallion at a good pace, whinnying out in pain and causing Meg to fly off the saddle. The reins slipped through her fingers and she grasped at them to catch herself. She prepared herself to hit the ground hard when something grabbed the back of her kirtle. Montgomery hauled her onto his horse.

"Well, if it isn't little Meggie from the well, now married to the Laird of the clan."

"Nay," Meg's voice was little more than a whisper, and her whole body trembled in fear. *Had they killed Duncan?* Her mind raced. *Will they kill me? What of the babe?*

"Oh, aye, wee Meggie," the man drawled in a decent Scottish burr. "You have not been as fruitful as we would have liked. When your father assisted us, we received pathetically little in the way of how best to remove your kind, but once you were interred in the manse, *then married to the Laird,* for Christ's sake, we should have learned how best to run your small clan off the land with little noticeable bloodshed. But, Meggie, you proved to be quite a poor spy. Your poor father. So now we have little care of how your clan leaves this land, so long as you leave it. That is where you come in."

The tall blonde reached over and clutched her around the waist, sitting her in front of him on the stallion. Meg batted at his hands as he lifted her into place.

"We ride!" he yelled back at the men who had dispatched Duncan, and the horse took off at a fast clip.

Wide eyed, Meg grabbed the pommel of the saddle, in shock over her situation.

Kidnapped! she thought. *What will become of me and the babe?*

Duncan sat at a table with a cloth over his head, covering a large, bloody lump. How he managed to climb atop his horse and ride home he did not know. He had been so dizzy, he thought he would fall off his horse on the way home, food for the scavengers.

Fortunately, Gavin rode out to meet Ewan, and when he said that he had not encountered Duncan or Meg, Ewan had a sinking sensation in his stomach. They found Duncan as they returned near the keep, barely clinging to his horse, his head a bloody mess. Ewan grabbed his brother and flung him over the front of the saddle. He turned his horse as Gavin took the reins of Duncan's.

Once Duncan was laid out in the main room, Jenny tended to his head and stopped most of the bleeding. She cleaned the wound, then placed a linen pad over it and wrapped another linen around his head to keep the pad in place. She worked silently, trying to overhear Gavin and some other men talk with Ewan near the door. She and the rest of the house help knew something was gravely wrong. With Meg absent, half of the clan lands on fire, and now Duncan's head opened and bleeding, they felt the wrongness of it all in their bones. It had been so quiet in the Highlands, a welcome respite amid all the warring that had happened. Blood coming back to the Highlands was not a good sign.

After Jenny secured the wrap, she gave her patient some whiskey. Hopefully, it would numb the pain in his head enough for him to talk. He said only "northwest," and Ewan nodded to Gavin, James, and Simon. Keith and Hamish had already left to tend to the burning crofts and care for the wounded, and Ewan wanted to keep the search party small to avoid notice. Just the four would go after Meg and the men who had, as of late, caused nothing but trouble.

After hearing Duncan's pronouncement, Ewan and his men headed towards their horses. Gavin saw Jenny standing near the kitchen door, watching them, wringing her hands in her apron. Against his better judgment, and for what reason he could not explain, he strode toward her quickly.

"What is it, Gavin? What has become of our Meg?" Gavin took one of her wringing hands in his own.

"She has been taken by these ghost-devils, these English. Yet, Ewan and I ken where they go when they disappear, and we shall go there now and retrieve Meg. Dinna be worrit. We shall recover her in good health."

Gavin made to turn away then stopped. His hand still holding Jenny's, he grasped her to him with his other arm and kissed her fully, moving his body against hers. As quickly as he kissed her, Gavin released her, and turning away, ran to his horse and mounted. The others were starting down the path, and as Gavin trotted to catch up, he raised his arm to her as goodbye.

⇢⇛⇛⟩ ⟨⇚⇚⟵

What Ewan and Meg did not know was that Connor Lachlan had been searching for an opportunity to speak to his Meggie, to tell her what occurred with him, the bind he had found himself in, and ask her to forgive him the sacrifice of his oldest daughter. He did not honestly think he would get forgiveness, but at least she would know he was so very, very sorry.

He grabbed his walking stick when Duncan and Meg departed and hobbled after them. He was doing a poor job of keeping up with the horses, slow moving as they were, and heard Meggie scream. His head snapped up and he ran ahead, only to discover Duncan on the ground and that bastard Montgomery hauling his Meggie onto a large chestnut horse.

As Montgomery rode off Connor ran to catch up as best he could. It was when two of them stopped for water at Meggie's little glen did Lachlan meet up with them. The Englishmen were preparing themselves to ride off, joking with each other, when Lachlan saw his chance.

While they were busy readying the horses, Lachlan popped out from the nearby bushes. He managed to crack one of the men with his walking stick but got his upper back and neck, not his head. When the man yelled out in pain, the other rushed over with his sword drawn. As Lachlan pulled his staff back for another attack, the second Englishman thrust forward with his sword, and Lachlan could hear the ripping sound his stomach made as the weapon went through him.

Lachlan dropped his walking stick, grabbed his gaping stomach with both hands, and collapsed into the dirt at the side of the road. The Englishmen watched him bleed for a moment, then one delivered a swift kick to Lachlan's leg before mounting his horse. For a crazed moment, Lachlan thought, *add insult to injury.*

His very next thought was of how badly his midsection hurt, followed by how he never got to say he was sorry to his daughter.

Ewan came upon Lachlan on the side of the road, slumped to one side. Blood had pooled on the dirt, turning it to a mucky clay that stuck to Lachlan's clothes and body. Someone had run him through with a good-sized sword, and his life, like his blood, flowed from him. Ewan dismounted and crept along the road. Bending low, he could hear the man still breathing, choked and shallow.

"Lachlan," Ewan's voice was barely above a whisper in darkening of dusk. "What happened to ye, man?"

"I had hurt my daughter enough, MacLeod. I had to do something to save her. I did this to her, and I had to save her. She's my daughter, ye ken." His voice began to trail off, and Ewan took Lachlan's plaid and wrapped it around his shivering body. "Let her know, MacLeod. Let her know it wasna my choice. I tried to do what was best. I didna ken what to do. Tell her how verra sorry I am."

Ewan shushed him. "I'll tell her, man. I'll tell her. Did ye see where they went?"

"I followed them. They rode toward the sea." A sudden choking fit cut him off, and Lachlan tried to talk through the blood. "Tell my family, tell my daughter . . ."

He was unable to finish and died on the side of the road, in the dirt, with words of his daughter on his lips. Ewan used his hand to close Lachlan's unfocused eyes and signaled Simon to retrieve him. They hefted the body over the back of the horse that shied a bit at the smell and feel of the bloody dead man.

"Take him back to the house. Have him prepared for burial." Ewan looked back at Lachlan, whose face was now covered with the plaid as well. "I'll tell them that ye love them, man."

He mounted his horse and signaled the men with him. "They headed for their hiding spot near the sea. Pray to God they are not sea-faring. We will find my wife, so I can tell her of the noble death of her father."

The English had killed his mother and his unborn little sister, destroyed and ultimately killed his father, shattered his close and loving family, and assaulted his people and his land. By God they were not going to have his wife. *As God is my witness,* he swore to himself.

Grabbing the reins, he swung his stallion around to ride towards the rocky cliffs on the sea when something long and glimmering in the last of the daylight caught his attention. He dismounted and bent toward the ground.

He reached out to touch it, and a small smile appeared on his lips.

CHAPTER SIXTEEN

A Knight in Plaid

FEAR. MEG HAD NEVER known fear such as she felt now. She had thought she knew fear, the first time she met this cold blond man at the well, but she was at home then, still safe, her father near at hand. She thought she knew fear then, but no.

Now, she knew fear. She realized that there was a lot more at stake than herself, her own pain, but also that of Ewan's and that of her babe's. She held this fragile child's life in her body and in her hands. Not only her life, but her baby's life hung in the balance while she rode with the Englishman. She knew fear -- it was cold, painful, brain-numbing. The whole world seemed separate from her and all-encompassing at the same time. She could feel the horse moving beneath her, the breathing of the man, the monster, behind her, the crunch of the ground under the horse, but it didn't seem real.

She tried to make herself small, to disappear, and twined one of Ewan's ribbons as she thought of the best ways to keep herself and her baby alive. The ribbon worked loose, pulling her hair as it fell into her hand. She felt the length and focused on it stupidly. Stupid ribbons, gowns, what were they worth when the life of her bairn was at stake?

Then, she had a flash of an idea. Thinking quickly, she pulled a ribbon from her hair and dropped in on the ground, praying someone, Ewan, would take notice of it. A few moments later, as they headed northwest into the late afternoon light, she dropped another satiny strand, lavender.

Too soon she only had one ribbon left in her hair, but it didn't matter. They were at the coast.

Meg had never seen the ocean before, though they lived close to it. The largest body of water she ever enjoyed was that pond where she had first met Ewan. Reflecting on Ewan like that, back when her greatest concern was completing her chores, brought tears to her eyes, and she blinked them away. *I willna let them see me cry!* she thought to herself. *I willna let them know they have made me feel so.*

She pressed one hand to her belly, saying a quiet prayer for her babe, fingering the last ribbon. They were on the rocky coastline and tracking the horses would be difficult here. Meg would have to make this last ribbon count if she wanted Ewan to find her. She dropped the last one where they began to pick their way down the rocks; this last ribbon would have to guide Ewan right to her.

She again prayed, only this time for Ewan to find her soon.

Once they reached the narrow, rocky shore, the horse picked along until the blonde Englishman reigned it to a stop. There was nothing but the sea on one side, with its warm, salty breeze blowing in the mild air of gloaming, and the rockface on the other side of them. She could see nothing on the sea or in the crags in the rock. Where were they going?

The Englishman led the horse to the rock face, then dismounted, dragging Meg down with him. He caught her before she landed on the rocks beneath them and bound her hands loosely with a length of leather. He tied the horse to a rough outcropping. Turning back to Meg, he stuck his hand out to her. She looked at it stupidly, then looked up at the man's face. Grasping her hand in his, the Englishman shook it formally.

"The name is Montgomery. Since we will be spending a bit of time in each other's company, I thought it best if you know my name, Meggie."

Meg cringed inwardly at his informal use of her name. This Montgomery seemed to enjoy making her uncomfortable, and she had no idea what he had in mind. But looking into those yellow eyes was like looking into the eyes of a monster, and Meg was certain she had a good idea of what the mind behind those eyes planned on doing to her.

Montgomery grabbed her by her bound hands and proceeded to drag her along the rocks. He kept looking into the rocks of the drop they had just climbed, as if he were searching for something.

A little way down, he stopped abruptly, reached up with one hand, then placed a foot on the rock. He was still holding Meg's hands in his free hand. Meg watched him wondering, *Are we now going to climb back up the rock?* The one step up was all the man needed, however, as he threw himself into a cavern that blended into the rockface. Had Meg not seen him go in, she never would have known the cave existed.

Suddenly she was hauled up by her bound hands, the side of her body scraping along the sharp rocks as she went. She cried out a bit, using her feet to buffer herself from the outcroppings. All too quickly she was pulled into the cave.

She had to act quickly; she didn't want to risk that Ewan could miss this cavern. Meg used her toe to push her slipper off her other foot and heard it drop into the rocks below. Hopefully, it would be enough for Ewan to find her.

The cavern itself was not very large. Montgomery had to slouch, so he did not strike his head on the low, overhanging rock. He threw her into the shadowy back of the cave, then turned from her to work with something on the ground. The cave brightened, and Meg saw that he had started a small fire. Not enough to keep warm in winter, but enough for light in the cave.

He came to her with a piece of leather in his hands. Grasping both of her wrists in one of his, he wrapped the leather around them, knotting it tightly, so her hands were bound twice. He stepped back as if to admire his handiwork and gave her that twisted smile again.

"Now, we wait," Montgomery said and disappeared from the rear of the cavern.

As they followed the path towards the shore, Ewan kept watching for signs from Meg. As they moved, he would find a pink ribbon fluttering on a bush, or a violet one trampled on the ground. His smile grew wider with each ribbon discovery for it told him two things: one, she was alive, and two, she was leading him right to her.

Meg's ribbon trail veered off the road abruptly, and Ewan had to rein his group in to follow it. Instead of staying with the road, the ribbons led Ewan into some rocky underbrush that led in only one direction, to the sea. Ewan cursed under his breath, then guided Fire Foot to pick his way to the rocky shore.

Their pace was slow, and Ewan cursed both the path and the Sassenach who had led them on this merry chase. After a while, the brush cleared away and all that remained were the rocks. Their pace slowed more until Ewan reached the sheer edge of the rocky outcropping. He couldn't risk looking over the edge on Fire Foot; the horse would fall over the edge for certain.

Dismounting, he picked his way to the rocky edge to better see what, or who, was on the shore. As he lay down to see completely over the edge, he noticed the ribbon, waving yellow in the fading light of day, and the smile returned to Ewan's face. He looked down and saw that the rock face was not a sheer cliff, rather a series of rocky outcroppings, almost like steps, if one followed the rocks in the right way. It was then he caught movement out of the corner of his eye and scrambled back to his men.

"What is it?" Gavin asked in his sharp whisper.

"There is a way down. The rocks can serve as steps if we are careful. And careful we have to be; there are English on the shore. Do they know we are here? I dinna ken. But 'tis near dark, so we have the advantage."

Ewan led his men down the rock face. Gavin followed immediately after, knowing that Ewan would want to break free from any fighting as soon as he was able to find his wife.

Just as Ewan reached the rocky shore, three men appeared, followed by two more. Ewan grasped his claymore from his back and brandished it with both hands. He did not wait for the English to attack. With a loud yell, he lunged forward, Gavin on his heels, and entered the fray. He slaughtered the first man immediately, which told Ewan these were not men used to fighting.

Once Gavin was joined on the shore by James and Keith, all four armed themselves against the English. Ewan nodded toward Gavin, who nodded back, then used the pommel of his claymore to bash the closest *Sassenach* on the side of his head. The man dropped like a log, and Ewan took off running in the direction from whence the men came. Ewan knew Meg had to be near these rocks. As he ran, he prayed they had not put her on a boat.

Ewan slid to a stop when he saw something that did not belong among the gray rock -- a barely visible, fine piece of green. He regained his balance and approached the green. It was a slipper, his wife's slipper. Ewan regarded the shoe, confused. Why would she drop her slipper here? What was she trying to tell him? He looked at the rock face in front of him, then searched farther down the shore. When he turned his head back, he noticed an odd gash in the rock. He dropped his claymore to climb up and get a better look.

He was shocked when he looked around the front of the rock and saw an entrance into a cave. Had he come from the north, he would have seen the entrance plainly, but from the south it was disguised to resemble nothing more than the rock face.

He stepped lightly on the rocky outcroppings to reach the mouth of the cave, then hauled himself in. It was too light in the cave for it to be empty, and he realized he left the claymore on the ground outside. He cursed once again, removing his dirk from his legging and tucking it into his belt under his plaid for easy reach.

Ewan rounded a curve of the cavern toward the approaching light. A woman was bound at the back of the cave, sitting near a small, smoky fire. *Meg*. Seeing Meg bound in the corner, he threw caution to the wind and went to her. He called her name harshly and bent to remove the bindings from her hands, ignoring her whispered utterances. His sole thought was on removing Meg from the cavern, which turned out to be a grave mistake. He realized this when he felt the cool steel of a dagger against his neck. Keeping his head still, Ewan quickly palmed his own dirk from his waistband into his hand.

"Like the saying about leading a horse to water, and you definitely did try to drink, MacLeod."

Montgomery's loud voice filled the cave, even with the sounds of battle outside. Ewan fleetingly wondered how long before Gavin could find his way in and cursed his own stupidity at the same time.

"Ye have me now. Ye can send her home," Ewan argued.

"Yea, I could. But *I will no',*" he said in a mocking tone.

Keeping the knife on Ewan's neck, he reached over to Meg's chin, and cupping it in his palm, shook it roughly.

"You see, she was bait, very good bait. The leverage we needed to finally get you away from your home and off your land. With you and your *amour* dead, and your brothers really too young to take over leadership, I can easily run everyone else off the land. Problem finally solved." Montgomery snorted in derision. "Really, this little project took far too long for my tastes. You should have succumbed to your ill luck much sooner. It would not have come to this. As it stands..." Montgomery trailed off, rising. "Put your knees on the ground and keep your head bowed," he ordered Ewan.

He kicked the knife from Ewan's hand, and the weapon skittered across the floor of the cave with echoing resonance. The sound of metal on stone hurt Meg's ears, making her cringe.

"Now I could give you a choice, MacLeod. If you choose your lovely wife, you forsake the land, your clan, all. Or, are you the type of man to choose your people over your wife, over your very own life? I wonder, which would you pick?"

As Ewan was forced to kneel, Meg could not believe the utter stupidity of the man named Montgomery. For all that he was supposedly a "superior" Englishman, a clever and sly one to boot, he underestimated her.

While her hands were bound, true, he tied them in front of her person, giving her arms plenty of latitude. She wriggled farther into the cavern, a bit out of Montgomery's vision, thinking, *Being a woman made me too ignorant and weak to work within my bindings? Do the English think so little of the Scots?* These thoughts ran through her head as she searched the cavern for a good-sized rock. If it worked once before, it should work again, was Meg's logic.

She heard Montgomery say to Ewan, "You Scots are a heavily religious lot. Are you prepared to meet your maker, MacLeod?" before she brought the rock down on the back of his head, where it resonated with a sickening *Crack!*

Montgomery fell harder than the rock itself, and before Meg could blink, Ewan was atop him, stabbing his dirk into Montgomery's neck. Blood spurted over Ewan, staining his pale tunic crimson in the dwindling firelight. The air was noticeably chilled, and Meg tried to repress a shiver.

Ewan sat back on his haunches and peered up at Meg. He pulled his dirk from Montgomery's bloody neck and rose to sever Meg's bindings. As he slit through the cloth, he leaned close to Meg and said in a jagged voice, "Remind me never to get ye too mad, *mo leannan*. Ye are fair wicked with those rocks."

He then pulled her to him and held her tightly until Gavin entered the mouth of the cavern, himself fairly bloody.

"Christ, man!" Gavin yelled. "I have to do your dirty work outside whilst ye cavort in here with your wife? Could ye no' have given us a hand, ye lazy lout? What has marriage done to ye, anyhow?"

⤜⤜⤜⤜ ⤛⤛⤛⤛

Ewan carefully lifted Meg from the mouth of the cave and carried her to his horse. He placed her atop his stallion, swinging up behind her. He left instructions for Gavin, James, and the other men to bury what Englishmen they had killed, including Montgomery who lay in the cavern.

While Ewan did not think they would have any more trouble with these English, what with their leader dead and their secret usage of the rock cliffs and sea exposed, he still told his men to be safe and keep an eye out. If the Duke of Argyle did want to align with the English and maintain a foothold in the Highlands, he would try again. However, for the moment, the English were off MacLeod land, and Argyle was Robert the Bruce's problem now, not his. His greatest concern now sat in front of him on the horse.

They rode home slowly and quietly, with Meg trying to blink back tears at her ordeal. Once they were on the road heading south, Ewan took a cleansing breath. He had so much to tell her – how worried he was for her, how sorry he was that he had not been there when she was taken, and most of all, about her father and his final words to his daughter.

They neared Broch Lochnora. Meg let out a shuddering sigh of relief when she saw the gate. They dismounted, and Jenny, who had been waiting by the door, ran to them with Davey, who returned that afternoon with Meg's brother, still bandaged, at her heels. Jenny lunged at Meg, clasping her in a tight hug.

"Ye are safe! Ye are safe," she chanted over and over. Meg took the opportunity to whisper into Jenny's ear, "Aye, and Gavin is also. He will follow soon enough."

At that, Jenny let out a small cry and released Meg to return inside and ready herself for Gavin's return. Meg then turned her attention on the small boy who had found a special place in the heart of her home and clan.

"And ye, Davey? How do ye fare?" she asked him. He threw his small arms around her thighs and squeezed.

"I'm so glad ye are back, milady. Everyone was sore worried for ye!" Davey exclaimed in his little voice.

Meg reached down and gave him a large hug, nodding to Fiona and her brother James, who now watched from the door. Davey lived with Fiona now, and Meg was certain that any fears Fiona had for Meg were made worse by the fear of how Davey would react as well. Fiona placed her hand on her heart and nodded back to Meg, just as her own brother grasped her in an embrace.

While Meg was occupied with her brother, Fiona and Davey, Keith came up to Ewan and spoke to him in a low voice. Ewan nodded his head in understanding, patting Keith on the back to send him on his way. Ewan turned his attention back to his wife.

"Come now, Davey," Fiona called from the door. "I am certain milady would like a bath and some warm food now, love." Davey kissed Meg's hand then trotted obediently over to Fiona and, with James, followed her into the keep.

Fiona had a bath brought up to their chambers. Ewan helped Meg undress, washing her back as she sat in the warm water. She sighed with relief at the feel of the warm water on her back, casting off the dampness of the cave and the film of fear-induced sweat that covered her from head to toe. The scent of the water, lavender, and sweet grass helped to ease her mind and for a moment reminded her of the secluded glen before she was wed to the Laird MacLeod.

She leaned back into the tub and closed her eyes, and Ewan moved his ministrations to her neck, chest, and belly.

"I can tell your breasts have changed a bit. Fuller, ye ken?" Ewan spoke softly in the dim room. "Can ye notice a change in your belly?"

"Nay, 'tis no' larger. But harder, methinks, like there is a small bowl under my skin." Meg's voice was also soft, but raspy was well from the strain of the day.

"What did Keith say to ye when we returned?" she startled him. He bowed his head low, pretending to focus on the washing job at hand. After a moment, he spoke.

"Well, 'tis no' important overall, ye ken. But ye may be interested."

"To ken what?" she lifted her head and opened her eyes to study his face.

"Elayne is to be married," he said. Meg's response was not quite what he would have expected.

"Weel, thanks be to God," she spoke in a stressed tone, then laughed to herself. "Who is the poor man she is to wed?"

Ewan burst out laughing right along with her. He couldn't stop to answer her question, and tears of laughter rolled down his cheeks. When he finally regained control, he used the wet linen to wipe his face and regain himself.

"Keith mentioned the Laird of clan MacCollough, east of here."

"I dinna ken the clan. Is he a good man?" she asked, curious.

"I am no' certain, myself. However, methinks the farther away from here, the better."

"I could no' agree more," Meg responded, lying back onto the tub again. Ewan lifted her leg and washed it gently, placing a kiss on the bottom of her foot. Her toes curled inward, and she giggled a bit at the tickle.

With her bath completed, Ewan dried her with a large piece of linen. She tied it around her chest, right above her breasts. Then she helped Ewan out of his clothes which, in truth, looked quite worse for the wear. Meg picked up a fresh linen as Ewan stepped into the tub.

He tried to relax to the feel of Meg rubbing the cloth about his head, neck, and shoulders, but he could not. He had yet to tell her about her father, and he had to do it before he took her to bed. He did not want to keep that information to himself.

He wondered for his wife's sake, and Lachlan's, if she could grant her father his last wish. Ewan hoped she could forgive her father for what he had done and love him for what he tried to do that got him killed.

"Ewan, are ye there?" Meg's quiet question broke Ewan's reverie, and he knew he had to tell her now, before another moment passed.

"Nay. I am no'. Meggie, *a leannan*. I have something to tell ye, and I dinna ken how to say it."

Meg straightened up at his statement, her body tense with apprehension. She remained silent, waiting to hear what it was Ewan had to say.

"It's your father, Meggie."

Meg's eyes opened wide, but she said nothing.

"When he heard what happened to ye, that Montgomery had ye, he knew afore us all. He ran after them, Meggie, with naught but a small walking stick to protect himself against them. He was coming to save ye, Meggie. Do ye ken what I am saying?"

Ewan brought his head up to gaze at Meg directly in her somber green eyes. He touched her jaw with a wet finger and continued.

"He went after ye, he did. And he caught up wi' some of the *Sassenachs* near your glen. He tried to fight them off alone, but there were too many. Your father was caught in the belly wi' a shortsword by one o' the English, and they left him there in the dirt, bleeding. We came up on him no' long after. He asked..." Ewan paused and dropped his gaze back to the cooling water of the tub. "He asked that ye forgive him. Your father was only trying to keep ye safe, and when that failed, he was determined to save his eldest child. He asked me to tell ye that he is sorry, and he loves ye verra much."

Ewan stopped and let Meg take in the weight of his words. Meg stood, dropped the linen into the tub, walked over to their bed, and sat. Her eyes were unseeing as she fingered the damp linen towel she was wrapped in. The tears started slowly, rolling in giant drops down her cheeks, followed by her body shaking in silent wracking sobs, and she covered her face with her hands.

Ewan climbed out of the bath and moved to her, gathering her in his wet embrace, trying to soothe her. He did not have to tell her Lachlan was dead; she knew it when he told her of the wound to the stomach and the apology. Otherwise, Lachlan would have apologized to his daughter himself.

Eventually her sobs lessened, and she tried to rein them in with a loud hiccough. Meg took a few deep breaths and looked at Ewan sharply.

"My mother?" she asked, her concern showing plainly on her face. "Does my mother yet ken of my father? I should be wi' her--" Meg started to rise, and Ewan caught her hand.

"Aye, ye should. I sent Simon to your family to tell them of this eve's events. Let me help ye dress, and we shall ride to your mother's."

Meg threw her arms around Ewan, hugging him tightly. Surprised at this unexpected action, he put his arms around her as well.

"What's all this?" he asked her.

"I thought ye would tell me to stay here – that I was too weak or too tired from the day. Thank ye, Ewan, for your understanding."

"Weel, I do have some experience with a parent passing into the next world. I would have ye wi' your family, love, as I was wi' mine."

He helped her dress, then donned his plaid and escorted her downstairs. They rode out to Lachlan's croft, and Elspeth met her daughter in the yard, both crying on each other for what they had lost.

⇶ ⇷

They buried Lachlan two days later. Most of the village turned out for his funeral, and he was buried in consecrated ground after Ewan conversed privately with Father MacBain. Once the priest heard Lachlan's attempt to save his daughter caused his death, Father MacBain agreed that the man had asked for forgiveness to atone for his grave sins.

Melancholy rain fell on the day Lachlan was laid to rest, and the day seemed even more somber for Meg who covered her hair with a dark veil for the solemn occasion. After the burial, Ewan asked Meg, Elspeth, and the rest of Lachlan's family to follow him. They left the kirk and walked the muddy road to the edge of the village, not far from the Laird's keep. A mostly-built croft stood, built with new wood and fresh grasses and peat on the roof. It was fairly large, bigger than Lachlan's croft, and Ewan gestured for everyone to go inside. Meg's eyebrows rose in suspicion.

"What is this, Ewan?" Meg asked once inside the croft.

"I did no' think ye and your mother should be so far apart now that your father has passed. She and your family can live here. 'Tis larger and closer to the keep, and ye. We should have it finished in less than two days."

At that, Elspeth and the children shouted with elation, a bright spot on a woeful day. Meg took Ewan by the hand and pulled him to her, kissing him fully. He pulled her veil from her head, letting loose the golden sunset glow of her hair, and ran his fingers through it. It made his heart sing to see Meg happy; Meg was happy to be with Ewan.

CHAPTER SEVENTEEN

Epilogue

SHE WAS IN HER full pregnancy when they walked together to the fateful glen where they first met. Ewan was wrought with worry that she would bear the babe there on the road and pleaded with her not to walk such a distance, but Meg merely pushed him and, leading the way, strode matronly out the door as only a woman in her ninth month can.

They walked quietly, making small comments to each other, both wrapped in furs and plaid to ward off the winter's cold. When at last they reached the glen, it was a different sight than when they had last been there in early fall. Now the leaves were gone, replaced by snow-tipped laurels and rowans, the gentle loch dark with ice. She stopped near a tree and gently touched a finger to the fragile branch.

"Why are we here, love?" Ewan sounded cordial, but his insides were riled - both scared she would begin to labor now, and angry that she would risk her health and that of the babe's by making this onerous trip.

His eyes were hooded as of late, trying to hide his anxieties at the coming babe and responsibilities forthwith, the possibility of losing the babe or, God-forbid, Meg in childbed. He felt the weight of the world on his back; after all they had been through this summer, the precariousness of this newly-forming family he cherished more than his own life grew frighteningly clear.

"Hush, Ewan. Ye worry for naught. I would no' have come here had there been any cause for worry."

Ewan was amazed that she seemed able to read him so well, almost able to know his thoughts, and if he had met her now, he would have agreed with Elayne's claim that Meg was a witch. The further she went in pregnancy, the better she became at it, too. It was maddening, and he hoped it was a trait she lost when she delivered.

She broke a small piece of the branch off the tree and handed it to Ewan. He glanced at it in his palm, then looked at Meg with his question in his eyes.

"Land, my love, is like a woman - to men. It is something to covet, to desire, to own. If ye are nice to her, kind to her and treat her well, she gives back. She provides life; she suckles future generations; she is ample to those who treat her well. She is a mystery. Ye do not know when she will kick up a storm, turn cold on ye, or let ye bask in her heat. As much as ye try to read her, she changes on ye day to day, year to year. There is only so much of her for everyone. Many men will want her, but only one can claim her for his own. And sometimes, men will try to take her from ye, because they are jealous of what ye have. But like a woman, men dinna want to share. What is man's belongs to him alone, and he will not let others take what he has rightly won."

She paused and stroked his hand, moving the bit of branch as she spoke again.

"This past summer, ye took both a wife and land as your own, to lead and provide for both. When we were threatened, you guarded us with your life. Like me, who carries your son, the branch holds the key to the future as well. Within these buds are the makings of new life, just like a woman. Ye have cared for both well, and they will care for you in return.

"I want ye to know, Ewan, I ken. I ken your pressures, the weight of the clan, your family, and the guardianship of this land that was hard-fought and won. When there are times when ye want nothing more to do with her, when ye are angry because she rains on the new harvest or bakes the grass in her heat and ye rail at her, she still returns with clear water, fresh fruit, and fat beasts for the slaughter. She always returns, my love."

With that ending, she kissed him in the falling snow, then pulled back suddenly, before he could fully embrace her. He could feel the oppressive weight he had been carrying ease away.

"Mayhap I canna yet read well, but ye did no' marry a fool," she told him.

Six days later, the newest member of the clan MacLeod was born. The child was a black haired, blue-eyed girl, with a shriek that rivaled a banshee's. Cheers went up around the hall, then the grounds where people held court to the Laird's firstborn daughter.

Elspeth wrapped the child in soft cloths and handed her to the new mother, who gleamed like the sunrise despite just giving birth. She then took the child from Meg and handed her to Ewan. He held the newborn like she was made of glass, awestruck at the child he created with Meg. Once Meg was cleaned and propped up on the bed, Ewan gave the child back over to her mother for her first nursing. Elspeth and Jenny straightened the room and ushered everyone out.

Ewan gazed at his wife, who looked drawn from the ordeal of birth but very happy as well, and at the firstborn child she held. Love surged through him at the picture they made, and he could not imagine his life without them. How fragile life was, that they both could have been taken from him.

Ewan moved to the bed and sat on the edge, curling around his wife and child, reassuring himself that they were both here, both real, both his. Meg took his hand in hers and gazed up at him, her eyes full of unshed tears.

"'Tis greater than I could have imagined," she whispered to him. Ewan only nodded in agreement. They fell asleep together on the bed, Ewan holding his family in the safety of his arms.

⤜⤜⤜ ⤛⤛⤛

They baptized the baby the very next day. Father MacBain presided over the celebration at the keep, and the village came out in the swirling snow to see MacLeod's daughter join the clan and the family of God. Father MacBain beamed as he blessed the little girl, who let out an astounding shriek when the priest poured the water over her head. The priest then asked the new parents for the child's name.

"Caitir Margaret," they answered in solemn reverence.

Father MacBain nodded in approval and announced the blessing of Caitir Margaret MacLeod to the masses. A cheer went up in those walls. Laird MacLeod then invited all those present to a celebratory meal in the main hall at the keep and seated his family by the warmth of the hearth.

The celebration lasted long into the frigid night, and it was late when Jenny escorted Meg upstairs with the baby, followed by the anxious father. Meg handed the babe to Jenny, who changed the swaddling and prepared her for bed. Ewan helped Meg into their bed, and Jenny handed Caitir to her.

"I think I can handle it from here, Jenny," Ewan told her. Jenny smiled softly at Meg and the babe, then quietly left the chamber.

Gavin stopped Jenny as she walked through the chamber door. He paused with his hand on her arm, looking into the room at the picture the Laird's family created.

"I'm no coward, Jenny," he whispered, his head bent low. "I'm practical and very closed. I dinna wear my emotions. But I saw the fear Ewan felt months ago, and I see how he has let it go now. I know now that, for all the fear, all the horror, there is something greater that God gives us, if only for a short time. And if ye will have me, I would be honored to be your husband."

Jenny moved closer to him, pressing her face near his. He turned his lips towards hers and moving his hand to the back of her head, kissed his future wife. They clung together passionately, and the world was new, open, and wonderful.

CHAPTER EIGHTEEN

Bonus Ebook

DON'T FORGET TO GRAB your bonus ebook about Gavin and learn what happened before he and Jenny met? Click the image below to receive *The Heartbreak of the Glen*, the free Glen Highland Romance short ebook, in your inbox, plus more freebies and goodies!

Click here: https://view.flodesk.com/pages/5f74c62a924e5bf828c9e0f3

CHAPTER NINETEEN

Excerpt from The Lady of the Glen

THE SCENT OF A fresh fire kindling at the hearth overrode the less pleasant smells of the hall as he returned. Declan watched his oldest friend, probably one of the largest, hairiest men in the Highlands, awake and poking at the fire, encouraging it to flame. Torin Dunnuck may be hairy, but like Declan, he found the Highlands cold and took every opportunity to complain about it. He was also the only man in the house who would deign to light a fire. On this morning, Declan was grateful.

"Are ye cold already? 'Tis only October, ye chilly fiend," Declan taunted.

Torin stood, his frizzy brown hair almost touching the beams of the room and smirked at Declan.

"At least I have mine arse out o'bed before daybreak, ye lazy lout." He tossed the fire poker to the side where it clanged against the hearth and reclined on a bench near Declan, shoving some dirty rags to the side. "And ye are the one always complainin' about the cold!"

Torin flicked his eyes to Declan, not bothering to hide his present opinion of his Laird.

"Have ye put more thought to your half-crazed idea?" Torin continued. "Ye know that most o'the clansmen will not take kindly to changes. Unlike us reasonable men," Torin raised his bushy eyebrows to Declan, "most men enjoy drinking binges and free reign."

Raising an eyebrow at Torin, Declan guffawed at the taunt. No one more than Torin wished for the rough ways of the clan to remain; he was the Laird's most staunch opponent to the idea of civilizing the clan.

The hall slowly warmed, brightening with the fire and daylight, which did little to improve the appearance of the room. Disgust filled Declan, and again he pondered how his home, his land, his clan had fallen into such an abject state, which only reinforced his conviction that the step he was about to take was the correct one. The solution, however, would cause more strife than the dirt and decay of the hall.

"I received a letter," he told Torin. "I dinna ken if 'twill amount to anything, but I have heard the woman is a force to be reckoned with, and I think, I know, that is what we need."

"But," Torin hesitated, "ye do not even know the lass. Don't ye want to find a woman ye love? What if ye aren't even attracted to her? What if — " he paused a moment, choosing his words wisely. "What if she leaves like your own mam did? Are ye no' concerned with history?"

Declan reclined on a cot near the hearth. The fire and daybreak chased away the morning chill, and Declan collected his thoughts, scratching absently at his golden beard. His oldest friend might understand his motives but still vehemently disagreed with the idea. Declan knew without a doubt that the rest of the clan would likewise not be convinced. Declan turned his pale hazel eyes to Torin's dark ones, trying to explain his motives.

"I ken that women are often used as pawns in power struggles between clans, and men of power usually have the upper hand when it comes to a choice of brides. It should be that way for me, but when I see my clan in such condition, I know I must choose a wife who can help me get my life, my home, my clan in order. If she can do that, then I will love her no matter her reputation, or her appearance."

⤙⤚⤙⤚⤙⤚

"I wrote a letter, Lanie," Laird James MacNally admitted to his daughter.

"A letter?" Her dark eyebrows rose.

"Aye, a letter. Do ye know of the clan MacCollough, east of us?"

"MacCollough? Ye mean the dark and dirties?" A look of revulsion crossed her face as she noticeably recoiled.

Her reaction was not what MacNally hoped for. As a neighboring clan, MacNally was familiar with the reputation the MacCollough clan garnered over many years. Nevertheless, James MacNally was familiar with the new Laird, having heard accolades of the young man from other chieftains; some praise passed straight from the King himself. MacNally found several avenues of opportunity with Clan MacCollough. In strengthening that clan, he would assist a neighboring clan and ally, and perchance find a more significant opportunity for his headstrong daughter as well.

"Well, I would not quite call the clan that," he rolled his eyes. "But it is a clan in need of some, um, female involvement. I know Declan. He is a good man in a rough place. He has spent the last several years at the side of the Bruce. BlackBraes could be a great clan but has lacked a woman's hand for generations, and the rough men are a testament to that."

He paused to scratch his beard. "The MacCollough has heard of ye. And ye, my lovey, ye are the strongest woman I ken, stronger than many men. I think, the MacCollough is astute in his request — ye can help bring his keep and his clan into a more reputable state. Ye will have a maid or two, and Senga can go with ye." Laird MacNally would never design to send his daughter to a man's house without a chaperone.

Elayne pressed her lips together in a tight, shrewd line. "Why father, are ye playing matchmaker? Are ye hoping that the Laird MacCollough will so appreciate my overbearing ways that he will fall madly in love with me and attempt to wed the harpy, as you have so callously painted me?" She threw her head back and barked out a short laugh. "Why father, ye have more gumption than I gave ye credit for."

MacNally laughed as well, in spite of his daughter's foul humor.

"Ye see, Lanie? It is that behavior, gumption as ye say, that is needed. I think it will be good for ye. It will allow ye to explore the world, use your skills in a way much needed, and if ye wed a man, a laird, well, the more's the better, aye?"

Elayne tipped her head to the side, measuring out her father's words.

"What did ye write in the letter?"

"Do ye want to read it 'afore I send it?"

Elayne shook her head, her dark hair falling about her shoulders. "Nay, father, a summary of the letter will suffice."

MacNally cleared his throat. "'Tis a short letter, truthfully. I merely responded that I was aware his clan lacked a woman's care, that cleanliness and medical care may be needed, and confirmed my daughter was exceptionally skilled at both. I wrote that ye were looking for life experience and adventure, and mayhap he would find your companionship useful for a time."

Elayne cut her eyes toward her father, sharing the same smirk he presented her earlier.

"Useful, eh? I sound like cattle."

"Nay, my Lanie, ye sound like a prize."

The Lady of the Glen

https://www.amazon.com/dp/B07KVQYWH6

CHAPTER TWENTY

An excerpt from the Celtic Highland Maidens series –

THIS NEW SERIES WILL take us back in time, to a place where the Ancient Celts, the Caledonii tribe, fought for their land and their people against the Romans in 209 AD

The Maiden of the Storm

CHAPTER TWENTY-ONE

The Maiden of the Storm
Chapter 1

Northern Scotland, north of Antoine's Wall, Caledonii Tribe, 209 AD

Rumors circulated of Roman Centauriae extending their patrols north beyond Antoine's wall, what they referred to disdainfully as cnap-starra. And her father's tribe watched from their secluded positions as those soldiers behaved in stupid, overly confident ways. If they wouldn't have risked giving away their positions, the painted men might have laughed at the ill-mannered soldiering of these weighted-down Romans.

Ru was chieftain of his tribe, a remote relative of the great King Gartnaith Blogh who himself managed to run the Roman fools from the Caledonii Highlands. 'Twas said the king laughed with zeal as the Latin devils, in their flaying and rusted Roman armor, scrambled over the low stone wall. As though a minor cnap-starra could stop the mighty Caledonii warriors from striking fear into the heart of their Centauriae. Fools.

But speculation blossomed of rogue Roman soldiers venturing far north of the wall, a reckless endeavor if Ru's daughter, Riana, ever heard one. Warriors from her father's tribe and other nearby tribes traveled across the mountainous countryside, through the wide glen to meet them.

Thus far, the soldiers had remained close to the wall, fearing to leave the false security it provided. Ru's warriors had struck down one or two that meandered away from that security, wounding them, perchance fatally, with a well-aimed throw of a spear. The diminutive Roman soldiers, even clad in their hopeful leather and metal armor, were no match for the powerful throw of a Caledonii spear.

This most recent Roman soldier, however, appeared less resilient, less aggressive than his previous counterparts. Though clad in full Roman military garb, he wasn't paying attention to his surroundings — distracted as he was. The Centauriae had traversed the low mountains and lochs to their hidden land. And he was alone. Ru noted his lean-muscled build and made an abrupt decision.

"Dinna kill this lad," he whispered to Dunbraith, his military adviser and old friend. "We should keep him, enslave him. Melt his iron and armor into weapons. And use his knowledge against these pissants. Give them a bit of their own medicine."

Dunbraith's face, blue woad paint lines mixed with blood red, was fearsome and thoughtful. "Severus is defeated," his growling voice responded. "The Roman lines are scattered. 'Tis a safe assumption they will not even try to retrieve the lad."

A frightening smile crossed his face, one that Ru knew well. A cruel smile that didn't reach his eyes.

Ru nodded his agreement and waved his hand at his Imannae, a young Caledonii eager to prove his worth. The young man positioned himself just beyond the leaves of the scrub bush in which he hid, narrowed his eyes at his prey, and launched a strong-armed throw of his sharpened spear.

The Imannae's throw was perfect, catching the young Roman's upper arm in a sharp drive. The lad cried out and dropped to his knees in pain and shock. Ru and his warriors moved in as silent as nightfall.

The Maiden of the Storm

https://www.amazon.com/dp/B08DQY62JD

Acknowledgments

A thank you to my readers –

I would like to extend a heartfelt thank you to all of you for taking a chance and reading my first romance novel. Even with some extensive writing experience – even teaching others how to write! – actually completing a novel and publishing it involves the writer opening herself up, exposing herself in way that is challenging. That you, dear reader, took the chance to read this romantic tale makes the risk worth it.

Please note, since this is fiction, I have taken some creative licensing. First, kilts as we know them really weren't worn like kilts until the late 1500s. But, the Scots did have plaids, tartans they wore as capes or wraps or blankets. I merged the two and presented the kilt early. I love my Highlanders – I just can't imagine them without kilts!

I also gave the Scottish War of Independence a bit of a break, less war and conflict on a large scale to focus on the MacLeod's on a small scale. And while I do try to keep the story as historically accurate as possible, any other anachronisms are purely mine for the sake of the story.

I would also like to thank my kids and family in general for always supporting me. They always assumed writing was my real job. To my encouraging children, Mommy has always been an author. And my mom, who saw her daughter get a degree in English, of all things, and made no judgements, and instead remained confident that her daughter would be successful even with such an inauspicious field of study.

Finally, I would like to thank Michael, the man in my life who has been so supportive of my career shift to focus more on writing, and who makes a great sounding board for ideas.

If you liked *To Dance in the Glen*, please leave me a review!

About the Author

Michelle Deerwester-Dalrymple is a professor of writing and an author. She started reading when she was 3 years old, writing when she was 4, and published her first poem at age 16. She has written articles and essays on a variety of topics, including several texts on writing for middle and high school students. *To Dance in the Glen* is her first major fiction novel. She is also working on a novel inspired by actual events. She lives in California with her family of seven.

You can visit her blog page, sign up for her newsletter, and follow all her socials at: https://linktr.ee/mddalrympleauthor

Also By Michelle

As Michelle Deerwester-Dalrymple
Glen Highland Romance

The Courtship of the Glen –Prequel Short Novella

To Dance in the Glen – Book 1

The Lady of the Glen – Book 2

The Exile of the Glen – Book 3

The Jewel of the Glen – Book 4

The Seduction of the Glen – Book 5

An Echo in the Glen – Book 7

The Blackguard of the Glen – Book 8
The Christmas in the Glen – coming soon
The Celtic Highland Maidens

The Maiden of the Storm

The Maiden of the Grove

The Maiden of the Celts

The Roman of the North

The Maiden of the Stones

Maiden of the Wood
The Maiden of the Loch
The *Before* Series

Before the Glass Slipper

Before the Magic Mirror

Before the Cursed Beast
Before the Red Cloak –
Glen Coe Highlanders

Highland Burn – Book 1

Highland Beauty – Book 2 coming soon
Historical Fevered Series – short and steamy romance

The Highlander's Scarred Heart

The Highlander's Legacy

The Highlander's Return

Her Knight's Second Chance

The Highlander's Vow

Her Knight's Christmas Gift

Her Outlaw Highlander
Outlaw Highlander Found
Outlaw Highlander Home
As M.D. Dalrymple - Men in Uniform

Night Shift – Book 1

Day Shift – Book 2

Overtime – Book 3

Holiday Pay – Book 4

Undercover – book 6
Holdover – book 7 coming soon!
Campus Heat

Charming – Book 1

Tempting – Book 2

Infatuated – Book 3

Craving – Book 4

Alluring – Book 5

Made in the USA
Columbia, SC
11 February 2023

11688731R00136